exhibitionism

TOBY LITT

PENGUIN BOOKS

PENGUIN BOOKS

Published by the Penguin Group
Penguin Books Ltd, 80 Strand, London WC2R ORL, England
Penguin Putnam Inc., 375 Hudson Street, New York, New York 10014, USA
Penguin Books Australia Ltd, 250 Camberwell Road,
Camberwell, Victoria 3124, Australia
Penguin Books Canada Ltd, 10 Alcorn Avenue, Toronto, Ontario, Canada M4V 3B2
Penguin Books India (P) Ltd, 11 Community Centre,
Panchsheel Park, New Delhi – 110 017, India
Penguin Books (NZ) Ltd, Cnr Rosedale and Airborne Roads,
Albany, Auckland, New Zealand
Penguin Books (South Africa) (Pty) Ltd, 24 Sturdee Avenue,
Rosebank 2196, South Africa

Penguin Books Ltd, Registered Offices: 80 Strand, London WC2R ORL, England

www.penguin.com

First published by Hamish Hamilton 2002
Published in Penguin Books 2003
1

Copyright © Toby Litt, 2002
All rights reserved

The moral right of the author has been asserted

Set in Monotype Bembo
Printed in England by Clays Ltd, St Ives plc

Sex

And Other Subjects

Versions of the following stories appeared in the following places:

'A Higher Agency' in *Neonlit: Time Out Book of New Writing Vol. 1*; 'On the Etiquette of Eye-Contact During Oral Sex' in *The New English Library Book of Internet Stories*; 'The Audioguide' in the *Idler*; 'tourbusting' in *New Writing 8*; '"Legends of Porn" (Polly Morphous) Final Shooting Script' in *Piece of Flesh* (ICA); 'Unhaunted' in *The Time Out Book of London Short Stories Vol. 2*; 'Story to be Translated from English into French and then Translated Back (without reference to the original)' in *The Time Out Book of Paris Short Stories*; 'Alphabed' in *Girlboy* (Pulp Faction), and on the *babyLondon* website; 'My Cold War [February 1998]' in *Fortune Hotel*; 'The New Puritans' (as 'The Puritans') in *All Hail the New Puritans*.

The author would like to thank the editors.

www.tobylitt.com

Dreamgirls

Monday

The first words I said to her were these: 'You are the girl of my dreams.'

And she *was* – she *was* the girl of my dreams; and no other girl will ever be that quite so completely again – and thank God for that.

I should've guessed something was up, right from the start. I've never been someone to whom good things happen; not unless it's for something very bad to happen very soon afterwards.

Yet there she wonderfully was: sitting, arms wrapped around her knees, atop a groyne, nearby the West Pier, Brighton beach, exactly eight long days ago – as if for all the world she'd always been awaiting me.

She looked the spit of my ultimate-ever dreamgirl: Louise Brooks in *Pandora's Box*, b/w, dir. Pabst, 1929. The murder trial scene. The veil-lifting sequence. She was wearing a black velvet dress of the simplest cut. And when I saw her, I thought – *Save yourself the pain of even thinking of trying to talk to her.* I knew with utter certainty that, in the whole of my future life, there would never be another stranger I would more regret not having approached. *You've been through this before: even at parties where there was a theoretical chance you might be introduced.* I knew that I would not be ten steps past her, five, one, before a great swathe of depression would swoop down into me – a huge ghost-dark bird. *Just keep walking.* But because she was the girl of my dreams, this wasn't what happened – this, in fact, never stood a chance of being what happened.

'Aren't you even going to speak to me?' she said, just as I was about to pass her. 'I've been waiting such a long time. Let's –'

This was when I spoke, when I told her who she was: 'You are the girl of my dreams.'

To which she replied: 'Yes, and my name is Cluny.' And so it had to be, for I've always thought Cluny of names the most beautiful.

But before I go on, I have to go back – to the instant I chose to speak; for what Cluny had said was the most astonishing of all, of ever:

'Let's –'

The word wasn't even there: we, that is us, that is two people who are united – *we* were half-curled up into an apostrophe, like a tiny embryo, asleep, not even conceived yet, merely an idea, an agreement, perhaps unspoken, between the two heads, soft-pillowed and drowsy, smiling and sex-muzzed, of its lost-in-love parents-to-be. *We*.

('s: could a word be any less, any more?)

And what was even more wonderful was that she did not stop there, or after announcing herself as Cluny, but continued, saying, 'You are the man of my dreams. I'm so glad you're finally here. Let us go somewhere warm and cozy and just *be* together.'

And I helped her climb down off the groyne and kept

hold of her hand as we walked off down the beach and into what should have been the rest of our lives and for ever and ever, amen.

Before the end of the day, Cluny had moved in with me – into my cramped, top-floor flat. Miraculously there had been no obstacles to this: Cluny was staying with an unjealous female acquaintance, and Cluny's few possessions fitted in a single calfskin suitcase.

Already I needed to have Cluny around me all the time – her warmth and smell, her sudden movements and abrupt stillnesses. When I had a bath, Cluny had to sit on the edge of the tub; when I went to the loo, she had to talk to me through the door. We held hands constantly, and kissed with every other breath. Preparing our evening meal became the culinary equivalent of a three-legged race: if Cluny added salt to the boiling water, I must add the olive oil; if I opened the wine, Cluny had to pour it. Everything got spilt: wine, water, Parmesan, bolognese. We clinked glasses and smiled and laughed and *knew* our luck would hold.

As we lay all a-spoon, after the greatest sex ever (both of us exploding into orgasm just as the legs fell off my never-before-so-ill-treated bed), I told Cluny I would always love her no matter what and Cluny at the exact same moment told me the exact same thing using the exact same words.

And that was when our problems began.

Tuesday

That night, I had the most marvellous dream: the girl of my dreams was in it. In fact, it was a dream about meeting the girl of my dreams. But – devastatingly – the girl of my dreams was no longer Cluny. For how could she be? The girl of my dreams had to be *in my dreams*; Cluny was now *in my life*. A vacancy had come up, and had already – in only a few hours – been filled.

The new girl of my dreams had long red hair which glowed in the sunlight and freckles dappling her nose and forearms. When I met her, I was dream-walking down a fragrant country lane. The new dreamgirl awaited me there, perched inevitably on a five-bar gate. She was wearing very tight jodhpurs on her long supple legs and carrying a riding crop in her slim-fingered hands.

'Hello there,' she said, in a creamy Somerset accent. 'You're from that new family at the vicarage, aren't you?'

She introduced herself, confidently. She was called Lizzy.

My Lizzy dream lasted all dream-summer, and it was a long swelteringly sexy dream-summer. There was barn after barn of hay to be climbed up into and rolled in; there was leafy glade after leafy glade to be discovered and beromped.

When I woke up, I found Cluny looming over me – propped up on one elbow, black bob zagging around her face.

'And who is Lizzy?' she fizzed.

'No-one,' I said. 'Someone in a dream.'

'I came from a dream, too,' she said.

'Yes, but she's only a fantasy.'

Cluny smiled flirtatiously, dreamily.

'I thought I was your fantasy,' she said.

'You are,' I said. 'You are.'

We had a late breakfast, after Cluny had spent the entire morning doing her very best to be my fantasy.

★

4

It was late Tuesday evening before I left the flat again. I thought I'd escaped, but *there* Lizzy was – waiting for me on a low wall beside the corner shop. Cluny had desired post-coital cigarettes and, suddenly, I had too.

'Hello, Mr Handsome,' said Lizzy, in the same sweet cidery Somerset tones I'd heard in my dream. 'You live in the top flat, don't you?'

The long red hair was there, and the jodhpurs, and the riding crop, and the hands – such hands.

'Look, Lizzy,' I said, 'I can't deal with this now.'

She showed no surprise I knew her name.

'I understand,' she replied.

'Can you wait a minute?' I asked. 'I need to buy some cigarettes.'

'These?' said Lizzy, holding out a pack of Marlboros.

I wanted to say, 'What?' and to ask, 'How?', but I already knew What and I knew that I would never know How.

Lizzy smiled, dragging me back in imagination to our sweet summer of shag.

'I live in Flat D. I've just moved in. I'm a linguistic philosopher. I'm always free – night or day. I'll be watching out for you. Come over. *Soon.*'

She brushed fragrantly past me. I watched her unlock the front door of my building and go in.

It was all I could do not to follow her right then. But I was loyal to Cluny. I went back to her with the cigarettes and we smoked ourselves to sleep.

Wednesday

When I woke up, Cluny was slapping my face.

'You're disgusting,' she said. When I asked why, she

refused to tell me, and went off to fume in the living room.

There was a knock at the door. I went to answer it.

Standing on the top-floor landing was a thin young woman in thick glasses. There was something Germanic and '70s about her – as if she'd been a peripheral member of the Baader-Meinhof gang.

'Hello,' she said. 'I am Anne.'

In an instant, I adored and remembered her. For we had spent the whole of the previous dream-winter (i.e., the previous night) passionately plotting the overthrow of World Capitalism. To be honest, I remembered the passion rather more clearly than I remembered the plots.

'Sorry I am to bother you. I moved today to the Flat D, with Lizzy. And I feel need to have long discuss of Mao Thought.'

'Right,' I said, feeling that that was exactly what I wanted, too.

'Lizzy said would you to come round for lunch, yes?'

'Oh, good,' I gulped.

'And we can together all afterwards have sex.'

'I'll be there,' I said, without thinking.

I spent the morning trying to persuade Cluny to go out. But even the prospect of shopping for thicker mascara or silkier stockings couldn't rouse her. Her sullenness deepened, her eyes darkened. I felt as if I were watching a terrible thunderstorm boiling up. There was nothing I could do to prevent it – all I could do was watch and wonder and wait and then, when it broke, get soaked. Eventually, she said: 'You've dreamt of another girl whom you love more than me.'

From somewhere her calfskin suitcase had appeared. I

6

glanced down at it in shock, and when I looked up Cluny was wearing a 1920s travelling hat.

'I loved you more than anyone I've ever loved,' she said. 'But I just can't take any more.'

She picked up the suitcase, flung open the front door and thunderstormed out.

Such passionate declarations from this, the original girl of my dreams, made me feel deeply horny indeed.

However, in many ways, I also felt relieved; for the simple reason that – if she'd really been playing to character – she would have thrown all my stuff out the window before departing.

Just then, there came another knock at the door. Hoping it was Cluny, already contrite, or Anne, wanting me to come early, I opened it – only to find myself facing a policeman holding a broken version of my beloved Anglepoise lamp.

'Been having a bit of a domestic?' he asked. 'If I were you I'd come down and collect the rest before anyone nicks it. Not that there's anything particularly worth stealing.'

I followed him downstairs, and found – in confirmation of his words – every single one of my possessions lying dented, smashed or shattered upon the pavement beneath my bedroom window.

In the distance, I could just about make out Cluny's retreating figure – teetering on her patent-leather high heels as she tried to drag the calfskin suitcase along.

I spent the next hour or so carrying everything back upstairs – in whatever sorry state I'd found it.

I finished around a quarter to one, then had a quick shower before presenting myself at Anne and Lizzy's.

Hard as it is to imagine, the afternoon more than made up for the morning.

And things continued to improve as the day continued.

When I staggered back into my flat, having been both erotically (Lizzy) and ideologically (Anne) overwhelmed, I found that Cluny had returned – and, what's more, that she had either managed to mend or replace everything she had earlier defenestrated.

'Even my Anglepoise,' I said, marvelling at the perfect replica she had found.

'It was in one of the shops in The Laines. When I saw it, I thought of you, and I just stood there and started weeping. How could I ever have thought of leaving you? You are the love of my life. You *will* take me back, won't you? It hasn't been too terrible, has it?'

'Oh,' I said. 'Awful.'

Cluny promised to make amends, and did a pretty good job.

I have never been more exhausted than when I collapsed back on to my downy pillow that night.

Thursday

Which may explain why I dreamt a terrifyingly vivid dream: I was in hospital, being attended by a beautifully efficient nurse. Her uniform was as crisp as her vowels, her shoes as sensible as her manner, and her blonde bun as tight as her arse. Her forearms spoke of enemas and other terrifying eviscerations. She was known to everyone as Nurse Smith – and although I asked up and down the dreamwards, I never even heard speculation as to a Christian name.

We fell in love whilst she administered my first barium meal. It was a passion she fought passionately to overcome. But, in the end, she could but submit.

I dreamt the whole affair. It was midnight on an almost-empty ward. Nurse Smith came quietly in. The curtain was drawn. The bun undone. The uniform crumpled. The sheet lifted.

Next morning, I awoke to find Cluny sobbing silently beside me.

'What is it, my darling?' I asked.

'This,' she said, passing me a brown envelope.

When I looked inside it, I saw a pair of gifts: from Anne, a copy of Lenin's pamphlet 'What is to be done?' and, from Lizzy, a small corn dolly.

'Don't think I don't know what it means,' sobbed Cluny, 'because I do.'

I couldn't stand to see her like this. I too broke down.

'Something's happening,' I said. '*You're* the girl of my dreams. I only want to be with you. But now you've come into my life, some kind of barrier has been broken. I can't help it: I have other dreams, they have other women in them – and, because you broke the barrier, they are flooding out into my life.'

'Then we must escape,' said Cluny, desperately. 'We will run away.'

'With you,' I said, 'I could run away from anything. But I can't run away from my dreams.'

Somehow, a jangling pianola seemed to be playing in my bedroom – and I realized that, for the last minute, I hadn't been speaking out loud but mouthing the words in complete silence.

When Cluny replied, to the crash of further chords, I realized what was happening: a board of black appeared in front of her face, with white words printed upon it.

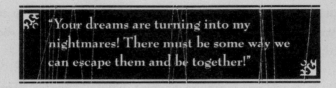

We were back in the Silent Era, from whence Cluny had in the first place sprung. Under the accompaniment, I could hear the hum of a projector and the crackle of old celluloid.

Looking round, I saw the room had turned into a scratchy-jumpy black-and-white print of a reality that had never existed.

Silently, I spoke: 'But the nightmare has only just begun! Last night, I dreamt I was in hospital! I dare not leave the flat, for I may be injured!' And a moment later, my view of Cluny was blacked out by the back of a board.

Cluny's board appeared a few moments after I'd failed to lip-read her words:

She threw herself at me, arms wide – and, in the process, knocked my head back against the wall so violently that I on the instant lost consciousness.

Saturday

When I came to, Nurse Smith was at my side, as were Cluny and two other women. Everything was hazy. I could hardly make out the women's faces. One of them looked familiar, but I couldn't place her.

'Where am I?' I said, and was relieved to find I could once again hear my words.

'Hove Hospital,' said Nurse Smith, attempting to suppress her emotion. 'You had a nasty knock on the head. You've been unconscious for two days.'

'How many nights?' I asked.

Nurse Smith looked puzzled, but no doubt she'd seen them through with me – squeezing my hand as the ECG beeped her the message of my heart.

'Who are you?' I asked the first new woman.

As I spoke, the haze cleared a little. I noticed that she had a baby in her arms which she was just starting to breast-feed.

'Don't you remember me?' she said.

I wanted to say *No*, but, at the moment I tried to speak, my mouth started to gush milk. The only way not to drown seemed to be to swallow, as fast as I could.

'I nursed you when you were ever so small and helpless. When I saw you small and helpless once more, I came back to be your Wet-Nurse again.'

The other women – Cluny, Nurse Smith, and the vaguely familiar one – gathered round the Wet-Nurse and cooed over the infant.

Still the milk kept flowing into my throat – until, just at the moment the Wet-Nurse's fat nipple was removed from the baby's mouth, it ceased altogether.

I felt an overwhelming sense of bereavement – as if the world had entirely lost meaning.

The Wet-Nurse put the baby on her shoulder and patted its back. An enormous burp erupted from deep within me, shortly followed by a gush of milky puke.

'There's a good boy,' said the Wet-Nurse to the baby.

Something in her tone was so reassuring that I, and the baby – who, by now, was fairly clearly another version of myself – began to bawl.

Waah!

The relief was immense. It was as if, for years, I'd been denying myself access to this wonderful sound I could make.

The gathered women smiled and, feeling myself deliciously appreciated, both me and baby-me fell asleep.

A few minutes later, I woke up. I felt totally enlivened. I wanted to crawl around, touch things, put them in my mouth.

'He's awake,' said the Wet-Nurse, looking down at her cherubic charge.

Cluny and Nurse Smith gazed at my by-proxy self as well.

But the vaguely familiar woman was now sitting on the counterpane holding my hand. She had a Mary Quant hairstyle and was wearing a bright orange miniskirt in Draylon.

'Who are you?' I asked.

She smiled, beatifically.

'Don't you remember me, either?' she said.

'No,' I said. 'Sorry.'

'You should know,' she said. 'No-one ever forgets their –'

And, just as her mouth formed the word, I knew what

it was going to be and joined her in saying, '– mother.' / 'MOTHER!'

'Yes,' she confirmed. 'I'm your mother just as I looked the day after you were conceived.'

Now that she said it, I could remember her – beautiful in the wedding photos, radiant in the honeymoon snaps.

'*I'm* the girl of your dreams,' she said. 'And I always will be.'

Just at that moment, Cluny stood up from the baby, turned round and confronted my mother.

'I disagree,' she said, '*I* am the girl of his dreams. He may want to sit there holding hands with you, but I'm the one he wants to spend the rest of his life with. I mean, he's hardly going to fuck you, is he?'

'What does that matter?' said Mother, gently but relentlessly. 'You see, he's already been inside me in a far more profound way than he'll ever be inside you.'

'Bitch,' shrieked Cluny, and grabbed my mother's lustrous helmet of hair.

'*Please*,' said Nurse Smith, instantly trying to intervene. 'Think of the baby.'

Cluny and my mother separated.

'He's mine now,' hissed Cluny. 'He'll never be yours ever again.'

'He'll always be mine,' cooed Mother.

I thought they were going to start back up, but just at that moment, in walked Anne and Lizzy. Lizzy had brought a basket of ripe English Pippins; Anne, a single-volume edition of *Das Kapital*.

'You can only stay for a short while,' said Nurse Smith. 'I'm going to have to sedate him very shortly.'

Sunday

When I saw Her first, I was standing in a strangely symmetrical garden. Everything around me – every straight-lined thing – plunged off towards an emphatic vanishing-point. The branches of the trees were loaded with formal-looking birds. They did not sing. In fact, the whole place was entirely silent. I was standing upon an elaborate mosaic in marvellous, marzipaneous colours. No wind was blowing, and the air smelt faintly of turpentine. She – she with a capital S – did not walk towards me, but somehow She seemed to draw nearer and nearer. It was as if She were on rollerskates, and someone was pulling Her along with an invisible rope. Her dress was of purest, palest blue. A golden light streamed from a source somewhere either above or behind Her face. Her eyes were downcast, Her demeanour modest. She had Her fingers ornately clasped to Her bosom, as if they were a bird's nest full of dainty, speckled eggs which She was carrying back to the tree from whence they had fallen. A smile of inner satisfaction, of pleasure greater than pleasure, curved Her exquisitely rendered lips.

I'd known who She was from the moment I caught sight of Her.

As She approached, I fell down upon my knees in simple adoration.

'Hail Mary,' I said, 'Mother of God.'

In my piety, I lowered my eyes to the mosaic. But, by some mysterious force, I felt them being lifted until I was once more gazing at Her.

She must have some message to convey to me, I thought – a message for the world.

My prayer was already faltering by the time I saw exactly what Her message was: She raised a single candle-white finger to Her perfect mouth, *shhhing* me.

I shhhed.

A slight crinkle of displeasure was discernible in the arch of Her brow. Perhaps She hadn't, after all, meant me to shut up completely.

'The Lord is with Thee,' I whispered.

'Oh, shhh,' the Virgin Mary said, with definite pique. 'Do you think I don't know that by now?'

'Oh,' I said, looking round, terrified. 'Where is He?'

'You mean —?' said the Virgin Mary.

'The Lord,' I said.

'He's with Me,' She replied. 'But then again, He's with you and everyone else, as well. That's His most essential characteristic.' She yawned the most delightfully small-mouthed yawn. 'You just can't get away from Him.'

'Well,' I said, 'if He's watching, I'm sure He won't be too happy if I don't sufficiently adore You.'

'Oh,' said the Virgin Mary. 'I'm bored of being adored.'

'God,' I said, involuntarily. The mosaic seemed to crumble a little beneath me, and get hotter.

'I'd be careful what you say around here,' said the Virgin Mary. 'Contrary to popular belief, He takes blasphemy rather seriously.'

I bowed my head again.

'Surely, Holy Mother, You can't be bored of being adored. Isn't it what every woman wants?'

'I suppose so,' said the Virgin Mary. 'But now and again it would be quite refreshing if someone just plain fancied Me instead.'

Here was a challenge. I started to get up off my knees, and

– at the exact same moment – the mosaic beneath me tumbled away.

I was beginning to fall through when, all of a sudden, the Virgin Mary miraculously took my hand and lifted me out of the scalding Infernal hole.

When She put me down again at Her side, showing no sign of physical strain, the grassy ground seemed firm enough.

'Nice try,' She said, 'but that particular sin's mortal.'

'Thank You and bless You, Holy Mother,' I said, resuming my adoration pose.

'Call Me Mary,' the Virgin Mary said.

With my head bowed, I could see down through the ruptured mosaic. A reddish light shone out through smoke that smelt horribly of brimstone. I heard the sound of fardistant screams.

'Come on,' said the Virgin Mary. 'Let's go somewhere equally unprivate.'

Again without walking, She led me towards a quiet bower slightly nearer the vanishing-point.

'Tell Me about sex,' the Virgin Mary said. 'You seem to have had rather a lot of it, this past week.'

The grass felt awfully spongy under my feet.

'I'm sorry, Holy Mother, but I'd rather not risk it.'

We had reached the bower. It contained a wide bench-like swing, entwined about with bright blue cornflowers. We sat down upon it, side by side.

'Put your arm around Me,' said the Virgin Mary. 'As if we were in the back row at a cinema.'

I reached my arm out, at which point a louder-than-ever scream came out of the Hell-hole in the mosaic.

'I'd love to,' I said. 'Honestly.'

The Virgin Mary looked sweetly peeved.

'I don't know why I even try any more,' she said. 'It's never going to happen.'

'I'm sorry,' I said, then tried to make amends. 'You are the girl of my dreams, though.'

'Well,' said the Virgin Mary. 'I suppose that will have to do.'

For a moment, we both sat with our separate thoughts.

'As there isn't anything you can do for Me,' the Virgin Mary finally said, 'is there anything I can do for you?'

'Oh, yes, Holy Mother,' I said. 'I'm sure I don't even have to tell You it. You must already know what I'm going to say.'

'Of course I do,' said the Virgin Mary. 'But humour Me for a moment, won't you?'

Even as the words formed in my head, I could feel Her tickling through my thoughts like a single, solitary beam of sunlight passing through a secluded waterfall.

'I'd like,' I said, 'a beach. An empty beach. Brighton beach would be perfect.'

'And are you sure you don't want anyone to be waiting for you *on* the beach?' the Virgin Mary asked.

'Yes,' I said. 'Quite sure.'

She smiled at me and I smiled back.

'But I would like them to be waiting for me when I get home.'

'What?' said the Virgin Mary, in pretend shock. 'You don't mean *all* of them.'

'All but one,' I said. 'Unfortunately.'

A Higher Agency

I am a writer; I write screenplays. You know, like for films before they are made.

I first became serious about this during the eternal summer of stoned fucking that followed my last term at Uni.

For five years I tried to interest agents and producers in my work – and, in all that time, there was no serious interest: I would send off customized letters, well-researched and personable; back, six months later, along with my now-totally-tatty script, would come a formula rejection.

About a year ago I finished what I felt was my best screenplay yet. Unfortunately, I am not at liberty to discuss it in any detail. I *can* say – I think – that it is set in West London, that it is very violent, very strange and that the ending still makes me cry.

When I finished the script I sent it off to the agent whose formula letters had always come back fastest. His name was Mr Harold Oliver, and he was a partner in the Sykes-Oliver Literary Agency. All I knew of Mr Oliver was his address, his promptness in reply and the thick black ink of his fluid signature. But I felt, somehow, that we had a relationship: he respected me, and I him.

At this time I was living in a top-floor bedsit half-way along a litter-strewn street just off the Shepherd's Bush end of the Uxbridge road. In the last days before I finished the script, I noticed a sign up in the window of a nearby Italian restaurant:

DISH–WASHER WANTED
APPLY WITHIN

I needed work, any work – the social were on my case big-time. My script had taken all of nine non-jobseeking months to write.

Straight after sending the script off from the Post Office, I went along to the Italian restaurant.

From the outside there was nothing special about it: a back-lit red and white sign above a large glass window with an aluminium-framed door in the middle.

As I couldn't afford to eat there I walked in and went straight up to the till.

'I'm here about the dish-washing job,' I said. 'If it's still going.'

The Co-Manager – whose real name I'm not at liberty to give – was, as it happened, working the till.

He was a dark-complexioned man, burly and broken-nosed, with no trace of an Italian accent.

'Do you have any experience?' he asked.

'Well, I've washed dishes before,' I said, jokily.

'How many?' he asked.

'I never counted them.'

'Roughly. How many at one time?'

I remembered a large dinner party at Uni, then multiplied by three.

'Thirty-six.'

'Do you have stamina? I need to know. I can't introduce you to the Manager if you haven't. Thirty-six isn't that many.'

'Well, it's all I've done. Take it or leave it.'

The Co-Manager leant over the till. 'Show me your hands,' he said.

I lifted them, palms upwards.

He made me turn them over then inspected my finger-nails very closely, one by one.

'Come with me,' he said.

He ducked out from behind the till and walked between tables to the back of the restaurant. Parting a beaded curtain with his boxer's hands, he led me into the noise and heat of the kitchen.

We approached a man in a dark suit who stood with his back to us.

'What do you think?' asked the Co-Manager.

The man glanced at me over his shoulder.

If possible, this man was even broader and more blunted-off than the Co-Manager.

'What do you think?' he asked back. He too had no Italian accent.

'It's been five days,' said the Co-Manager.

The broad man looked me up and down.

'Go with your instinct,' he said.

The Co-Manager put a hand on my shoulder and pulled me away.

'That is the Manager,' he said – and, even if I were at liberty to tell you more, which I am not, I never heard the Manager referred to by any other name.

The Co-Manager rumbled into my ear: 'Respect the Manager.'

'Does that mean I've got the job?' I asked.

'Come back tonight at seven.'

The Co-Manager walked me to the fire door and pointed the way back onto the Uxbridge road, past overflowing and sour-smelling dustbins.

'Come in the back way when you come back,' he said.

Just before I left he shook my hand – and I took this as a good sign.

Back in the communal hall of my bedsit building I saw that one of my ever-changing neighbours had left me a note – pinned up on the greasy corkboard by the phone.

CALL OLIVER SOON.

Another hand had added, in a different coloured pen:

and your mother too.

While I went to get Mr Oliver's number from my top-floor room, I left the payphone off the hook – hoping that this would warn everyone off from using it (and also, of course, prevent any incoming calls).

The payphone was still free when I got back downstairs.

I dialled, excited – no agent had ever phoned *me* before.

'Mr Oliver,' I said – and gave my name (which, as you'll already have guessed, I am not at liberty to give you).

'This script is just fantastic,' he said. I loved his low cigaretty voice straight off. 'I've already talked about it to some people,' he said. His voice made me think of Orson Welles and my dead-Dad and God. 'Interest is already firming up, I have to say – but we'll need to go to a second draft as soon as possible.' These were the words I had been waiting five years – and all my life – to hear. 'It would be an honour and a privilege to be your agent – and to make you very rich and very famous,' he said.

I had an erection, and I said: 'Yes, Mr Oliver. Please.'

'Call me Harold,' he said, and put the phone down.

As I had no-one else to tell I phoned my mother.

'Mr Oliver is famous throughout the industry,' I said. 'Everyone has heard of him.'

She said, 'Oh, really?' and 'That's nice' and 'Will you be coming home for Easter?'

I needed to do something to celebrate.

Back in my room I counted my money and decided that now – probably – I could afford a bottle of decent vodka.

I had honestly forgotten about the dish-washing job until I was walking past the Italian restaurant on my way back from the off-licence. In my joy, I had strolled past the first time without even seeing it.

Being a decent sort, or so I like to think, I didn't want to just disappear and never see them again – not when they'd been so kind as to take me on in the first place – so I decided I'd go in and tell them, Thank you very much, but I no longer need the job.

This time it was the Manager who, squat as an impacted British Bulldog, was standing behind the till.

'Didn't the Co-Manager tell you to come in the back way when you came back?' These were the first words he addressed to me.

'Yes, he did,' I replied, 'But –'

'You're early,' said the Manager. 'That means you're keen to start, does it?'

'Not really, you see –'

The Manager reached over the counter and grabbed the off-licence bag from my hands.

'Staff are forbidden from drinking on the premises,' he said. 'Unless expressly invited to by the Management.'

'No, this isn't for –'

'We can't have you dropping plates because you're pissed. Now, get in the back.'

'But I'm not working here,' I finally managed to say. 'I don't need the job.'

'You don't *need* the job?' the Manager said, turning overtly nasty for the first time. 'You don't *need* the job? Well, what if the job needs you?'

'You see, I've had a very lucky break. I'm going to –'

'I don't care *what* you've had, you agreed to do a job of work for us – in the back, now!'

I felt like turning round and walking out but the thought of all the money I'd spent on the vodka held me back. I decided that the Co-Manager might be a little more approachable.

After only a slight pause to see if the Manager would relent I went down the aisle towards the rear of the restaurant.

As I walked into the kitchen, the Chef was just barricading the fire door. The Co-Manager pressed his ear close to the phone. He looked at me as the beaded curtain fell back in place behind me.

'He said *that*?' he said. 'To *you*, the Manager?'

He shook his head ruefully. I'd seen actors do this in movies – this was the sadness before violence.

I skipped over to the sink, pulled on an apron and gloves, and started washing dishes.

Six hours later I was finished.

In all that time I'd hardly dared look over my shoulder.

I *had* listened, though – I had listened to the Chef shouting at the Waiters and the Waiters shouting at the Chef.

The Co-Manager had been there – occasionally on the phone, more often than not talking about me.

I had listened and cowered.

The Waiters had kept bringing me greasy crusty charcoaly dishes – dishes with cigarettes stubbed out in them – dishes with blood-soaked tissues on them – dishes with phlegm slopping across them.

Finally, when no more dishes came, I took off my apron and gloves and tried the back door.

'No, my friend,' came the Manager's voice. 'Come out *this* way. We're all having a night-cap.'

I turned to see his face poking broadly through the beaded curtain.

Out in the restaurant the Chef and the Waiters were sitting up and down on either side of a long table, smoking and drinking.

Bottles of House Red stood in pairs on the red gingham. My vodka bottle was present, too – intact and at the head of the table.

As I walked in there was a round of applause, led by the Manager. He picked a full glass up off the table.

'To the best bloody Dish-Washer we've ever had.'

'Hear, hear!' said everyone else, then applauded.

The Co-Manager came over and stuffed a wodge of crumpled notes into my hand.

'Great job,' he kept saying. 'Really great job.'

'Sit down,' said the Manager.

I took hold of my vodka and got ready to make my excuses.

'Please,' said the Manager, pulling back a chair – with just the hint of the hint of a threat.

I sat. The Co-Manager sat on my left-hand side, the Manager on my right. We sat.

The Manager poured me out a glass of House Red.

'Cheers,' he said.

'Cheers,' I replied, unable not to.

'Cheers,' everyone said.

We all took large loud glugs.

For a moment afterwards we just sat there, tired and smiling. Then the Co-Manager said, 'Speech.'

'Oh yes,' said the Manager. 'A wonderful idea.'

'Really,' I protested.

'Speech!' cried one of the Waiters. 'Speech!' chorused the rest.

'Go on,' stage-whispered the Co-Manager, nudging my elbow.

I stood up, unsteady on my feet through fear and exhaustion. My hand grabbed the vodka bottle for support. I looked down the two lines of brightly lit, heavily fleshed faces.

'Well,' I began, having no idea whatsoever what my speech was meant to be about. 'First of all I'd like to thank the Manager and Co-Manager . . .' There were lots of hear-hears: I seemed to be on the right track. '. . . for all their help and encouragement – and for giving me this great opportunity in the first place. And I'd also like to thank the entire Waiting Staff, each and every one of them, for their . . .' A word was fluttering round my head like an injured bird. I grabbed it. '. . . forbearance.' There was laughter and heavy-handed applause from the two Managers. 'I must also mention the Chef, whose innovative and expressive use of some of the most obscure areas of the English vernacular has kept me most entertained.' More applause. ('Most entertained!' gasped the Manager, as if I'd told the joke of the century.) God, I was almost enjoying this. 'And finally I'd like to say how much I've enjoyed working in this fine –'

'Enjoyed?' said the Manager, all hilarity gone.

'Past tense,' said the Co-Manager.

They both stood up. It was like being between two sides of beef in a refrigerator.

'Is leaving?' said the Manager.

'Thinks is leaving?'

'Yes,' said the Manager. 'But isn't.'

'How could he?'

'It's a vocation.'

'A gift from God.'

Again I looked down the table at the Waiters, at the Chef. They looked back – but not at me, at Judas.

'To leave would be a travesty.'

'Almost blasphemous,' said the Co-Manager.

'As near as makes no difference,' said the Manager.

'Look,' I said, 'I'm really sorry, but you'll have to find someone else.'

'There is no-one else,' said the Manager, almost distraught. '*You* are the Dish-Washer.'

'I'm a writer,' I said, weakly.

'What you do in your spare time is no concern of mine,' he said.

'A *full-time* writer.'

'Well, then,' he said, 'what have you been doing for the past six hours?'

'That's –'

'What have you been doing?' There was the hint again – and the sadness.

'Washing dishes.'

'Yes,' the Manager said. 'And what will you be doing for six hours tomorrow?'

I didn't dare hesitate.

'Washing dishes.'

Hilarity instantly returned. There was another round of toasts. My back was mercilessly slapped. Another grubby note somehow found its way into my pocket.

It was half-past two before I hit the cool quiet air of the Uxbridge road.

There was no time to work anything out on the short walk round the corner and home.

It was clear that, for some reason, the Managers had decided to make me stay on. Perhaps only until they found someone else, though it didn't seem that way.

I could always not go in the following evening – but somehow I felt sure that the Managers would make me suffer for this: the restaurant was on my route to the Tube station, the off-licence, the launderette, everywhere. I could always avoid it by walking round the block, but I would bump into them in the end – and it would be a very very hard bump. And the end might really be the end.

I could go and stay with my mother, but that was always a last resort.

Still undecided, I went to bed.

The next morning I woke up late – achy-armed and slightly hungover.

I tried to get started on the second draft of my script, but my brain just couldn't click into focus. Desperate, I went out for an inspirational walk.

As I hurried past the Italian restaurant, I saw that they had taken down the Dish-Washer Wanted sign.

That vacancy was filled.

Seven o'clock found me back in the kitchen.

I had been terrified going in, but the Managers greeted me like the proverbial prodigal, the Waiters called me by my first name and the Chef promised to think of a good nickname for me.

Eventually he came up with Emu – because, he said, I was good at keeping my head down. (He meant ostrich, but I didn't correct him.)

The hours sloshed past – dish after dish after dish.

The orders thinned out. The orders stopped.

Standing in the propped-open-by-a-broom fire door, the Chef had a cigarette.

In came the Co-Manager to pay me, filthy cash.

Out I was again in the cold air – free and not free.

This routine carried on for a week.

On the way home I would think of escaping; in the morning I would be unable to work; come evening I would be back in the kitchen.

My mother called but I didn't call back.

And then Mr Oliver rang.

'Hey,' he said, when I made it down to the payphone, 'how's that second draft coming along?'

'It's a bit difficult,' I said.

'Creative work is never easy. But the rewards . . .'

'No, you see – I've got this job I can't seem to give up.'

'What? You love it so much?'

'No, it's dish-washing. I hate it.'

'Why can't you just give it up?'

For a moment I thought I'd be able to control myself, then I started sobbing – right there in the communal hall.

Mr Oliver was very understanding. He asked me where the Italian restaurant was. He said he was sure the whole thing was a silly mistake. He mentioned someone very important he needed to consult.

When I asked him what I should do that evening, he said: 'Go in just as normal. But I promise you, it'll be the last time.'

God, did I hope it was.

My hands were raw from rubber and my elbows covered in cuts.

The Chef's emu-jokes had become more and more elaborate. Now, he reckoned, emus only stuck their heads in the ground because they loved taking it up the arse.

The Waiters were starting to booby-trap dishes with olive oil and broken glass and glue and faeces.

The Co-Manager was pinching my bottom and the Manager was ignoring me completely.

At about midnight, just when we were usually starting to turn customers away, my agent walked in.

I knew the moment he was there because he shouted my name in the loudest, lowest voice I'd ever heard.

I walked towards the beaded curtain, but the Co-Manager stepped into my path.

'Let us deal with this,' he said, and grabbed and squeezed my balls – hard, very hard indeed.

Winded and dizzy, I fell to the floor.

From this position I found I could see under the bottom of the beaded curtain and into the restaurant.

My agent, Mr Oliver, was standing beside a very tall, very thin man – a man I'd never seen before but who I assumed to be Mr Sykes. (Unless it was the other way round – which I soon found out it wasn't.) Mr Oliver was also tall and thin, but not so tall and thin as Mr Sykes. Both of them had skin that, in the dim light of the restaurant, looked luminously blue.

The Manager stood before them, barring their way into the kitchen.

I decided to stay down – it seemed the safest place.

Mr Oliver shouted my name again, loud and low.

Obviously, I didn't appear.

Mr Oliver and Mr Sykes conferred for a moment, then Mr Oliver called out to the Manager: 'I'm sure we can come to some arrangement acceptable to both parties.'

'The boy is mine,' said the Manager. 'I am not giving him up.'

'We have a prior claim,' said Mr Oliver.

'Do you?' said the Manager. 'Well, we have a stronger claim.'

From his inside pocket Mr Oliver produced a gun. 'Stronger than this?' he asked.

'Oh,' said the Manager. 'Much.'

As he said this I looked round and saw the Chef reaching for something far back in a steel cupboard: a double-barrelled shotgun. Once he'd grabbed it, he tiptoed over to the Co-Manager and handed it to him.

I looked back out into the restaurant. The Waiters and customers were clinging to the walls.

Mr Oliver hadn't moved.

But Mr Sykes was now also pointing a gun at the Manager, who had raised his hands over his head.

The Co-Manager quietly clicked the two firing-hammers back into position.

For the first time Mr Sykes spoke up: 'The boy is ours – give him back to us or face the consequences.' His voice was a strangely penetrating hiss.

'I'll tell you what I'm going to give you,' said the Manager, and dived to one side.

Immediately on cue the Co-Manager stepped through the beaded curtain and fired off his rounds. But Mr Oliver and Mr Sykes had been prepared for this. They were already diving for cover behind tables on either side of the aisle.

The Co-Manager, sensing his exposure, turned to throw himself back into the kitchen – but too slowly.

The first shot pumped through his shoulder. The second lodged in his gut. The third ripped open his throat.

Bits of the Co-Manager spatted down onto me where I still lay on the kitchen floor.

Hidden by the till from Mr Oliver and Mr Sykes, I could see the Manager pulling his pistol out of an ankle-holster.

'Mr Oliver!' I shouted. 'Be careful! He's armed!'

Then I felt the Chef sit down on top of me. For a moment he allowed me to examine my reflection in the broad blade of his favourite meat cleaver. 'Shut up,' he whispered.

The Co-Manager's blood was soaking up into my trousers, from my hips to my knees.

Out in the restaurant the Manager started firing. He was trying to cover himself as he made a dash for the kitchen.

The tactic failed miserably. Without him noticing, Mr Sykes had crept under one of the longer tables.

When Mr Sykes shot the Manager, he was practically aiming up his nose. And, if this was – in fact – where he *was* aiming, then Mr Sykes was a pretty good shot, for the nose, along with the chin and forehead, was the first part of the Manager to hit the ceiling.

As the Manager snapped forwards in total pain, Mr Oliver shot him a couple of times in the stomach. But somehow the Manager kept firing – completely at random, waving here and there.

The window at the front of the restaurant shattered.

Mr Oliver dodged from side to side, trying to outguess a blinded dying man.

A fifth bullet, a sixth – they all went wide.

Then, cleverly, Mr Oliver dropped to the floor. All the remaining bullets would go over his head.

But he hadn't reckoned on Mr Sykes, who – in an attempt to save Mr Oliver from further danger – had all this time been planting bullets up into the Manager's chest and guts. Now, though, he tried a shot to the ankle.

The Manager crumpled – and his last living bullet got Mr Oliver through the left eye.

There was a period of calm during which two of the customers dashed out the front door.

I was completely soaked in the Co-Manager's blood.

The Chef whispered in my ear: 'Stand up.'

I did so.

He pushed me through the beaded curtain and into the restaurant, the cleaver close to my throat.

'You can have the boy,' he said. 'Just let me have the restaurant.'

There was a silence. I looked for Mr Sykes, but he'd hidden again.

'That's all I want,' said the Chef. 'The restaurant.'

'Yes,' said Mr Sykes. 'We can do that.'

Mr Oliver groaned and died.

'Let him come forward,' said Mr Sykes, from somewhere on the left.

'I'm trusting you on this,' said the Chef.

He pushed me forwards.

Mr Sykes' voice hissed: 'Walk towards the door.'

I did, leaving bloody footprints behind me.

When I reached Mr Oliver, I stepped to one side so as not to tread on him or his blood.

Crack – and behind me the Chef went down.

The bullet must have missed me by nothing.

Crack – Crack – Crack.

The Chef slumped back through the beaded curtain and fell on top of the Co-Manager.

'Come on, boy,' said Mr Sykes, standing up from behind a table on the right and placing his thin hand on my shoulder. 'We've got to leave, quickly.'

'But the police –'

'You have work to do. We have to get away. To a safe place.'

'Where?' I asked.

He didn't reply until we were in the car, moving.

'You know,' he said. 'Your mother is very proud of you.'

I looked at him closely.

'Very *very* proud,' he said, deadpan.

On the Etiquette of Eye-Contact During Oral Sex

Posted: alt.sex.oral
Heading: New FAQ

Woman-on-Man[1]

Due to the physical construction of men, and the natural curiosity of women, it seems obvious that *accidental* eye-contact is far more likely during woman-on-man oral sex than woman-on-woman or even man-on-man. (See below.)

We, the authors, will therefore use this combination to examine the perils and pitfalls of a number of varied situations.

During Casual Sex

In our experience, we have come to regard this as potentially the trickiest of all situations. However, most of the most obvious difficulties are removed if one is aware – at the

---

1. We, the authors, have – for reasons that soon shall become obvious – decided to divide this section of *The Universal Guide for the Innocent and Unsure* into gender/gender-specific subsections. This policy should not be taken as implying a 'hidden agenda' of any sort. My co-editress and I are quite in agreement upon wishing to emphasize this point.

time of the fellatic act – that this is casual sex *qua* casual sex.[2]

To a certain extent, we feel, eye-contact during oral sex during casual sex doesn't matter at all. This is because no ongoing relationship is at this juncture being established. When one looks into one's casual partner's eyes, one is not looking into one's future. Therefore we should suggest that one should indeed look – as this will be one's only chance. Also, in casual sex, any clues as to the success or failure of one's performance are welcome. Remember, there may be no cosy post-fellatial chat during which to establish or confirm mutual satisfaction. It could just be bye bye baby bye bye.

At the End of a First Date

We feel that this is often the situation in which the stakes are highest. As whatever one does on a first date one will almost certainly be expected to repeat throughout the ensuing relationship. For years and years afterwards. For ever, maybe.[3] It is important, therefore, to establish in one's own mind a clear set of principles long before one has encountered the specific situation.

We would suggest that one writes down one's 'ground rules' on a piece of paper and gives them for safe-keeping to

2. If one is in some doubt as to whether one will see the sexual partner again, then one should refer to the following sub-subsection: At the End of a First Date. But one should not, of course, refer to this sub-subsection during the sexual act itself. Reading during oral sex was permissible only in the Age of Empire – and then only the Letters and Obituary Pages of *The Times*.
3. My co-editress, in particular, would like to emphasize this point – although I begged her not to, I really did.

an intimate friend – or perhaps to one's mother. Then, following the date, one's related obedience or disobedience can objectively be gauged.

We realize that many things occur 'on the spur of the moment', but one must be careful not to be pricked by that spur. (Not, of course, unless one wants to be. In regards to this, consult the sections elsewhere – particularly those entitled On the Etiquette of Screaming at Orgasm and On the Etiquette of Horseplay and Pony Clubbing.)

At the End of a Second, Third or Fourth Date

Clearly, if one reaches this stage without having performed oral sex, one is hoping for a serious committed relationship. We would strongly suggest that you discuss the matter with your potential partner beforehand. Perhaps in the restaurant, over coffee and liqueurs. If one is in a group of close friends, or even merely within hailing distance of a couple of vague acquaintances, then the opinions of one's fellow diners are always worth gleaning.

At the End of a Fifth to a Thirteenth Date

One should, by now, have a fairly clear idea of the potential partner's interest or lack thereof in oneself. For the would-be fellatress: if he has up until now shown no signs of desiring sexual intercourse, then he is probably impotent or carrying an STD. We would advise you to steer well clear. For the fellatee: what are you waiting for? A papal dispensation? Hannukkah to end?

In an Established, Committed Relationship

In many ways, this section should be redundant. The sexual behaviour of any couple is – in the vast majority of cases – established during the first eighteen to twenty hours they spend together in bed.[4] So, as far as eye-contact is concerned, either one already does and will continue to do so or one never has and never will.

However, in an attempt to galvanize a post-spark relationship, one may start doing things in bed (or outside it) that are unprecedented. Offering oral sex may turn out to be one of these. Making eye-contact during oral sex might be another. Winking or making a comic "gagging expression", we would advise strongly against.

On Your Honeymoon

In the words of Primo Levi: If not now, when?

During Extramarital Sex

All extramarital sex is, we feel, defined in relation to the intramarital sex which it is *not*. It is likely, therefore, that one's instincts will be to compensate with one's adulterous partner for what is lacking with one's tedious partner. We have no major problem with this. (Consult the section On

---

4. Including sleep, but excluding holiday intercourse. This involves two entirely different people to the ones you are at home. Two nicer and more exciting people, frankly.

Leaving No Clues Behind Even if Your Partner *is* a Forensic Pathologist or Sherlock Fucking Holmes.) However, one should be aware that a certain amount of honesty (or very expert deception) is always required when looking into another human being's eyes. If one is conducting an affair in which one is lying to one's partner about one's marital state then it may be advisable either to avoid eye-contact altogether (for fear they should see one's guilt) or to practise in the bathroom mirror (for a few minutes, say, every other day).

After the Birth of Your Firstborn

After childbirth, certain difficulties are almost bound to occur in sexual relations. We have found that the most common one to be involved with oral-sex eye-contact is the desire to bite the penis off out of hatred for the immense pain which that member has inflicted upon one. If one believes this to be a possibility, then one had better avoid eye-contact altogether. The look on that smug sperm-slinging bastard's face may be more than you can stand without immediately chomping his dangly bits off. [5]

During Sex with Your Doctor
(or Any Professional Man)

Of course, we acknowledge that sex in this relationship will be a total power-abuse trip. And surely most of the pleasure to be had out of such a desktop kinkfest will be to do with 'looking up' to the professional, as one did to one's father. (See the subsection entitled During Sex with a Blood

5. My co-editress is nodding in agreement. She has a fine set of gnashers.

Relation.) We[6] strongly advise you gaze long and hard into his steely blue eyes.

During Sex with a Member of a Religious Order

Supplication is a major part of all the world's religions. Therefore, to look adoringly up into the eyes of any of its celebrants, whilst at the same moment tonguing their circumcised or uncircumcised love salami, will drive them wild with blasphemous desire. A must.

During Sex with a Blood Relation

Fathers, uncles, brothers, cousins, second cousins, it makes no difference. Incest is a consciously committed sin and an illegality to boot. To hide from consciousness of it, whilst performing it, is immature and petty. Gaze deep, sickgirl. What the hell – you're already burning.

During Sex with an Animal[7]

The mechanics of the thing rules this out in the case of most animals – unless some pretty damn ingenious use of mirrors is made. We would suggest that this is only worth while if one finds it, in fact, the whole point of the sex in the first place.

6. My co-editress in particular suggests this. Which I find slightly worrying.
7. Had we not received a great deal of mail on this subject following our first posting, we would not think it worth mentioning.

During Sex with a Family Pet

While the issue of the greater intimacy of the relationship may be worth considering, we would still refer you sick puppies back to the section entitled During Sex with an Animal.

During the Making of a Hardcore-Porn Video

Yes, definitely.

But not only that. In this situation it is imperative that one also make eye-contact with the eventual viewer, through the intermediary which is the video camera. The viewer's pleasure in one's performance will be enhanced a hundredfold if one transfers to them via one's glinting gaze one's own intense delight in the act.

During an Orgy

What is the point of an orgy, we ask, if not to see and be seen engaging in depraved sexual activity? A person with their eyes closed at the orgy is like a blindfolded blind person, alone, in the National Gallery, at night, when all the lights have been turned off and the pictures removed. Get a grip.

In a Public Place

It is always advisable in this situation to keep one's eyes out for members of the constabulary. The fellatee may, we admit, be in a better position to perform this task than the fellator. However, vigilance should not be allowed to impinge upon pleasure.

With the Lights Off

Don't be silly.

During Sex in the 69 Position

Join the circus, freaks. (You're obviously living in the Hall of Mirrors, anyway.)

A Further Note for the Short-Sighted

The wearing of glasses during oral sex is a moot point between us, the editors. I myself feel that it is a good thing – particularly in situations where the fellator is rôle-playing (as secretary, nun, school-teacher). My co–editress, who has just popped out to walk the dog, asserts that the many advantages of contact lenses should not be overlooked. But she's wrong you know – utterly wrong.

Man-on-Woman

In most cases the sub-subsections above deal perfectly adequately with any given situations – being written to deal with the generalities rather than the specifics.

Woman-on-Woman

Given the difference in male and female anatomy, it is far less likely that accidental eye-contact will occur. A certain effort – a certain straining of both necks – is required to achieve a woman–on–woman gaze.

The innate structural equality of the relationship establishes a further balance. Eye-contact may be less of a turn-on, given that the power thing isn't as important (unless artificially created) and there isn't quite as much to look at, narcissistically speaking. (This, we have to admit, is another moot point. But some people like looking at clouds and some hills.[8]) However, eye-contact may be more of a turn-on, given that one is – in a sense – doing exactly as one would be done by.

Man-on-Man

The doing-as-one-would-be-done-by point also holds true here. For anyone requiring further clarification, we would refer you to the popular website Tip-Top Tips for Top-Tip Licks.

---

8. And some like both. But my co-editress hasn't yet come back with the dog, and it's almost two days . . .

The Audioguide

¶ Allow us to welcome you to the Gallery of the Museum of Your Head. We hope that this audioguide will enrich the experience you have whilst visiting our gallery, which is also your Gallery. At the end of the tour please return this Audioguide to the Museum Guard sitting behind the desk beside the EXIT door. If you have any further questions relating to the Gallery, or to Your Head, please do not hesitate to ask. And please also if at any time you feel like stopping the tape and taking the time to pause and reflect without our voice – voices – incessantly describing and iterating and reiterating and delimiting in your ears – please feel free to attempt to do so. Of course, our voice – voices – will not go away – they never do, do they? And if the Museum Guards observe you progressing through the Museum – or the Gallery – with the headphones – call it what you will – off, then you will be objected – excuse me – you will be ejected from the Museum – with all impossible haste – the Museum of Inside-Your-Head – with all unnecessary violence – and now we come to the first room. ¶ Room Number 2 – Here we have a series of works, thematically grouped under the heading – what you will – "Hearts & Flowers" – this is a cool meadow-land rather like the Alps through which poets and composers –

notably Mahler but also Bruckner – might wander at their
ease – Wordsworth, for instance – once – in hopes of
finding again the fresh-bursting springs of inspiration – the
works contained within this room – the works' outing –
these works are so-to-speak – hypocrites – the public face of
your Head – as if – as if, indeed, there is any public display
to the contents of Your Head, except in polite
conversation: for instance, with your mother – talking with
your mother – in which case, this room – Room Number 2
– we're talking – this room would be the room to which
you referred – we're talking with your Mother – this room
has hardly any real relevance to the rest of Your Head –
what do we talk about? – it is, in fact, an entire lie – entirely
untruthful – but it is necessary for you to possess the idea of
such a room as this in order that you not scream merely –
she tells us things about you – scream when you are asked a
simple question by your lover, for example, such as, 'What
were you thinking of, just then?' and you – in this situation
– in this fix – will play for time, saying, 'When?' and they,
he or she, will say, 'Just now, when you were looking at
me?' – she tells us about you at school – And you reply
– Your Mother does – referring to Room 2 – about the
changing rooms – 'I was thinking about how beautiful you
looked.' On the wall facing you immediately is a still-life or
nature morte, *Daffodils in blue vase on red tablecloth in sunlight
near Riviera in France circa 1910*. To your left – oh, *Daffodils
etc.*, is by a minor-happier follower of Van Gogh – to the
immediate left of this is *Abstract restful work in pastels*. On the
far wall is *Landscape: My homeland in all its glory* – we're still
in the Changing Rooms – a splendid urgent splurgent
emergent work – and here is *The happy relationship I'm
having at the moment* – oh, it's handholdy and lovecuddled

up in there – there is astringency, however, for further
developments see Room 3 – how long have we been in the
Changing Rooms, now? – and here is – with your mother,
with your mother – here is the largest work in this room
The rewarding and fulfilling job I do – it's a gusher – it shows a
desk, moddled mollycoddled modelled out of excreta – dark
brown and light – just in case your mother asks if you're
still having trouble digesting – the energy upkeep – and you
can show her by reference these lovely solid grown-up
healthy healthy – flush – turds that you do now – these days
now – no eating disorder, no excreting disorder – spash
– splash – splashflush – because of course she may ask – her
voice echoing off the tiles in the showers – 'What have I
told you?' – DECENCY – the smallest work in Room 2 –
Room *Number* 2 – Room *Bumber* Two – INDECENCY – for
we're nothing but clear, here – the smallest room, it is – and
hence, it has a pure white canvas entitled *Isn't the weather
nice/awful?* Alternate title or theme for this entire room, The
Nice Place – Niceness – this painting of clouds is by
Constable; not the famous Constable, unfortunately Your
Head cannot afford originals – everything here in the
Changing Rooms – everything in the Gallery is,
unfortunately, for example, a reproduction, a copy, a fake,
or at best a work either studio/workshop of, circle of,
follower of, manner of, after, the mood-artist concerned –
the Moog artist – the Constable in question here is actually
Police Constable Audrey Wilson, of whose paintings
no-one has ever said anything but that – beyond – her
paintings are paintings, they fill the canvas – it *is* canvas –
from top to bottom and from side to side – they function
as they are meant – minimally – to function – minimally
– to function – and that is all that ever *has* been said of them

– mummily. ¶ Walking slowly out of Room Two –
strolling, for example – we enter Room 3, a far lighter affair
– Here on display is kitsch – we are suffering from – 'we'
meaning you – suffering from a certain amount of anxiety –
we don't like repetition, do we? – anxiety plus happiness
placed under scrutiny has a tendency to produce works of
kitsch – here is a series of cartoons entitled *The emotions
falsified* by Waldo Dizziness and his studio – it is not known
whether Waldo himself ever actually set eyes upon these
particular cartoons or, in fact, upon his studio – and Waldo
Dizziness may himself be entirely made-up – here we have
Mock-anger, Faux-jealousy, Amour-à-la-Ursatz, Fake-hate –
again – mothermother – these are presentable to the general
viewing public viewing, but if you place your face closer to
the paper you will see that – up against the wall – that the
cracks – cold against the tiles of the shower wall – the
cracks are beginning to zag in the hencebackward smooth
surface – for your greater pleasure the Inside-Your-Head
Museum/Gallery would like to introduce some background
music onto our – here are the gentle lulling strings of
muzakians Autumnal Reverie – the puppies multiply on
the wall to your left – not sexually – not by mating –
individually – cold – by budding – like amoebas –
amoemarimbas – all of them by Geoff Coons – on your
right is something we would advise you to ignore – of
course, you've already seen it, haven't you? – you little
tinker – but why is a crucifix – a Buddha – Mohamet – the
Torah – why are these things here? – "You still go, don't
you?" – you still say you go, at least – if you look around
the edges, you will see the bulbs and fluourescence –
fluourescenes – also, a slot for entering coins – your religion
these days is entirely hypocritical or midnight – your

requests these nights are entirely craven or petrified – we
are impatient – on the floor. ¶ Into Room 4 – which is
dark – the wet floor – This is more like it, more like You –
like *you*? – like you – seeping through the cracks in the
floor – it is dark dark dark – the cracks between the tiles
– we can't see very far – the tiles of the shower – in fact we
can't see your hand in front of our face – the shower in the
Changing Room – s – and so we advise you to stumble
forward – s – in as straight a line as possible – ss – the
changing rooms in your school – towards the dim glow –
sss – the school in your area – where did you lose your
gorm? – in the middle distance – in your village – which
may or may not be the door – in your town – we're not
exactly sure – your city – there are, it has been conjectured,
artworks upon the walls of Room Four but no-one has ever
dared walk off away from the dimness into the dark in order
to find them and feel their frames and forms, for, of course,
no-one comes into their own Head – the Museum-Theatre
of their own Head – equipped with a torch – you are nearer
to it, now – this is the room you refer to when you feel that
life isn't worth living – obviously you feel it *is* – worth
living – because you are still being drawn on by the dimness
– the crudeness – the light at – the crudeness of the conceit
– and here it comes now. ¶ Out, and into Room Six –
there is no Room 5 – room-size – you have sunk entirely
through the floor of and are now beneath the floor, in
whatever is beneath the floor of – in Room 6 there are very
interesting paintings on the walls and sculptures in the
middle of the floor, perhaps the most interesting works in
the entire collection of In-Your-Head but unfortunately
you are distracted from them – that person – that presence
– because they're there, aren't they? – over there – that

presence, that person – wandering idly around grotesquely idly the gallery of your head – the paintings are dark and light oblongs – the sculptures are spikes and blobs, upon which you are unable to focus – approach them – all your senses are directed toward – s – that person – for you, sir, male; for you, madam, female; for you, sir, female; for you, madam, male – I think that just about covers it – get close – they are wearing the clothes to entice – get clues – the line of their body suggests the greatest lovemaking, conversation, game of chess – whatever you desire is there, gratifyingly – if *only* you could see their face! – for they are looking closely at all the paintings on the wall in the Gallery of 'Your Head' – and it is terrible – from them they must be learning all about you – the pictures – but they must know all about you, anyway – and the sculptures on the floor in the museum 'Of Your' head – they must know because they are here already – in in-your-head in your head – they are learning about you – under the floor – even to even be here, they must love you – love – ssss – they are loving you and not even knowing it's you they are loving – approach closer – see how they move in long and short lines – this is the person you have always lived to be loved by – oh believe you lived to be beloved by her-him/him-her – they are walking slowly away – he-she/she-he – your beloved and they don't even know you – please eject the tape-cassette and turn the tape-cassette over, please – slowly but still somehow managing to move faster than you – you're running to catch them – you can run – you're running in the Museum – PLEASE EJECT THE TAPE-CASSETTE AND TURN THE TAPE-CASSETTE OVER, PLEASE! – a Guard intervenes – you shouldn't run in a Gallery, not even in Your Head – 'It is dangerous,' says the Guard –

48

'For your own safety, please refrain from running in the Museum of In Your Head.' – there is an entrance, an exit, a door – through it goes your love, you old romantic – you go after them – exiting Room 6 – never to go back – never to see the art that for all you know may or may not be on the walls and floors. ¶ Room Seven is empty – Room 7 is *not* empty – but your beloved is somehow not in Room 7 – impossibly – you old romantic, you – you go back into Room 6, where Your Beloved still strolls unknowing of you and who you are (*their* Beloved) with their face turned away from you and of course you pointlessly run but slowly they elude you and even as you sprint towards them they are walking through the opposite door out they go apparently into Room 4 again but you follow them out of Room Six only to find yourself back in the emptiness of Room 7 – crushed – for a desperate experiment, you zigzag across in and out of room 6, no longer longingly looking at your beloved-who-eludes, no, running in terror from the impossibility of Room 7 to the greater impossibility of Room 7 again – running between the twin impossibilities of Room 7.1 and Room 7.2 – after four or five times you decide your head is your head and has ever and anon been odd and you've always been what people have often seen as an awkward sod. ¶ Room 7 is music merely, the soothe of the good life, an installation of sorts – with a camera upon the wall in the crannyspider Y of the corner. ¶ Room Eight shows the emptiness of Room 7, as viewed through the camera – although, in fact, for example, there is some time-lapse, as you can see yourself, yourself just leaving ¶ you go back into Room 7 and wave at the camera, smiling – then ¶ duck back into Room 8 to see yourself waving and smiling at the camera back in Room 7 a few seconds beforehand –

this is good – this is your favourite work so far – you
wave ¶ and return ¶ a few times more – you're enjoying
this – until the time-lag grows and you see yourself – no –
coming in and exiting and you get lost as to where you are
and how far back and whether you're catching yourself the
time before or the time before that – disconcerted, you stop
and watch, waiting for your enterexiting to stop – it doesn't
– *get out now*! ¶ Room 9 – you are attacked – a form that
vaguely resembles your Beloved is all over your face with a
wetness like something cold and slimy being dragged slimy
yet gritty over your face cold like slug mixed with sand and
mixed with placenta mixed with dead insects mixed with
thick white snot – the curtain parts on either side of your
face as you try to bat your way through, flannelled, in the
baby bath, in the school showers again, into Room 10. ¶
Relief – the relief of room ten – it is patterned that is about
all we feel it necessary to tell you – as you begin to walk
across it you are excited but your excitement soon turns to
boredom – it is a desert of abstraction – even missing the
beloved was better than this, even the gritty slime was
preferable to this – you are in an installation called
*Milliseconds Seconds Minutes Hours Days Weeks Months Years
Lives* – you made it yourself, during your nihilist period –
more accurately: your nihilist coffee-break – there are
stripes of black and white running entirely through it – top-
to-bottom&side-to-side – but strangely you never catch
the vertical or the horizontal lines crossing – at least from
this room you have a choice of doors – Room Eleven and
Room Twelve, presumably – you go left. ¶ Out onto a
stage where the performance has just finished and the
applause – oh the applause! – it's so prolonged – and it's for
you – and you are on the stage – it's your performance –

the smiling faces – you were great – and you walk back into room 10 as they cry encore encore and you don't know what to do – what can you do again that they loved so much last time? – you re-enter as the acclaim continues – huge – you oblige with a little soft-shoe shuffle – you can't tapdance – the ovation ascends – you sing a note, badly – la! – the cries get louder yet – you back out, bowing – though it seems to make no difference whether you bow or not – you try Room Twelve just for a change. ❡ Here the crowd is throwing things and booing – they are hissing – stamping their feet – you stand, bewildered – you begin to recognize faces and realize it is the same audience as in room 11 – you back out, narrowly avoiding being hit by a rotten courgette – jeté. ❡ Across in Room Eleven the audience still loves you – the same people – your old maths teacher, for example – they applaud you – acclaim you – but that's how it is here – hurrah in one room and howl you down in the next – in the Theatre of In Your Head – for no apparent reason – for safety's sake, and for ego's, you go through the door at the opposite end of the stage in Room 11. ❡ It is pure Self-Disgust – you can't see anything for occupation – apart from the preoccupation of looking at yourself – the walls and floor of the room and probably the ceiling are your own back and arms and legs – as you walk – stumble – out into the middle of the room you feel yourself walking up your own nauseating back, and in the feeling of that feeling you feel small footsteps up the back of your back – you retch – you wretch – you back out of out of on your back – you return to ❡ the applause which salves you – just before you left you noticed a door at the opposite end of the room of self-disgust – perhaps Room Thirteen? – but maybe you've left numbers behind – you saw a door – the

ovation restores – out into room 10 – ¶ then dash across
room twelve, the missiles missing – ¶ into pure pleasure – it
is love – Self-Love – you are stroking the nerves inside
yourself with a warm, soft wave of delight – as you move
forward – s – you feel a shiver within your groin – it's too
much – you demand maximum contact, maximum
stimulation – it's not enough – you lie down on the floor –
you like lying down on the floor – the pleasure inside you
lengthens, and within that pleasure a smaller pleasure lays
itself down – your clothes feel removed – Adamic, Evine –
you squirm against your squirming – your half-closed eyes
see a door on the other side of the room – the far side – so
far away – it hardly seems worth the crawl – but if you go
it's only to see if there is the possibility of anything better
than what you already have . . . – what you have having
awakened you to the possibility of better betters than you
had previously imagined being able to imagine – it is
perpetual growing ripening orgasm as you slide across the
floor – moving like a nymph over a nymph – there can
surely be nothing beyond this delight – out the other end
door and you ¶ start to worry – where are you? – you
worry that if you don't go back and see what you would
have found through the door at the other end of the room
of Self-Disgust – if you never go through that door you will
never know what's through that door and if you never
know you'll never know if it could have been an even
better better than that – that pure pleasure you've already
found. ¶ You crawl back across your sensual, sensuous self ¶
sprint past the hate-audience ¶ round the tedious corner ¶
and stroll past the audience-*d'amour* ¶ into the self-disgust
room. ¶ It's so creepy you can hardly move – but you go
forwards – force yourself – somehow – and finally make it

through – over – the fresh flesh field into the new room.
❡ Where you worry about what has happened to the room
of self-love whilst you've been away – perhaps it's
disappeared – things *that* perfect never last – it's much nicer
than this worry – there is a single door at the end of the
Worry Room, black and upright – you worry about what's
behind it – but you worry more about the disappearance of
the Room of Self-Love – you turn ❡ and hurrycrawl back,
back through over-determined self-disgust ❡ applause ❡
Room dull 10 ❡ anti-applause ❡ self-love is still there, self-
love is still there – you stay awhile a long long while – you
crawl out merely for respite into ❡ The Worry Room – at
the end of it is the door you noticed before – immediately
you begin to worry whether this Worry Room is the same
as the other Worry Room – you worry that if you go
through this door you might never find what's through the
door in the other Worry Room – it might be like the
applause & anti-applause, the self-love & self-disgust – it
might be like that only for the rest of your life – and so you
go back but first you leave something of yours on the floor
to the left/right of the entrance to the Worry Room #1
conjectural. ❡ You hurry back – through self-love etc
❡ ❡ ❡ as fast as you can go. ❡ In the Worry Room # 2
Conjectural the thing you left before is still there but is it
the same thing maybe it isn't maybe it was there all along &
you just never noticed it – so you mark it, the thing, scratch
it – and ❡ you ❡ rip ❡ back through to Worry Room #1 ❡
where you find the thing and the thing is marked just as
you marked it when you marked it – and suddenly all your
worry evaporates – fizzes off – there is only one Worry
Room and that you will always be able to find your way
back into the Room of Self-Love – you in fact ❡ ❡ ❡ ❡ go

back into the room of Self-Love for another lengthy session
– the Gallery is closing – I'm afraid it's that time – late –
later than you think – THE MUSEUM IS CLOSING! ¶ You go
back into the Worry Room – solitary single unique, you're
sure – worried you'll get locked in the Gallery of the
Museum of In-Your-Head but also secretly hoping that
you'll get locked in so that you can spend a whole night in
the self-love room – you go to the EXIT Door, what do you
expect to find through the EXIT door? – you expect to find
yourself back at the start of the cassette-tape of the
Audioguide of the Gallery of the Museum of the Theatre
InYourHead – you expect also a reference to a book, a
book you have been reading but which has never referred
to itself & has instead pretended to be an Audioguide – you
expect this referring now to refer also to itself – you expect
these self-references to go on for quite some time and to
become rather boring – you also expect to be presented
with the conceit of 'the rest of your life' – indeed –
whatever – for example – for the rest of your life – if you've
got this far – you have no choice – everything else you do is
framed by – named by – claimed by – defamed by – the
happycrappy – framing – maiming device – crude and
conceited – of 'The Audioguide of the Gallery of the
Museum of In Your Head' – you expect you expect you
expect a Gift Shop – you expect the tiles in the shower in
the changing rooms in your school in your town in your
time in your childhood – you expect your mother – you
expect the Guard sitting behind the desk beside the EXIT
door – they are there – they are waiting for you to give
them the Audioguide – so the gallery can finally close – sssss
– you expect them, him or her, to be your doppelgänger, in
an ill-fitting uniform – expect away! – but whatever else

you might expect, you know for certain that you will –
Please leave the Gallery, the Gallery of the Museum of the
Theatre of the Audioguide In Your Head is now Closing –
you know for certain – Please *leave* the Gallery, the Gallery
of the Museum, the Museum of the Theatre, the Theatre of
the Audioguide, the Audioguide In Your Head – you will
hear these words in your head, "And you opened the EXIT
door out of the Museum Gallery Theatre Audioguide of
your head and you –" And you hand over your Audioguide
to the Museum Guard sitting behind the desk beside the
EXIT door. ¶ And you – ¶

Map-Making
among the Middle-Classes

90 G4

Along with the dinner-party invites, Josh Withers had enclosed a photocopied page of the A–Z. (Thick black arrow. We Are Here. Exclamation mark. Exclamation mark.) The location of their, his and wife Selina's, new house (Putney) was much much better than their old (Balham). This, rather than any anticipated difficulty in his guests finding the place, was why Josh had found it necessary to provide them with maps. (It was April. Tonight was their first entertainment; these, their closest friends.) There was little danger they would get lost, either whilst driving (Michael and Fumiko) or walking from the Underground (Ian). However, he wanted to be quite sure that they knew, before they arrived, *just* how close his new house was to the Thames and *just* how far from the South Circular. This stunning location would therefore form the sole topic of conversation for at least some percentage of the evening. The time remaining, or so Josh hoped, would be almost entirely spent in babytalk – after, that is, Selina had spread the glad tidings of their much-attempted and finally achieved pregnancy. His wife had *insisted* that she be the one to make the announcement, and as Selina rarely insisted upon anything – and then seemed always to choose utterly trivial points on which he could not possibly consider capitulating – he had decided to indulge her. Their glory would therefore be delayed, fudged. Howsoever, his would be the greater part: she was 28, he 41.

What Josh *did* in order to be able to afford an almost-riverfront townhouse in Putney was obscure even to Selina. As far as she could tell, he made money through the time-dishonoured method of making money make money.

Earlier in his life/career, Josh had been more adventurous with his capital. During the late '80s, in the broking heart of The City, he opened a luncheonette called 'Wimps'. But no-one got the joke (at least, not his intended clientèle), and the 'whole concern' went 'belly up' due to 'lack of proper financial backing'. Following this failure, Josh had given up on both serious entrepreneurship and on anything approaching a sense of humour.

SE16

The first of Josh and Selina's guests to set out for their dinner-party was, logically enough, the one who lived furthest away: Ian Flaherty, 37. He had recently split up with his very non-serious girlfriend, Connie, 23, and for the previous fortnight had been pretending, to himself as much as to others, that he lived in dread of the coming evening's delights. In actual fact, he was secretly looking forward to renewing his circuitous courtship of Selina. She was fair game: Josh was utterly incapable of flirting with anyone. This, Ian somehow knew, was why Selina had married him. Their last serious encounter had taken place during Josh and Selina's Christmas party. But Ian's memory of the entirety of that evening's events was clogged in cobwebs of frozen vodka.

Just before he set off, Ian had been working on a paper. He was an interdisciplinarian, a sociologist, whose subject was the interaction between people and architectural spaces (and, reciprocally, between architectural spaces and people). Ian's main contribution to knowledge – so far – had been the slight modification of an older colleague's theory as to why so many 'young people' went to 'raves' to 'large it' to 'techno music'. The reason for their attendance, the colleague (who had never clubbed, taken E, or listened to more than two minutes of bangin' happy hardcore) speculated, was that – in England's office-bound post-industrial society – the 'young people' were attempting nostalgically to re-create the conditions of a Victorian factory floor. He cited as evidence a club in Blackpool called 'The Furnace'. Ian's slight modification of this theory (more accurately described as a wholesale trashing) suggested that, as the 'young people' were perceiving their environment through the virtual reality (spot the post-trend) of drugs, a straightforward sociohistorical interpretation of the club environment was impossible. Far closer to the truth (though he avoided that particular word with great scrupulousness) was that attendance at 'The Furnace' and other similar clubs, combined with the ingestion of randomly bought and dubiously concocted chemicals, was a metaphysical gamble: to go to a club was to enter purgatory, and by the end of the evening one might end up either in Heaven or in Hell. Ian did not mention, in his article, that Heaven usually took the form of a sweaty seventeen-year-old shop-assistant's bedsit, and Hell was a five-deep scrum of rained-upon munchie-mad Mancunians in front of an about-to-close kebab van.

UPSTAIRS BEDROOM

Josh finished tying his shoelaces, stood up and looked at himself in the full-length mirror. He was thinking about Selina. He had found himself married to her after indulging the idlest of curiosities – a desire to know exactly *how* unattractive she would look without clothes on. (She *would* be unattractive, of that he'd been certain; once she was naked, unorthodox patches of bristly brown hair would be revealed – her eyebrows promised this quite explicitly.) His courtship of her had been, almost, a series of bets with himself: Could he really ask out such an obvious social and sexual inferior? Would he be able to endure the tedium of her secretarial conversation? Had he the sheer willy-power, during sex, in her disgusting flat, to maintain a facetious erection? Was he brave enough to resist fleeing in the face (podgy) of her mother? Could he get through the wedding ceremony without laughing out loud at the obscenity of it all? Yet, at some level, he was aware that he was the only person laughing at the joke he had made of his life.

His worry now, though, was that somehow Selina had overheard him – had got the joke (the joke that was on her, the joke that *was* her). Perhaps pregnancy had gifted her with the necessary added insight. Or perhaps the knowledge of his impending fatherhood had caused his deadpan to crack. Whatever it was, he sensed her sometimes, in bed, looking sideways at him – trying to decide if he were asleep or pretending to be asleep. And as he was only aware of this whilst pretending, it was fairly certain she also did it whilst he was unfeignedly sleeping. This thought worried him.

CIRCLE LINE

Ian felt like getting very drunk this evening. He was taking along two bottles of insultingly bad red wine. Whatever Selina served up as a starter or a main course, he knew one thing was certain: he would be the afters (not, though, a sweet). Gooseberry was inevitable, double gooseberry; but gooseberry fool or gooseberry crumble? If the alcohol took him up, he would be foolish. Proposals of marriage would be issued; encouragements – only quarter-unserious – to elope. If the alcohol took him down, he would crumble. The dinner table would be invaded by his well-known *alter ego*, The Oracle of Nihilism.

He thought he might lose either Josh-and-Selina or Michael-and-Fumiko as friends. It wasn't clear to him if this was something he would really mind. Although, on principle, he liked all of them as individuals (particularly Selina, to whom the most fervent marriage proposals would be issued), the structures of their existing social interactions – the condescension of their patronage – made it inevitable that, over the lengthening period of his bachelorhood, he would come to despise them.

Would tonight be conclusive? He really didn't himself know – and that was because he really didn't know himself.

To only very few is it given to predict their own unpredictability. Among these lucky souls are drug addicts (for whom it is chemical) or accountants (for whom it is rigidly seasonal: Christmas party, summer holiday).

He sat back in his seat on the Tube. Only another half an hour to go. He considered cork-forcing one of the bottles with his thumb.

KITCHEN

Selina was taking the opportunity of the onions for a good weep. Nowadays, the only places she could with impunity cry were her therapist's greenhouse and the slow lane of the health-club swimming-pool.

'Oh, don't be such a wet and a weed' – that was what Josh would say to her, if he caught her. Part of the reason she was weeping was that she couldn't bear the idea of having a child, and having it grow up, and then hearing Josh say such unkind words to it as well. She didn't want him to be the child's father; and the blessing was, he wasn't. Ian was the father. She was convinced of it. There had been an incident, a fumbling encounter, a few months before. It had taken place during their Christmas party, after Josh had fallen asleep in the company of armchair and armagnac. The whole thing had been so quick, so minor, that Ian had probably forgotten it completely. He'd been drunk. Almost incapable.

DINING ROOM

Michael Xut, 40, was an award-winning neo-minimalist architect and interior designer. Unfortunately, so chastely neo-minimal was the living space for which Michael had won his single award, and in which he and his partner, Fumiko, 34, still had their existence, that there was absolutely nowhere at all (no bourgeois mantelpiece, no dust-gathering bookshelf) for him to display the award itself – a transparent perspex octagon, mounted on a screw of steel.

Fumiko: Japanese by birth, Californian by upbringing: compact, black hair with deliciously premature streaks of white: overtly quiet in public, allegedly passionate in private: exclusively *Commes des Garçons*, ostentatiously dirty finger-nails.

Within ten minutes of their arrival, an argument (the first of the evening, the latest of dozens) had started up between Ian and Michael. Ian, intimidated by Michael's wealth and wife, was, as usual, the aggressor.

Selina was still in the kitchen. Josh was looking out some wine in 'the cellar' — actually the attic.

'But surely you'll admit that the designers of almost all contemporary interiors — lofts and the like — are concerned with creating large areas of mock-sacral space.' Ian had thought of the hybrid "mock-sacral" earlier in the week, and had been looking forward to using it ever since. As Michael was the only person with whom Ian could *have* this sort of conversation (and it had been Michael who had directly inspired the train of thought that had destinated in the bastard coinage), Ian had decided to make sure he got it in early — before he got drunk and lost three-quarters of his usual vocabulary (whilst gaining access to a fearsome fifty words that he never otherwise dared utter).

Michael glanced at Fumiko, eyebrows aloft. They had, although they hadn't mentioned it to each other, been expecting this: they were architects, after all, and so couldn't meet a new person or even take a taxi without being sociologically *j'accuse*'d. More specifically, Ian always ended up losing arguments to Fumiko that he'd started with Michael. Fumiko disarmed him with a logic so transparent, so perspexy, that he couldn't see its edges, and so assumed it didn't have any, conceded she'd said everything that needed to be said, gave up. After which, however, he'd go away, have a think, decide he'd been right all along, come back and start in again on Michael.

'Yes,' said Ian. 'You –' (The onslaught had been focused down to the personal more rapidly than ever before. Ian, it was clear to Fumiko, certainly hadn't got laid since last time they met – about two months ago. She caught Michael's expression. His eyebrows were now higher than a drag queen's in a planetarium.) 'You are merely attempting to construct religious-type spaces in which there is no chance whatsoever of anything religious taking place. I mean, I could understand it if – in the middle of your vast floors, looking up at your huge windows – you had a congregation and some choirboys and a priest. But nothing religious, nothing ceremonial is ever going to take place in those secular cathedrals.'

'Life is ceremonial,' said Fumiko, with a mild smile.

'Instead,' Ian went on, though he knew – from Fumiko's tone – that he'd already lost, 'what's going to take place is the usual bourgeois routine of breakfast, lunch, dinner and TV.'

Selina, who had been in the kitchen putting finishing touches to the starters, came through carrying them. As she'd arrived just in time to hear Ian's last sally, she decided to attempt a witticism.

'Well, if anyone can bear the usual bourgeois routine of it, here is my humble attempt at sushi.'

As soon as she said it, she felt doused in scalding shame: now it appeared that she had joined everyone in ganging up against Ian. Although he *was* a little tedious, it hadn't been her intention to make it quite so clear this opinion might be entertained out loud. Her shame became all the more scalding when she became aware that Josh, holding two bottles of goodish South African plonk, was standing directly behind her.

Perhaps she needn't have worried: the awkward moment was buried beneath a rapid piling up of middle-class exclamations: *lovely* (Fumiko), *wonderful* (Michael), *good good good* (Josh).

Selina set the sushi down in the middle of the table and went off back into the kitchen to get the pickled ginger, wasabi and soy sauce. (Josh stood back out of her way, treating her with a far more exaggerated caution than before she'd become pregnant.) She'd thought about but refrained from saying anything apologetic to Fumiko. To suggest that Fumiko might have more to do with sushi than anyone else around the table would be to risk racism. That, however, didn't mean that Selina wouldn't consider Fumiko's praise – if it came – as of higher currency than that of the others (which, unless she served them steaming piles of turd, was quite inescapable).

Meanwhile, in the other room, the object of Selina's anxiety, making a preemptive gesture of cultural and gastronomical disownership, turned to Michael and said: 'We haven't had sushi in *ages*, have we?'

Ian was, as yet, not belligerently pissed enough to force their talk straight back round to how crap Michael's architecture was. He would save that for later, calculating that any loss he might in the mean time suffer, vocabulary-wise, would be more than compensated for by a redoubled vehemence. All it would take to turn him into a Samson of the PoMo, bringing the entire empty edifice of Michael's carefully constructed career tumbling down around their ears, was a few more couply comments like Fumiko had made just then.

ENCOMPASSING DISAPPOINTMENTS

By a quirk, the Withers' dining table was perfectly orientated with respect to the points of the compass. It was a medium-sized oblong of pale Ikea maple, perfectly suited to entertaining six, but bound, with only five present, to leave a grinning gap: the empty space where Ian's wife/partner, had he had one, would have been. Josh sat at the head of the table, the northernmost point; to his left (East) was Michael, to his right (West) Fumiko. Ian was positioned immediately to Fumiko's right (South). That left the seat beside Michael free for Selina – who was therefore very handy for the kitchen.

IN THE REALM OF THE SENSITIVE

Within a very few minutes of their all sitting down at table, Fumiko was aware that something had happened to Selina. Whereas at previous dinner parties she had sat at the edge of their talk, silently fretting over her non-participation, this evening she seemed – equally silently, but more calmly and contentedly – to be brooding upon some withheld secret.

At first, Fumiko was inclined to think that Selina's affair with Ian had turned serious. Everyone (everyone except Josh) knew about their frantic Christmas fumblings. They had been overheard, although no-one now admitted to eavesdropping. But Fumiko decided that, knowing Selina as she did, this explanation was improbable: had an affair caused the alteration visible in her, it would have been a change for the worse, and this seemed entirely for the better.

Selina was, for the first time, wholly in possession of herself. Josh was beaming a battery of signals at her, but absolutely nothing was being reflected back.

Then she came up with the solution; and, as was quite often the case with Fumiko, it turned out very close indeed to the correct one.

Her first instinct was somehow to inform Michael of her discovery. Not because she particularly wanted him to know at this point *what* she had discovered. But because, when the moment came for disclosure to be made (by Josh or Selina), she needed Michael to know that she had already guessed everything. It was important to ensure his witness.

Fumiko cared more about being seen to be right than about being right *per se*. If she could have been consistently mistaken in her logic, but unerringly correct in all her deductions, she would have taken that as a fair exchange, and been ever afterwards perfectly satisfied.

The difficulty now was in finding some way to convey the information to Michael without betraying herself to those already in the know. It would be highly socially dangerous if Josh and Selina, but particularly Josh, caught her in possession of contraband knowledge. Somehow she must find a way of smuggling it through their heavily policed customs.

During the four years of their relationship, Fumiko had taught Michael a certain amount of bedroom-Japanese. He had also Berlitzed himself for a month or two, prior to visiting Tokyo and meeting her stone-faced parents. Fumiko was almost certain that his language skills would be adequate for the verbal drop safely to be made. Yet there was a minuscule factor of doubt, and to be caught gossiping in a foreign language – to leave Michael suspended, needing to evolve an unprepared lie – that was too much of a risk. And so, first of all, to create the necessary distraction, Fumiko spoke to Selina.

'This sushi is delicious. So authentic.'

In a single moment, Michael's attention was all hers. Only half an hour beforehand, driving their Ka down from Hoxton, they'd been discussing and disparaging an aesthetic based upon some falsely contrived notion of "authenticity". The example that had come up was the Delta Blues. A CD of Robert Johnson's 'Hellhound on my Trail' had been playing in the background. Michael had taken it out of the car-stereo slot and frisbeed it out the window onto Putney Bridge. Hearing her use the word now, he knew that she was being . . . inauthentic.

'I've always loved sushi. It reminds me of my childhood.'

Michael knew – didn't he just know? – that the only things which reminded Fumiko of her childhood were loud male shouting and intense physical pain (both of which – on occasion – she called upon him, at one and the same time, to supply).

'Thank you,' said Selina, hoping she didn't look too give-away-radiant.

Now that the sushi had received the commendation of the only expert present, everyone else turned towards the hostess to reconfirm it with their ignorant English encomiums.

Fumiko took the opportunity of this exquisitely contrived hiatus to say smilingly across to Michael, in school-book Japanese: 'The wife of the host is with child. I am sure. Keep quiet now.'

Luckily, Josh barged in with: 'What was that?'

As usual, he was coldly fishing for compliments for his wife. (Unusually, this time, it was compliments for his wife's cold fish.)

'I was just saying,' said Fumiko, eyeing Michael quiet. 'The Japanese equivalent of "Just how mother used to make it."'

Michael couldn't help but gasp/laugh in astonishment/acknowledgement at/of his wife's quick wittedness. Yet, a moment later, he was plunged into renewed terror at the thought of what she would be like to have as an enemy. He had done so many things that would, if discovered, antagonize her.

ON THE NARROW ROAD TO THE DEEP NORTH (OF IAN)

Ian kept quiet throughout the sushi. Fumiko's burst of Japanese had reminded him only too clearly that the language games of all couples were, essentially, private.

Often, Ian was tempted to call Fumiko *inscrutable* to her sallow-skinned, almond-eyed face, just for the hell. But he didn't consider her scrutability anything much of a challenge at all. He thought her banal. Her clothes, for example. It had been a while (at least since the Jesuit Brothers back in Cork) since he had known anyone so devotedly black-wearing. She *was* intelligent, though with a synthesizing species of intelligence, one that tended to bland things out rather than distinguish them. In its way, hers was as much a totalitarianism as Michael's Zen fascism.

Ian had known before he came this evening that he was the fall guy for them all. That, though, didn't make him view the drop as any the less vertiginous when, as he now did, he approached the precipice proper.

He felt sick.

IN ANGUS WILSON TERRITORY

Armed with this new information (host–wife–baby), Michael looked at Selina sideways. She wasn't wearing anything radically different than before: her dresses (bless her) had always looked like they were made from let-out-able maternity patterns. She'd exhibited a loyalty to Laura Ashley, even during the Disaster Years, that smacked of genetic predisposition (Selina's family hailed fairly heartily from Cheltenham): brown flowers, pinprick-sized, upon a darker brown background – that was Selina's trademark pattern. The only surprise (so dowdy her dress sense, so mumsy her mufti) was, Selina wasn't a charismatic Christian. In fact, Selina wasn't – and never would be – a charismatic anything.

Normally the only time Michael looked at her, other than when saying hello or goodbye, was when she spoke – and that was mainly out of surprise that she had actually opened her mouth rather than interest in anything she might have to say. Now that he troubled himself to make a far more careful than usual examination, he found he was at the disadvantage of having previously taken in scarcely enough to afford a comparison.

Selina did appear a little fuller of figure and fatter of face than did his scrambled-together mental image of her. If this impression wasn't illusory, he thought, it was most likely explained by the fact that he had most vividly taken her in not in the proportionate flesh but via a photograph of the two couples together (taken by Ian) the last time the party was assembled. (The five of them had formed a sub-party clique of greater, more frequent intimacy, amidst the trivial comers and goers of the Christmas do.) If he had noticed her then, it was because, for once, seeing her though Ian's camera-eye, he was surprised to discern that she could have been – given different clothes or the lack of them altogether – quite attractive. That he had *completely*, during the entirety of the intervening time, forgotten about this flash of fuck-worthiness, served only to bring it back to him all the more dazzlingly now: Selina was looking, for once, *sexual*. Her nose was more Val des Aires than ski-jump – giant slalom, not downhill. Her cheeks glowed with a reddish hint of pre-eclampsia in the offing. (Perhaps before her time came she could be "induced" to something more pleasant than a convenient birth.) Her eyes, now he deigned to notice their colour, were either bluey-green or greeny-blue – and as they were in truth neither (being either grey or gray), he chose the shade he most preferred (greeny-blue). Her breasts, to cap (or cone or conch or cream-cake) it all, were at least twice the size of Fumiko's microbosom. This – Selina's discovered sexualness – might not supply her with the ever-absent charisma, but it did endow her with the allure of ambition. She was, he all of a sudden saw, worth flirting with. Ian had succeeded last Christmas; why not he, some time before next? And then the thought came over him, triumphantly, that, for once, he was one perception ahead of Fumiko. Chronologically, and ironically, he knew who the father *must* be. This information he would have to suppress – for to reveal how he had deduced it would be to expose himself to Fumiko's suspicion: he could not allow her to believe he had *considered* Selina in any way at all. Fumiko took curiosity as commitment, interest as involvement, acknowledgement as affair. Her jealousy darted faster than the serpent's tongue, and was possessed of a venom yet more rapid still. Survival, not death, was the inevitable consequence of a bite – survival followed by total paralysis: months and months of being unable to act in any way.

In order to play dumb, Michael decided to reignite – as soon as the opportunity arose – the argument with Ian.

SEXUAL ORIENTATION

If one thing had always made Josh nervous in his relations with Michael, then that one thing was the memory of a certain night – twenty years beforehand, in Michael's rooms, at Trinity, Cambridge – when they had gone to bed together. This had been Josh's only homosexual experience, and he looked upon it as a blessedly unsuccessful experiment (though successful in so far as it conclusively demonstrated to him that he much preferred soft-slack women to the hard-hairy business with men). However, Josh had always had a sneaking suspicion that Michael would one day bring the subject up again. And, for fairly clear reasons, Josh was becoming more and more convinced that tonight would be the night. There was something about the combination of his achievements – job, house, wife, baby – which, in its very bourgeoisness, seemed likely to goad Michael into having a go at undermining it all.

Michael's bisexuality had been a known fact, right from – it seemed – matriculation, Michaelmas term, 1978. Josh knew nothing, and was very glad he knew nothing, of Michael's more recent gay affairs. There had been some rumour about a fashion designer – one too many photographs in the *Evening Standard* of the two of them, arriving at parties dressed in slightly too-colourful yet still inter-coordinated clothes.

Fumiko was known to have accepted this side of

Michael's sexuality. For this, she was in equal measure respected and derided. Men tended to wish their wives and partners might exhibit similar forbearance with regard to their own heterosexual affairs. (That this forbearance was almost universally unforthcoming was often given as a particularly fine example of the hypocrisy innate within contemporary sexual mores.) Women, on the other hand, suspected that Fumiko had extracted from Michael something doubly enviable in return. The promise, perhaps, that she would never be forced into sex when she didn't herself want it. Or a straight 50 per cent share of Michael's company. Or merely a graphic account of each non-adulterous encounter immediately after its completion.

Josh didn't know why he so feared the possibility of Michael's blabbing: no-one could question his heterosexuality; certainly not after this evening's announcement. His entire life was proof against such suspicions. But it would be typical of Michael to make some throw-away comment after Selina's announcement. (Turns to Josh, bats eyelids: 'Well, whoever would have thought it!') Josh couldn't stand it when Michael turned camp. He felt offended by it, but knew that there was no way he could make his disapproval public. To face off against the effete was to put yourself in a no-win situation – that's why the buggers had invented camp in the first place. The bitchy comment to be let loose as the policeman shut the cell door upon one's bruised face. The final verbal flourish before the gay-bashers introduced you to the joys of concrete and steel toecaps. In such a soft-core environment as this dinner party, the wasp could easily outbuzz the humble dumbledore.

For once, Josh was grateful that Ian was present. Whatever else one might say about him (stolid, dull, oafish when drunk, bitter), he never camped it up. Ian was straight – in every imaginable way.

Selina was now clearing up the plates and heading off to finish preparing the main course: roast venison fillet with apple pureé and rosemary sauce, peas and celeriac mash.

The menu, he would have admitted, was rather eccentric. But the kitchen must for ever remain Selina's unquestioned domain.

IN THE PRIVACY OF THEIR OWN HOME

In the past few moments, Michael had become worried that the reason Fumiko had so quickly noticed Selina's pregnancy could be ascribed to her recent hypersensitivity on the subject. Just after Christmas she'd had a miscarriage – all the more distressing for being the first indication she'd had that she was pregnant rather than (as happened more and more frequently) stress-relatedly late. They had decided not to upset their friends by publicizing their grief. Something about the very idea of a prematurely but accidentally terminated pregnancy didn't square with the large plain white surfaces of their lives. (An abortion, paradoxically, might have fitted in perfectly: the aesthetic of antisepsis, the assertion of total life-control.) That dark dense little splot of blood and tissue would stain – they agreed, though not in such language – the image of themselves that they had meticulously conveyed to their friends and clients. Michael was sure that he hadn't forced this decision upon Fumiko. Like everything else between them, it had been 50/50.

At the time of the miscarriage, he had been . . . Well . . . his affair . . . one of his affairs had got out of hand. Within the very same hour he had received an ultimate ultimatum and made a life-saving hospital dash. Afterwards, Fumiko had steadfastly refused to blame him for what had happened. She did not want children, she said. Her body, at some level, knew that she did not want children. Her body had made a mistake (everybody makes mistakes), which it had acted quickly to rectify. Nothing more, really, need be said about it.

In fact, when he next tried to bring the subject up – aware that the level of his compassion might be being calibrated – Fumiko made it clear that silence was, as always, her greatest solace. Since then, he had avoided appearing even physically any more solicitous than hitherto. Surely, however, after they had got back home this evening (not whilst in the Ka, definitely not: the Ka was the place for loud-talk), there would be a necessity for him to say something.

All he could for the time being do was wait for the moment that Josh and Selina made their announcement. Seeing how Fumiko carried her congratulations off would give him some indication as to what he might get away with later in the evening.

KITCHEN II

Josh made his excuses (more alcohol, Selina) and popped through into the kitchen, leaving Ian and the male half of The Xut Architectural Partnership to their seemingly interminable argument about, as far as he could see, nothing more than why the two of them couldn't act like real men; take the argument outside, spill some blood, crack some bones, and have done with it.

Selina, when he discovered her, was standing over the hob – shaking and shuddering.

Josh realized instantly that now was not the moment to show irritation. But the fact that he must appear free from irritation, at this particular juncture, was what irritated him the most.

'What is it, my darling?' he said.

'Go away,' said Selina, thickly. 'I'm fine.'

'Then why are you crying?'

Selina had been asked this question so many times by her therapist that, hearing it now from Josh, she almost thought he was attempting a deliberate parody. What the therapist meant, though, was, *Can we attempt to trace the absolute most basic cause of your tears?* Whereas what Josh meant was, *Can't you put a brave face on it at least for the time being?* The former was part of a process that had already been going on for three years, and would continue for the foreseeable future; the latter, an attempt to get through the present evening without anyone noticing that any getting-through had been going on.

A scene was what Josh most wanted to avoid. Yet Selina felt her life wasn't so much a scene, more Wagner's entire *Ring* cycle being enacted by four rival ensembles (one for each opera) simultaneously upon a single stage. (Josh hated opera: 'All those declarations,' he used to say. The declarations being, of course, what Selina yearned most achingly towards.) There was no dignity in her drama: the music was a cacophonic catastrophe, the four conductors had all flounced off in implacable strops, the four assistant stage managers all believed they were Adolf Hitler come to re-create the Reich, the lighting booth was a fistfight-frenzy, the opera singers kept bumping into each other and knocking each other over – several of them, she knew, had been killed by getting caught when the scenery unexpectedly moved (her mother being only the most obvious example).

Josh, having got no answer the first time, repeated the question: 'Why are you crying?'

Selina laughed: the panorama of possible answers was so vast, the whirl of elements to be framed beyond all but a J.M.W. Turner. (Josh hated Turner: 'All that formlessness,' he said. The formlessness, of course, being the aspect of the paintings that Selina found most piercingly accurate.)

'It must be morning sickness,' she said, for want of – the entirety of everything ever; for want of love.

Her sobbing became exaggerated. Perhaps even audible in the dining room.

'You'll feel better once we've told them,' said Josh. 'Would you like me to do it?'

'No,' said Selina, turning round. 'You're *not* taking *that* away from me, as *well*.'

As she spoke, she gave added emphasis to her words by making downstrokes with the potato-masher.

'I won't ask you what you mean by that,' said Josh. 'Mrs Plinkton said we could expect a certain amount of emotional turbulence during the first three months.'

The Complete Guide to Conception, Pregnancy and Birth had been Josh's bedside reading for the past couple of months. (Selina's reading had been Lawrence's *Women in Love*. Josh, of course, hated Lawrence. 'All that phony closeness-with-Nature guff,' he said. But Lawrence only needed to mention leaves, earth, light, water for Selina to feel as if she were amongst those things – being penetrated by them – finding it impossible to tell where she ended and they began.)

Josh, Selina felt, now knew the inside of her body better than she did. He had shown her cartoon illustrations of what size 'it' was during weeks five to six. He had lectured her about the mysteries of cell division, symmetry and reciprocal organ development. And Selina's thoughts, right from the beginning, had been twofold: her first had been, *It's mine*; her second, *It's not yours*.

To try and protect herself from the declaration she knew Josh would one day force from her – the making public of her second thought – the assertion of her total separateness – she told him to go back into the other room.

After reminding himself that the kitchen must for ever remain Selina's domain, Josh backed slowly out.

CARPET AS CARTOGRAPH

Re-entering the dining room was not made any the easier by Fumiko's almost instant inquiry: 'Is everything alright?'

'Oh, fine, fine,' said Josh. And then, he couldn't resist any longer. There was glory here to be had, and Selina wasn't in the proper mood to appreciate it. 'This is quite a big night for us – bigger than usual. It'll all be clear in a little while.'

Ian and Michael had stopped arguing, halted by the quality of Fumiko's attention to Josh. They were both aware that she disliked him extraordinarily: so, anything which might bring her and Josh together into intimate confab was instantly fascinating.

'What's that?' asked Michael.

'Oh, nothing,' said Josh. Then capitulated once again to the temptation of himself being the one to translate the blaze of delight within his and Selina's marriage into a general conflagration of congratulation. He wanted to be the Putney Prometheus, bringer-of-fire to cold, huddled, failing dinner parties such as this present. Selina would stand there, flubbing match after match as she always did. Selina was no torch-bearer, no Olympian like himself. 'Well, not really nothing – something quite major, actually. Life-changing. But I'm going to leave it to Selina to make the actual announcement.'

Josh sat back, watching as the flames of enlightenment and the heat of curiosity illuminated the faces of his conjured audience.

Behind him, having entered just upon the word *announcement*, stood Selina – holding the dish of roast venison fillets in her oven-gloved hands.

All four of the others looked at her: Josh, alarmed at the infernal possibilities that his words had called into being; Michael, delighted at Fumiko's soon-to-be-proven perspicacity; Fumiko, enjoying examining Selina as closely as she had ever examined anyone; Ian, plummeting down through the vodka-cobwebs of his memory, down past a back-flashing calendar of calculation, down towards the only fall-breaker that seemed to exist: the blue carpeted floor of the master bedroom in Josh and Selina's old house during Josh and Selina's Christmas party.

For a moment, everyone remained perfectly still. It was as if, whilst Selina had been out of the room, they'd all been playing Musical Chairs. Her entrance had been the silent cue for them to drop down into the nearest seat.

'You *told* them,' said Selina. Carefully, she put the venison down upon the sideboard – ignoring the fact that it would almost certainly leave a scald-mark there. 'You bastard, you told them.'

Raising her hands to cover her face as she started once again to cry, Selina slowly sank to her knees.

Everyone stood up, except Ian; everyone, apart from Ian, made a plaintive noise.

Selina went down onto all fours, in an attempt to prevent herself from sinking through the floor. She felt deeply elated – there was now no longer any reason for her not to leave Josh, for her not to grant herself a total collapse.

Ian quietly and deliberately slid his chair back, dipped under the table and, ignoring the various reactions of Josh (snarling), Michael (yodelling) and Fumiko (giggling), slowly began to crawl upon hands and knees through the forest of the table-legs and across the wide steppe of the carpet towards truelove Selina (sobbing).

It was a long journey, he knew, but he was sure he would get there, eventually.

tourbusting

'Wouldn't the coolest thing now be to be Japanese?'

Syph is speaking. We are in Rotterdam, Europe, lost in thick fog together.

'A bridge over a river next to a church. Haven't we walked past this once before?'

That's me, name of Clap, dissecting the bridge-river-church interface. With me, Nippo-theorizing, is Syph.

We are from Seattle. We are in a band called *okay*, lower case, italics. We are on our third European tour.

'I mean, think about it. We can't match those copycats for hipness. No way. You see, Clap, we've completely forgotten how to be ourselves. But *they* know how. They know that it's about choosing who you want to be, not being destined to be anyone in particular. And they are better at choosing than we ever were.'

'Can we sit down for a minute?' I say. 'I'm not feeling too great.'

'When the Japanese are punks, they are the greatest punks ever; when they are rockabillies, not even Elvis can touch them.'

Twenty days in.

This is it – we have reached the point of self-annihilation. So much of what comprises who one is has been left behind.

Jackson Browne found a phrase for it, 'Running On Empty'. In this non-state you can go for two days without having a single real thought. *How did I get here?* – that is the thought that most intrudes. The non-thought is always – *next, next, next*. Next gig. Next girl. Next goodbye. Aspects of it I do sincerely appreciate – I love the sense of left-behindness. You never use a bar of hotel soap more than once – if at all. (And if you're really sensible, you carry your own with you: so that's not a very good example.) But if you don't like something – a magazine containing a bad review, a tape that's gone fucked in your Walkman – you just drop it. Within seconds, it is miles away. Another country. (As the lyrics to my favourite of our songs go: 'I reach out in the dark to touch/something a thousand miles away.') Similarly, if you freak out some girl and she has hysterics at you, she's two towns behind before her slap even hits your face. You become impervious to pain – of a non-serious sort. Self-harm becomes a bit of a game. (Not that *okay* are great ones for stage-diving. It's not part of our image.) You eat nothing but shit. You look like a piece of shit. And you talk shit a hundred per cent of the time.

Twenty days to go.

'You see them,' Syph continues to talk shit, 'walking around downtown – children dressed like souvenir teddy-bears – groups of girls with their heads close together and their hands over their mouths – couples holding hands, each so cool you can't decide between them – serious young hipsters buying huge stacks of CDs – companymen, who break into a mild sweat as they move from the pavement to the road – senior citizens in beige and fawn golfing clothing.'

I am the drummer, Clap. Syph is the lead vocalist. We have a bassist, Mono. We have a rhythm guitarist, Crabs.

Our mothers did not call us by these names – though Syph's is starting to. None of us knows if she knows what it means.

'Do you remember when we were on tour in Tokyo?'

'I feel bad. I'm sitting down. You can keep walking.'

I sit down on a low concrete wall with black railings stuck in it looking out across a street of cobblestones and grey-green walls.

'Like, no-one gives blow-jobs like the Japanese. It's the kind of thing they probably have instruction manuals about that are a thousand years old. Like The Karma Sutra.'

'The *Kama Sutra* is Indian.'

I stand up, lean over the railings and puke into the hedge.

'They do ancient things with their tongues and with the roofs of their mouths.'

I hear a whining sound.

'Did you fart?' I ask.

Syph looks shocked. He can't remember.

'I don't think so,' he says. 'Was it in tune?'

I lean back over the fence and look beyond the hedge. I see a paw, an ear – black and white.

I turn back to Syph. I say: 'I think I just puked on someone's dog.'

'Are they Japanese?' he says, and does ancient things with his tongue.

'What are we going to do?' I ask.

'We need to score.'

Syph is right – we smoked the last of our stuff before the border. Syph is superstitious about carrying grass over inter-national divides. He says it has to do with Paul McCartney. But he is quite happy about having speed in his pocket while making passport control. Which means that, until we score some dope in each new city, he is unbearable. And because he is likely to speed his way into getting arrested, I always go with him to try and track something down. If we are lucky, there's someone from the local fan club to help us connect. But *okay* aren't very big in Rotterdam, as we are finding out.

'I'm going to have a look at it.'

'Whatever,' says Syph, and plucks his Marlboros from his suit pocket.

Members of *okay* wear suits at all times. We play gigs in suits and we play ice hockey in suits. It's part of our image.

Our music is slow and formal with lyrics about love and guilt. We also sing about the sea.

We sound like the Velvet Underground on quarter-speed.

Climbing over the fence feels surprisingly easy. I haven't eaten anything in two days. Maybe I am getting the better of gravity.

I fall into the hedge, branches digging into my legs through my suit.

With a flip of my arms I roll off onto a patch of grass.

'Are you okay?' says Syph.

'Dollar,' I reply, keeping very still.

Whenever one of us uses the name of our band in a context not relating specifically to our band, that person is required to put a dollar in the stash-pot. It is a band rule.

'You didn't break your back?'

'I'm fine,' I say. I haven't opened my eyes yet. I don't feel any pain in my body.

Then a warm wetness crosses my nose and I smell a bad smell. I open my eyes into the face of the dog.

'Hi,' I say.

It continues licking.

I'm not sure if the bad smell is the smell of the dog's breath or the smell of my puke, which runs all down the dog's back.

I roll away.

The dog tries to follow me, to carry on licking, but it is tied to the hedge by its lead.

'You've gone all quiet,' says Syph, then laughs. 'Is the dog Japanese?'

'Throw me your cigarettes and your lighter,' I say.

He throws them. I light up. I throw them back.

'Shit,' he says. 'That almost went down the drain.'

'Sorry,' I say.

I lie on my side on the lawn in Rotterdam, Europe, looking at the dog.

It is a mongrel, black and white. It doesn't look like anything much. Except thin. It looks kind of bony and shaky. Like Syph.

Syph got the job of lead-singer mainly on the strength of his hips. To this day, he's never been able to find a pair of pants that stay up. His mother used to make him wear dungarees or suspenders. At school we called him Wall Street.

The girls always loved him. Still do.

Some nights I get seconds and some nights thirds and maybe once a tour I'll settle for fourths. But Syph always gets firsts.

We drummers have our own distinct kind of girls. They are enthusiastic long before you are successful and loyal long after you're shit.

Drummer-girls tend to have long hair and large breasts and bring their own contraceptives and leave when asked.

Lead-singer-girls, from what I've seen and heard of them,

84

are model-like and neurotic and bring drugs and want to do really weird sex-things on you so that you never forget them.

Some nights Syph doesn't even get laid, because none of the girls in that town comes up to his high standards. But that is rare. Syph's standards vary from town to town. Sometimes he ends up with Little Miss Rancid-and-a-half. (And I end up with her mutant grandmother.)

'It's a nice dog,' I say.

I look down at myself. There are a couple of muddy paw prints on my shirt. There is a bit of puke on my lapel.

'I think it's homeless.'

'Hey!' I hear Syph shout. 'Hey! Yeah!'

'Yeah?' I say.

'Come over here, I wanna talk to you. Yeah, come on. Yeah. Hi, I'm Steve.'

Syph was talking to a girl. It wasn't hard to tell.

'What's your name?'

There is a giggle.

'I'm Inge.'

'Would you like a cigarette, Inge?'

'I have to go.'

'Hey, Syph!' I shout. 'Ask her if she knows whose dog this is?'

'Who is there?' Inge asks.

She was *so* beautiful. I just knew it was going to break my heart all over again to watch Syph closing his hotel door behind them as they walked in, smiling.

'That's my drummer,' said Syph. 'He's found a dog.'

Inge says, 'A dog?'

'Yeah,' says Syph. 'Woof-woof.'

Usually the beautiful ones laugh at Syph's less funny jokes.

And the more beautiful they are, the more they laugh. And the sooner that door closes behind them.

I decide to stand up.

'Do you happen to know where we might chance upon some blow?' Syph is now doing his comic Englishman.

When I get to my feet I find myself standing face to face with an angel called Inge, with only a vomit-covered hedge separating us. Inge is very slim with short-cropped white-blonde hair. Her eyes are dream-blue. And oh her skin . . .

'I'm Inge,' she says.

Syph rises to stand slim-hipped beside her.

'I'm Brian,' I say, hating my name totally.

'Where is the dog?' she asks.

'It's down here,' I point. 'Is this a garden or something?'

'I think it is a park,' Inge says. 'I will come round.'

Without turning towards Syph she starts off.

When she gets a few paces away Syph looks at me and mouths: *mine.*

I shake my head.

'Musical differences,' I say. This is the threat anyone in the band always makes when they take something so seriously that they are prepared to break up the band over it.

'I saw her first,' says Syph. 'You wouldn't even have said hi.'

'If it hadn't've been for the dog, she'd've walked off.'

'I tell you, if she goes for me I'm having her.'

Inge has found a way into the park.

'Hello,' she said, and holds out her hand to be shook. 'Brian.'

She has an angel's ankles.

'Hi,' I say.

We shake.

Then she turns her attention seriously to the dog, addressing it in Dutch or whatever language they speak in Rotterdam. She can't fail to notice the puke, but she doesn't seem to associate it with me. I reach in my pocket and take out some gum to chew, to get rid of the smell.

Syph climbs up on the railings, jumps the hedge and joins us.

'What does he say?' I ask. 'Does he belong to anyone? Are they coming back?'

Inge says, 'I think he was left because they did not want him.'

'Sometimes they have addresses on their collar,' says Syph.

Inge says, 'There is no address.'

Inge stands up.

'What were you going to do?' she asks.

I look at Syph. Inge's eyes follow mine.

'Well,' he says, 'we are actually going to score some blow. Do you know where we could find some?'

Inge turns back to me – a little shrug, eyes rolling to the heavens where she belongs.

I say, 'I was going to wait here to see if his owner came back. Then I was going to try and find a police station.'

And please can I kiss you?

'Give me your handkerchiefs,' she says.

Members of *okay* have handkerchiefs in the breast pockets of our suits at all times. It's part of our image.

'We must clean the dog.'

I hand over part of my image quite happily. Syph is flirting with the idea of refusing and of using his refusing as a way of flirting.

'Give it her,' I say.

Inge cleans most of my puke off the black and white dog with our handkerchiefs.

'Do you want them?' she asks.

Syph says, 'Nope.'

I say, 'Yep.'

Inge hands them back, and I wrap them in the handkerchief I always keep in my side pocket for real use.

'I will take you to the police station,' Inge says.

Syph looks at me with *no way* in his eyes.

'But we have to be somewhere else,' he says. 'Don't we?'

'I'll come with you,' I say.

Inge kneels down and unties the dog's lead from the branch of the hedge.

'But we need to score,' says Syph.

'See you back at the hotel,' I say.

Inge looks inquiringly at both of us.

'Come on, boy,' I say to the dog.

Inge speaks to it in the Rotterdam language.

We walk off, leaving Syph behind.

Outside the park gates we turn left into the fog.

'You are a drummer in a group?' Inge asks.

I am stunned. She's been paying more attention to Syph than she's let on. She really doesn't like him.

'Yeah. We're on tour. We're playing tonight at some club.' As I am half-way through the line, I go on with it anyway. 'Would you like to come?'

'Maybe,' she says. 'The police station here is very close.'

I hear footsteps running behind us in the fog. I don't need to look. Things have been going too well. It is Syph.

'I thought I'd lost you guys,' he says.

Inge leads us up to a door-way and into the police station.

Inge tells the policeman the story in the Rotterdam language. He then asks us to confirm a few details in English. It seems like Inge's left out any mention of the puke. I am glad of that.

We give them the name and address of our hotel.

Inge gives them her address and telephone number.

Inge and I say goodbye to the dog and watch the policeman take it off down a long white corridor.

On the foggy street outside the police station, Inge says, 'What is the name of your band?'

'It's *okay*,' I say. 'Spelt o-k-a-y.' And just so she knows, I tell her the name of the club we're playing at.

'Do you know where we can score?' whispers Syph.

Inge looks at him pitifully.

'Come on,' she says, and leads us off round the corner.

Unexpectedly, she stops, reaches into her backpack and brings out a clingfilm-wrapped chunk of dope. She breaks off a corner and hands it to Syph.

'God,' he says. 'The woman of my dreams.'

Inge turns to me.

'You are a kind person,' she says, and kisses me on the cheek. 'Goodbye.'

I watch as she walks off into the fog.

Syph doesn't even look. He is sniffing the dope.

'This is really good shit,' he says. 'Let's get back to the hotel.'

That evening the lighting set-up means that I am unable to see anything of the audience – it is just a sheet of white light which applauds whenever we finish a song.

Our set-list goes: 'Thousand', 'Blissfully', 'Jane-Jane',

'Motherhood', 'Sea-Song #4', 'Hush-hate-hum', 'Walls', 'Queen Victoria', 'Long Cold Lines', 'With Strings', 'Gustav Klimt' and 'Work'. We encore with 'Sea-Song #1' and our quarter-hour cover of 'Marquee Moon'.

Syph dedicates one song to a girl we met today. Thanks. For services rendered.

At the end of the encores, I walk straight up to the mike and say, 'Inge, if you're here, I'll see you in the bar.'

Two Inges show up, neither of which is the right one.

Back in the dressing-room there is a drummer-girl but I brush her off.

'I'm going for a walk,' I say.

'What?' says Mono.

'A walk?' says Crabs.

'See you back at the hotel,' I say.

'Maybe,' says Syph, who has one girl sitting in his lap and one opening him a beer.

For an hour or so, I wander about trying to find my way back to the park. But the fog has gotten even thicker and everywhere looks even more the same.

I stop a cab and tell the guy to take me back to the hotel.

Inge is sitting in the lobby with the black and white dog at her feet. As I walk up, the dog I puked on recognizes me and starts to strain on its lead.

'You didn't come to the gig,' I say.

'I was there,' she says. 'I left.'

'I asked you to meet me in the bar. Didn't you hear?'

'I thought you would get another girl. I wanted to see. I came to wait here.'

'What, you were testing me?'

'I don't know,' she says, smiling. 'Maybe.'

'Hi,' I say to the dog.

Someone has obviously given it a bath. And love. He licks the salty spaces between my fingers, looking up at me with wet eyes.

'Brian meet Brian,' says Inge.

'They let you keep it?' I ask.

'I went back and told them that the story we said before was a lie. I told them that I lived with you and that you didn't want the dog, so that you made me give it to them. I told them that we had split up and that I wanted my dog back. They didn't want the problem of a dog. They gave it to me without question.'

'Do you have a boyfriend?' I ask.

'No,' she says. 'I have a dog called Brian.'

I am very close to saying woof-woof.

Just then, Syph and his two girls, both Japanese, plus Mono, Crabs and their girls, plus several other girls and a couple of boys, come through the hotel doors.

'Great dope,' Syph says to Inge as he walks up.

His girls are already getting jealous. They touch him even more.

'Musical differences,' I say to the whole band. 'I'm afraid to say.'

'Nice doggie,' says Mono.

'Irreconcilable musical differences.'

'Really?' asks Crabs.

'You have dope?' asks one of Mono's girls.

'Yes,' I say. 'I think so.'

Syph says, 'No way.'

'Yoko,' says Crabs.

I smile at Inge and she smiles back.

'Let's go,' Inge says.
And I say, 'Okay.'

That last bit didn't really happen. It's just how I day-dreamed it the following afternoon on the tourbus. Cologne was next. Then Munich. Then Berlin. Nineteen days to go. What really happened was that I went back to the hotel, alone, only to find Inge not there. No sign of that dog, either. Then I went for a walk, to try and find the park or the police station. But I couldn't. I got lost again in the fog. Then I stopped a cab and told the guy to take me back to the hotel. That detail was true. Syph and the others were there in the bar with a group of girls. None of them was Japanese. But one of them I saw straight off was a drummer-girl. I think she had long hair and large breasts and brought her own contraceptives and left when asked. It's just, you meet so many and remember so few.

"Legends of Porn"
(Polly Morphous)
Final Shooting Script

Lee Perverse and Polly Morphous first met on
the set of the Kurt Spurt/Wolfgang Bang
VeryHardCorps ~~film~~ production, *Hey, Guys, It
Just Stopped Hurting XIV*.

[We open on an empty soundstage. Narrator
(t.b.c.) walks leonine towards camera, wearing
sharp acrylic junglewear.]

Back then, Lee was working under the name
'Sodeep Sodark' and Polly was known only as
'Extra, If Needed'.

Hey, Guys ... was Polly's first porno and
Lee's fiftieth. But, between them, on this
very soundstage, something clicked — and what
happened afterwards, well, that was *sexual*
history ...

[Cut to archive footage — baby-photos,
Yearbook-photos, amateur-photos.]

From the very start, their lives were
parallel. Born poor, raised hard — their only
way out from the tough streets of San
Francisco was through the sex industry.

[Cut to Narrator, on the tough neon-lit
streets of SF.]

Lee started off hustling outside local motels and diners; Polly got a very bad reputation in school, and was able to trade it up for a pole-dancing gig and what is ~~eumphemistically~~ laughingly called 'a modelling career'.

[Fade in on poolside interview: Kurt.]

It was Kurt Spurt who spotted the star quality in both of them:

"Obviously, you know, it's not easy to see whether someone is really going to get the viewers hot — I mean *really* hot. In order to make that diagnosis, you gotta see them in action — up close, up *real* close. I could see from the moment he unzipped his jeans that Lee was enormously gifted. But it was only when he took with so much gusto to the *submissive* role that I knew I had someone I could take to the top — and over it."

[Cut to Narrator, still on the soundstage.]

Kurt is lavish, too, in his praise of Polly:

[Cut to Kurt, on the tough neon-lit streets of SF.]

"When she walked on set, even though the production guys have seen a *lot* of flesh, they were begging straight off for bit parts. She had something about her — a kind of innocence; something that guys really wanted to destroy. She didn't *look* like a pornstar, not the old kind. I don't think a surgeon had been *near* her body. It was as if she'd somehow evolved into being just *totally* desirable. I knew the

moment I saw her that I had to team her up
with Lee."

And team up they did.

[Cut to VT, *Hey, Guys, It Just Stopped
Hurting XIV* — hall scene.]

During their first half-hour together,
nothing spectacular happened.

Wolfgang Bang, who was producing, recalls:

[Fade in on corner-office interview,
swingchair.]

"We weren't worried about Lee, you know. He
could handle himself. He had it down. Never
had a problem with Lee. Not one. But Polly
had to prove herself. If you watch it now,
even with a professional eye, there isn't
much in that first scene in the hall to tell
you that erotic magic is about to happen.
Lee has all the chops. Polly comes across
as a bit of a scream-queen. Let's face it,
she's a first-timer and she's trying too hard.
Lee should look like he's in control, and
he doesn't. Kurt called 'Cut', he and I sat
down, talked it through. He'd seen Polly
eyeing up the couch when she came in. He
figured, Hey, she might have something about
doing it on couches. We decided to give
her another chance, this time ... on the
couch."

[Cut to Narrator, sitting on "The Most
Famous Couch in Porn" — in the Museum of Porn,
Washington DC.]

Little did either of them know at the time,

but this was to be the most important decision
either of them ever made.

As Kurt said, afterwards, "I just had an
instinct.' And what an instinct it was ...

[Cut to *Hey, Guys, It Just Stopped Hurting
XIV* — couch scene.]

The scene started normally enough. Lee and
Polly enter the room. They are already naked,
having moved through from the hall. Seated on
the couch are Ursula Undress and The Rabbi.
She holds his cock in her hands, but nothing
much is going on. ~~As the Rabbi has been part
of the series since *Hey, Guys, It Just Stopped
Hurting IX* there is no explanation of his
presence~~. The scene develops as one would
expect, right up till the moment Kurt gives
Polly the direction — edited out in the
released version, but here dubbed back in:

"Give me more! Improvise! Come *on*! I want
something special!"

You can see the moment of ~~puzzlement~~ doubt
on Polly's face.

[Close-up, repeat, slow-motion.]

What can she possibly do that she isn't
already doing?

Then she, too, has her moment of
inspiration:

"Wow, I *really* like your *couch*. Where did
you get it?"

The other actors react in various ways, but
their professional skills allow them to carry
on, just.

4

Lee glances offscreen, towards Kurt.

[Close-up, repeat, slow-motion.]

[Voice over. Kurt, mumbling.]

"I could tell that Lee wanted to know whether he should go with this. I think I just shrugged."

The Rabbi raises his eyes momentarily towards heaven.

[Close-up, repeat, slow-motion.]

And Ursula Undress, being somewhat distracted anyhow, seems not to be taking it in.

[Close-up, repeat, slow-motion.]

[Cut to archive footage of Lee and Polly.]

[Interviewer, offscreen, asks them:]

"Lee, what did you think, that first time Polly mentioned the couch?"

"Well, to be honest, I hadn't really noticed the couch before ..."

[They laugh — Polly punches Lee playfully in the upper arm.]

"No, but seriously ... this was the first time anyone had really seriously challenged me to act while I was doing anal. What I came to see later was the aspect that Polly was trying to push the whole thing further, take it to another level. I had to think fast. *Did* I like the couch? Where *had* I got it from? And so I said ..."

[Cut to *Hey, Guys, ... XIV*.]

"It's new. I only bought it yesterday."

[Cut back to archive footage. Polly says:]

"And so I say ... "

[Cut to *Hey, Guys, ... XIV.*]

"You have realllly good taste. I love this couch. It's so soft and leathery-smooth against my skin."

[Cut to Kurt Spurt, outside a dive bar, ~~looking shifty — the guy wants a drink, bad~~.]

"Man, from that moment on, the whole thing just went wild. Everyone got in on the act. For the rest of the scene, they did all the usual stuff, oral, anal, double. But the whole while, they kept talking about the couch, the décor, the color scheme ... I can't deny, I was a bit *freaked*. I mean, how's this going to play? I could see the sound-guy snickering. But I've always been open to new things; and there was something *really* fresh about this, something real."

[Cut to *Hey, Guys, ... XIV*. The couch scene runs to the end.]

Rabbi: "I noticed it, too. It's really good quality."

Ursula: "I have a couch just like this at home."

Polly: "Perhaps we could go there some time."

Lee: "What a great idea."

Polly: "How did you get the idea to combine the pale leather with the pink throw cushions?"

Lee: "I've always had a certain visual flair."

Ursula: "You can say that again."

Rabbi: "I only wish I was so gifted."

Polly: "What kind of couch do you have, Rabbi?"

Rabbi: "Nothing special."

Ursula: "Hey, maybe we could all go down the couch store later and pick him something out?"

Lee, Polly, together: "That's such a *great* idea!"

Rabbi: "Well, I mean, if you'd really like to."

Lee: "We'd *love* to."

[Cut to Wolfgang Bang, driving a golf cart.]

"To this day I can remember the atmosphere on set when that scene finished. Everyone there was just stunned. What we'd seen was ... I don't really know how to put it. It was the breakthrough everyone had been looking for."

[Cut to Narrator.]

"Now housed in the Museum of Porn, Washington DC, this couch has become the single most visited item in the entire history of the sex industry. For on this couch, a pivotal moment took place. As Wolfgang Bang explains ... "

[Cut to Wolfgang Bang, piloting his Lear Jet.]

"We couldn't do much with that scene in *Hey, Guys XIV*. The script had already been written. We were on a tight schedule. And, besides, we needed to see what kind of a reaction it got. But we started work on a sequel straight away

— that night, even. Kurt and I went to my beachfront place, sat right down, and started typing out a scenario. That scenario became the first Polly Morphous/Lee Perverse flick *Looking for a Decent Couch for the Rabbi*. We finished at about five in the morning. Right away, we knew that what we had in our hands was a paradigm shift. We went out for a walk on the beach, smoking some fine Cuban cigars. It was like, History. We knew we could relax. Then *Hey, Guys ... XIV* came out, and was such a massive success — our biggest film to that point. We'd been sitting on the script of the Rabbi's couch, but now greenlighted it for production. Unfortunately, in between times, the original Rabbi had died of a massive heroin overdose, so we had to replace him. That wasn't too difficult. We'd always needed a second dick on hand, anyhow — circumcised. The shoot went real smooth. We hired a store one night and just took it over. By this time we'd come up with the idea for Polly and Lee's names. Everything just went click. You could hear it. Everyone could hear it. With that click, an entire industry began to quake."

[Cut to *Looking for a Decent Couch for the Rabbi*. Wolfgang continues in voiceover.]

"I mean, look, for a start, none of the actors took their clothes off for the entire first forty minutes of the film. That was unheard of. Instead, we just let them improvise. We got a hand-held camera and

8

followed them throughout the store. Polly was
totally in control. She led us from couch to
couch. And when we got there, she'd get
everyone to sit down on it and describe how
comfortable it felt. She had a wonderful
natural gift for scenic construction. The
film built from a fairly plain cotton-
covered couch in pink to a slightly larger,
more showy one, then to the tigerskin, the
white leather and wow-finally the calfskin —
which was, of course, the most expensive. The
Rabbi got more and more excited about how his
new couch was going to look when he got it
home to his apartment. We wrapped that day's
shooting late in the evening. The following
day, we had moved the couch (the calfskin
one) onto the set that was meant to be The
Rabbi's bachelor pad. And I have to say, it
looked fantastic there. We shot the final ten
minutes straight off, just as they stand. It
was wild. There'd been so much foreplay,
without it being really foreplay. All the
actors were just frantic. It was so real.
And, of course, we ended on that famous final
line . . ."

[Cut to *Looking for a Decent Couch for the
Rabbi*:]

The Rabbi: "Jesus, I love this couch!"

[Cut to the Narrator, browsing in a porn
superstore. He looks up, as if surprised to
see us there. ~~But he's relaxed. Hey, he's not
ashamed to be seen buying hardcore. He's that~~

kind of a guy. He picks a copy of *Couch* off of
the shelf.]

"*Looking for a Decent Couch for the Rabbi*
went on to become first the biggest selling
movie in VeryHardCorps' history and then the
biggest selling movie in the history of the
entire porn industry. What happened afterwards
has became a legend. Polly Morphous/Lee
Perverse became the most successful
syndication imaginable. And throughout the
industry sexual acts were relegated, for the
first time, to a subsiduary minor role in porn
movies."

[Cut to Kurt Spurt, in a bar, drinking.]

"We couldn't make them fast enough to
satisfy the demand. After *Looking for a Decent
Couch for the Rabbi* we did *Looking for a
Decent Rug to Match the Rabbi's Couch* and then
Looking for a Decent Couch for the Priest and
then *The Rabbi and the Priest Move in Together*
and then Couch films for the imam, the
Krishnas ... Then we did a bunch which were
Polly's idea. *Polly Morphous and Lee Perverse
Go Shopping for Curtains*. It was money all the
way. Perhaps we should have paid more
attention to who was making us that money."

[Cut to the Narrator, walking through an
idyllic graveyard.]

"The lives of porn stars are short, fast and
often end in violence."

[A gravestone comes into view.]

"That of Polly Morphous was shorter and

faster than most, but her death — at least —
was perhaps as she would have wanted it."

[Cut to Kurt, in the same bar, later — ~~he~~
~~looks bad~~.]

"Polly always loved the ocean. When she got
a little money, the first thing she did was
invest in scuba lessons. After the films hit
big, she got a huge schooner-boat, and a
private dive-coach. She was on at us all the
time to do *Polly Morphous and Lee Perverse
Swim with Dolphins*. One day ... she pushed it
too far. She wasn't experienced enough. She
went down too deep. I think that was her
problem all along: she always went too deep.
Man, I miss her."

[The Narrator stands in front of the
gravestone. We see the inscription. 'Polly
Morphous/Swimming towards the light/
Constantly.' He looks towards us, moved.]

"Everyone who knew her said that Polly was a
pure soul, too good for this world."

[The Narrator turns away from the grave, and
begins to walk towards the sea.]

"Lee Perverse left the porn industry soon
after Polly's death, and has not returned.
Although the two stars will always be thought
of in the same breath, there was never a hint
of offscreen romance. Lee rapidly made another
fortune, in the discount soft-furnishings
industry. L. P. Stores are a feature of every
Californian mall, and there are plans to take
the franchise nationwide."

[The camera pans round to gaze towards the glistening ocean.]

"But one can't help but wonder, how often does Lee Perverse think of the lost spirit that was Polly Morphous?"

[We close in on a dolphin, cutting nimbly through the surf.]

[Titles. Sad music. Out.]

Of the Third Kind

'But why didn't The Calling work before?'

'They have reasons we don't know.'

'But d'you think tonight will happen?' I said.

'I heard the man who made the film went up in a real UFO, but the government wouldn't let him say. It's going to happen.'

'Immaculate,' I said.

1978. Amplewick. Midfordshire. We were walking along the Prom. It was about ten o'clock, a July night, clear, expectant. The trees on the left side of us striped the path with big blue shadows. No-one else was on the path or the playing-fields. The houses were already behind us. Ahead was the War Memorial, encircled by holly bushes. We were going up the Furze.

'Tonight is immaculate,' said Robert, looking up at the stars.

I looked up as well.

'Yes,' I said. Robert, who was eleven, always thought of the things to say, and said them. If I ever thought of them, I thought Robert would think they were silly; so I either kept quiet or agreed. I was almost eleven.

'What do your scanners read?' asked Robert.

I clicked open my palm and moved it from side to side, making a quick pass across the sky.

'Negative read-out, Captain. Someone must be jamming their frequency.'

'No,' said Robert. 'It's if you travel faster than light, you don't send out signals. Not ahead of you, at least. They're coming in too fast.'

'Warp Factor 10.'

With a mouth-beep, I flipped the scanner shut and mimed putting it back in my pocket.

Robert stopped and looked directly up, between the branches.

'They are out there. Tonight, they are going to collect us and take us away. They were just waiting, before. Tonight, they will answer The Calling.'

'Immaculate,' I said.

★

We got on our speeders and hummed our way past the War Memorial. Robert made a loud electronic twang as he turned tightly to the left. I copied the twang as I followed him, but his voice had already returned to the hum.

The ground under our feet was the loose sand that all the mile-long hill of the Furze was made of. We sped down a path through the bracken and gorse. Silver birch trees whizzed by on either side.

The Calling Point was about a hundred metres ahead: a group of medium-sized trees, planted in a dense grid. To get to The Calling Point we would have to crawl under the bottom boughs and into the middle.

'Check for lifeforms, Lieutenant,' ordered Robert.

I brought the scanner out again.

'Negative read-out, Captain,' I said. 'The coast's clear.'

'I'm going in,' said Robert. 'You cover me.'

He unhooked an imaginary lightsaber from his belt and pretended to activate it. Through his teeth came the lightsaber's characteristic low fizzing sound.

I followed the soles of Robert's trainers until we came to the small clearing that he had decided, about a month ago, was The Calling Point. We had come to issue The Calling a couple of times a week ever since then. It was very dark in the shadow of the trees.

'Are you sure no-one is tracking us?' asked Robert.

'A-OK.'

Robert took out his scanner, just to double-check. It made a slightly lower beep than mine. When he'd finished a very thorough scan, he put his hand on my shoulder and said: 'Good work, men.'

I felt proud, like Robert always managed to make me feel.

'Are you clear on procedure?'

'Crystal, sir.'

'Good.'

He picked at a scab on his elbow and looked up. Whenever Robert scratched, I started to itch myself. If he got a bike for his birthday, I had to have one for Christmas. He made the long falling whistle of a bomb or a satellite dropping. The sky immediately seemed twice as big.

'What did you tell your mum?'

'I said I was round at yours.'

'Good.'

'What did you say?' I asked.

'I didn't have to say anything, I just escaped. They won't miss me.'

One of the things I envied Robert the most was that his parents didn't care about him, didn't treat him like a girl.

'Remember,' said Robert. 'You have to empty your mind of all thoughts. Just let them sense you are ready for them. If they come, you will go.'

If I knew anything, back then, it was that I was ready for them. After the hundred frustrations of my nothing-happening life, what I felt most was a total yearning. My whole body resonated at this particular frequency. What I desired, above all toys and treats, was that, one night, a UFO would descend and take me and Robert away – away from Amplewick, away from Midfordshire, away from school, away from grown-ups. I was more than prepared for them to do experiments on me. I expected to be scanned and probed, to wake up with blood seeping from my belly button. In fact, if they had come, and hadn't experimented on me, I would have been very disappointed. But, even so, as long as they took me away, I would have forgiven them almost anything. Anything, that is, except bearing the slightest resemblance to earthlings – especially, my mother. I desired aliens. I yearned for extraterrestrials. I wanted them so badly that I couldn't believe that they didn't feel my want. Somewhere among all their sensors, they must have had something to detect the yearning of young men. From my point of view, this yearning was so unmissable that it formed the background radiation to the whole universe. I would lie in bed at night, issuing what only now appear to me as what they really were – prayers. *Please take me away. Come before school tomorrow, please. I'm going to go mad if you don't arrive soon. This is the end, unless you pick me up.* When they did come – and they would, they must – I knew exactly what would happen. Robert and me would go into their blinding

light, we would be taken to the mothership, we would be
analysed, we would disappear off the planet. Our parents
would miss us for a few days, then forget us. The school
would soon deny we had ever existed. There would be a
government cover-up. On board the mothership, we would
travel the galaxies. We would see new stars and black holes,
Horsehead nebulae and supernovas. We would visit water
planets, desert planets, ice planets. With our earth knowledge, we would help the aliens solve some tricky problems.
They would thank us and honour us and trust us and listen
to everything we said. There might be some other earthlings
on board – pilots lost in the Bermuda Triangle, farmers from
the plains of Iowa. After exploring the universe and learning
all the secrets of space travel, we would be returned to earth
forty years later. Our parents would be dead or very old. My
mother and father would be together for the first time since
they split up. When we walked in, they wouldn't recognize
us. Then we'd explain and they'd be amazed and believe us.
The government wouldn't believe us until we'd proved by
our superior knowledge that we were telling the truth. We
would be heroes and meet the Prime Minister and the
Presidents of all the countries, especially America. Then,
when we got to twenty and didn't want to grow up any
more, the aliens would come back and fetch us – just as we'd
arranged – and we would set off again into space.

That's how I knew it would be. That's how it would be
tonight.

★

Robert climbed to the top of his Calling Tree, which was
slightly taller than mine. About ten seconds later, I was up
there with him. Our trees stood a couple of metres apart.

Too far to touch across or even jump, unless you were really good.

Robert didn't say anything. He was preparing himself to issue The Call. I could hear a car accelerating down the Noburn road. In the south of the sky was the orange glow of Newton. Behind me was the path that runs along by the School. Robert was breathing very deeply and slowly. I was still out of breath from the climb. I could see his eyes were closed. I closed mine.

After about a minute he said: 'To issue The Call, you must be pure. Are you pure, Martin?' He always said this. I don't know where he got it from.

'I am pure,' I said.

'Then issue The Call.'

I felt the tree sway slightly with my weight. There wasn't much of a breeze. A twig was sticking up my trouser-leg. I wasn't sure if I was allowed to move to stop it tickling me. Robert's breathing was the loudest sound I could hear.

For about ten minutes, the terrible *nothing* happened. There were no lights, no pulsar engines; there was no arrival and no escape.

'It's not working,' said Robert. I opened my eyes and saw that he was looking back at me. 'We've tried like this and it hasn't worked. They can sense we're not pure enough.'

'But I'm really trying.'

'I don't know what it is.'

'I keep getting tickled by the tree.'

'I think it could be our clothes.'

'Why?'

'I think they're interfering with our signals.'

'Really?'

I looked down at my stripy T-shirt and my khaki cords, slightly flared.

'You mean the metal in the zips?'

'Maybe,' said Robert. 'Or maybe it's just them altogether. Maybe The Call goes out from all of us. I think we should take them off and try.'

He immediately pulled his T-shirt over his head, gripping the trunk of the tree between his legs.

I hesitated, then said, 'We'll try for a bit.'

In order to take my clothes off, I went a bit lower down the tree – down to where it didn't sway quite so much.

'Don't touch the ground,' warned Robert.

'I'm not going to,' I said.

Getting my underpants off was quite a struggle, and it was a strange feeling – all the leaves against my skin. We threw our clothes down in the space between The Calling Trees. I remembered seeing an empty Coke can there, once before, and hoped my trousers hadn't landed on it and got sticky. I looked across at Robert, just to check he really had done it as well. He had.

Not surprisingly, I felt much more exposed now. But this, I thought, must be good. It must mean that my signals were going further.

With my eyes closed, I sensed the UFO plunging towards me through infinite time and hyperspace – as huge and unknown as the future.

I also sensed that Robert was occasionally looking over at me, to check that my eyes were closed.

*

We had been Calling for about five minutes when I heard something approaching. It wasn't an alien spacecraft, as it was making sticks crack and calling, 'Come on, boy! Come on!'

I did my scanner and said to Robert: 'Lifeforms approaching, Captain.'

'I know,' he said.

'Shall we wait for it to pass?'

Robert thought about this for a while. It was just possible we might be seen from the path.

'Negative,' he said. 'Mission aborted. Mission aborted. They won't come tonight.'

The voice got nearer. It had now been joined by a barking and a light scampering.

'We are under attack,' whispered Robert, starting to climb down. 'Take evasive action immediately.'

I jumped the last few feet and for a moment thought I'd twisted my ankle. My legs and arms felt scraped all over by the bark of the tree. Everything seemed darker, now we were out of the moonlight. There were no colours. Robert, a slim white shape, was already pulling on his underpants. It took me a couple of seconds to find mine. Putting clothes on felt funny, even after such a short time.

'Tracker beast,' said Robert.

I pulled on my trousers, could only find one sock. Robert was now in his T-shirt. I saw him pick up his trainers. The dog, which was small but loud, came through the trees.

'We'll have to split up,' said Robert. 'You go that way, I'll go this. Meet up back at base, tomorrow. I'll contact you.'

He crawled off, holding his trainers. The dog didn't follow him. It was looking at me, barking. I heard branches snapping behind it.

'What have you got?' said the man. 'Is it a rabbit?'

I finally found my sock.

'Come on, boy! Where are you?'

I scurried, on hands and knees, in the direction Robert had pointed, away from the voice, out of The Calling Point.

★

When I got home, I was out of breath.

'What did you do this evening?' asked my mother, in her interested-voice. She was in the kitchen, drinking coffee from the big mug.

'We played War,' I said. That was what I always said. Until we saw *Star Wars* and *Close Encounters of the Third Kind*, until we read *The Hitchhiker's Guide to the Galaxy*, it had been true. But now all we played was Space.

'Your trousers are dirty again,' she said.

I went to the sink and ran the water till it was really cold.

'We were in the garden,' I said.

'I wish you wouldn't play wars,' my mother said.

'He was the Germans,' I said. 'And I was the Africa Corps.'

'It's Cor,' she said. 'Not Corpse.'

I knew this already, but I also knew she'd be disappointed if I didn't make the usual mistake. She might even suspect I was lying.

'I won,' I said, after I had filled my glass.

'Well, that's something,' she said.

'I'm going to bed.'

She went to kiss me but the phone started ringing.

★

I was in the bathroom, putting toothpaste on my tooth-brush, when I heard my mother coming up the stairs, quicker than usual.

'Martin?' she said. 'Where are you?'

I had locked the door. I'd only started doing this recently – since Robert asked me if I did. I took private baths, now.

The door-handle turned. 'Open up,' said my mother. 'I'd like a word with you.'

I didn't do anything. I wanted to know why I was in trouble.

'Martin?'

As soon as I opened the door, my mother dropped to her knees and reached for my belt-buckle.

'Mum!' I said.

The first bit of the belt flapped back, slapping against the top of her hand. I put my free hand on her head to stop myself falling over. My other hand, the one with the tooth-brush in it, I held behind my back. The belt pulled my stom-ach in, tightly, then fell free. I reached down with my hand to undo the button, but my mother's hands were busy there. In a moment, the zip went down and I saw –

'Oh, shit!' said my mother, taking her hands back and putting them over her mouth.

I was wearing a pair of blue Y-fronts, with white stitches and a white Y. I had never seen them before.

My mother stood up. For a moment, she didn't do any-thing. I saw her sway a little. Then she placed her hands on my head and put on her gentle-voice.

'Martin, get your pyjamas on and come downstairs. I'll make you some boiled milk.'

She turned and went back down the stairs. I heard a click as she bit on one of her fingernails.

★

When I got into my bedroom, I leant back against the door after I had closed it. My dressing-gown lifted up off

114

the hook and fell over my head. I badly needed to speak to Robert. I needed to know what lies he was telling. Had he told his dad about us going up the Furze? Or had he made up some brilliant excuse? The excuse theory didn't seem likely, because if it had been *that* immaculate, his dad wouldn't have rung up. I knew Robert always told the best lies, but I couldn't see how it was possible to explain how we'd ended up wearing each other's underpants. He might have told his dad about going up the Furze, but he wouldn't have told him about The Calling Place. I was sure Robert had kept *that* secret.

Robert had told me his dad sometimes slippered him. My bum began to tingle.

'Martin!' called my mother, up the stairs. 'Your milk's ready.'

*

She was sitting at the kitchen table. There was a mug for her and a mug for me, both steaming. I had put on my dressing-gown. She looked at me and gave me a funny smile, one I hadn't seen before. It was as if she was sort of proud of me, but too sad to be proud. I touched my finger down on the surface of the milk and lifted the skin. It sucked up like a parachute. I dropped it into my mouth. I sat down.

'Martin,' said my mother. 'Do you know why Mr Jenkins phoned up?'

'No,' I said, deciding this meant the same as yes, in the circumstances.

'He was very upset. He wanted to know what you'd been doing.' She looked at the table-top and touched a little group of breakfast crumbs. I became aware of how quiet the house was. Something about the situation felt very grown-up. My mother never usually spoke that slowly to me, only to the phone. 'I want to know what you were doing.'

I heard her take a long deep breath, and then she managed to look at me. Round about this time her hair was permed and she wore hooped gold earrings. Her skin was always pale, but it looked particularly white now. She was wearing something patterned with little flowers.

'It's complicated,' I said.

'I thought it might be,' said my mother. She did her new smile again.

'I don't think you'd understand.'

My mother was a teacher, so she thought she knew all about kids. I usually found it funny that she got it so wrong so often. It amused me that she couldn't remember what being a kid meant.

Once more she was looking at the crumbs, picking them up on her fingertips.

'Try me,' she said. 'Try and explain.'

If I could go back now and sit opposite her, inside the boy that I was, I'm still not sure I'd be able to say anything. At that age, I didn't have the words – and the ones I did have, I wasn't allowed to use. There was no way I could tell her how much I loved her or how far away from her I wanted to be. It would have killed her.

For the first time in my life, my mother was prepared to listen to me as if I were an adult. But I was trying so hard to think of the best lie that, for several minutes, I completely forgot she was there. Finding the best lie was all that mattered. But the best lie wouldn't come. There was something in the way – something new.

Then, suddenly, I wanted to try and tell her the truth. But I didn't know where to start, because there was no start.

There was only the all-around yearning, the background radiation of my universe. There was only the UFO, now plunging away from me and Robert, out into the infinity of far-away space, leaving us behind, leaving us stranded on this terrible, incomprehensible planet.

Mimi (Both of Her) and Me (Hardly There at All)

See this. See it as it was seen (by me): Waterlow Park beside
Highgate Cemetery; two girls – twins? – girls; paler-than-
pale skin; dyed black-oh-so-black hair; black bra-straps
against white backs; twenty-five or -four or -six (maybe,
just); British Airways flight-bags, one each; black-red-black
tartan blanket; black combat trousers; bare white feet with
grass-stained soles; sunbathing on green grass in nice park;
skin so white, oh-so-white, hasn't seen sun all winter;
one, looking for something; other, informed; black sunglasses
– on, off, on; one, finding . . . cigarettes; red-and-white zig-
zaggy pack; both laughing at something intimately private;
both smoking; smoke; laugh; smoke.

I, too, am in the park – sitting alone, killing time before
the two o'clock guided tour of (and only way to get in to)
Highgate Cemetery West. After seeing them, I hope, for
fairly obvious reasons, they too will take the two o'clock tour.

Ten to two. Outside the cemetery's black iron gates
('Church Gothic', as the guide will soon inform us). They're
there.

They – The Two – stand to one side, each taking turns to
turn and whisper whispers in the other's ear. They know –

probably have for a long time known – the effect of their appearance(s): combined/duplicated. But whilst they are at some level aware of it, now, right now, it isn't the main thing on their minds.

Among the other people about to take the tour: an American couple (hetero), four acnefied Japanese girls, a probably-Swedish backpacker, and a dozen or so interested old ladies.

What would they see, all of them, were they to pay any attention to me? A young man, curiously shagged-looking. Once they might have put this down to excessive masturbation. However, in this case, my case, it is because I have been spending too long in the British Library (toilets – ha ha).

Of which more later –

'Please assemble under the colonnade at the bottom of the stairs,' said a Matronly woman, hook-nosed and wearing a frumpy dress in vertical blue and white stripes. She represents The Friends, a voluntary organization that now watches and wards the cemetery.

– more later is now: research (mine) has been progressing recently into the literary life of Dante Gabriel Rossetti, with special reference to the circumstances surrounding the publication of his first volume of poetry, *Poems*, 1856.

'Do you have a camera?' says Matron. 'That will be two pounds for a camera permit.'

The maybe-Swede pays; the Japanese confer and then buy two permits between them; the Americans resist.

Before we start off, Matron firmly tells the American woman that she must cover her bare shoulders if she is to go any further.

'This is the resting place of the dead, after all.'

Her tone suggests that the United States are without death.

When it becomes obvious that the American woman doesn't have anything else that she might put on over her shoulders, Matron fetches her a cardigan so manky it seems likely the graveyard cat (called Domino, we later learn) has been bedding down upon it for the past decade.

After we have forgathered under the colonnade, Matron gives us a brisk pep talk. We are warned not to smoke, eat, drink, chew gum, talk too loudly, collect souvenirs, or deviate from the path of the tour. We are told, if we are very lucky, and quiet, we might possibly see fox cubs at play. The interested old ladies coo. I check to see if The Two appreciate her *Bumper Book of Adventure Stories for Boys and Girls* manner. But their heads are down and their heads are turning – onespeaks, otherspeaks, shespeaks, shespeaks.

Matron finishes: 'Are there any graves you would like in particular to see?'

(I think later that the question is asked to forestall disappointment, and possible recriminations, half-way round the tour.)

'Yes,' I say, when no-one else speaks. 'The Rossetti tomb.'

Matron's sympathetic-face: on.

'Ah, yes. Well, I'm very sorry. But – as you know – the Cemetery is still a going concern. And a member of the Rossetti family was buried here only quite recently. So they've asked us to keep people away. I'm sure you'll understand. The feelings of the relatives must of course always be paramount.'

The Japanese girls are disappointed. They explain it to each other in Japanese.

The Two, my Two, don't seem to have heard. Their back-of-the-classroom gossip continues. I notice, with pleasure, that their inattention is annoying Matron. Not quite enough, however, for her to give them a legitimate off-ticking. I think she is too scared of them for that. Amid all the burgeoning greenery, The Two appear unmistakably vampiric – mmm. They have tongues and teeth and eyes and teeth. Matron leaves well alone.

I almost depart at the moment of disappointment. If The Two hadn't been on the tour, that's probably what I would have done. The rest of the cemetery, while of some general relevance to my period, isn't anything like time-worthy enough to have brought me here.

'That's very disappointing,' I say, loudly. 'I've come rather a long way.'

(Matron, I want a chance to get back at you.)

For the first time The Two look at me. It was worth speaking up, I realize, just for that. A flash of generational sympathy triangulates us: Matron, officious old bag, die.

'Well, I'm very sorry that you've been disappointed,' she smarms. 'But I'm afraid, as I say, there's nothing that can be done about it.'

The tour begins: up the stairs, and here's the first pausing point: a grave which Matron informs us 'is of particular interest from the point of view of the development of the history of funerary architecture'.

It is a little stone chair with a little stone cupola over it and a little stone robe carved-draped upon it.

Matron excrescently expounds: life, a garment, cast off, casually. She continues, triumphant, offering verification – the grave (records show) belongs to a woman who died tragically young. Pause (particularly among the interested old ladies) for general contemplation of death, and of Matron's exegetical expertise.

Others move on.

I am hanging back, disgruntled. The wasted library time is more and more irking. Couldn't they have put a sign up outside saying that Lizzie Siddall's tomb was unavailable for viewing? Surely, a high percentage of the cemetery's visitors came for her and her alone.

The 'any particular graves' question, coming after we'd all already paid, did suggest a certain pecuniary cynicism.

However, the day is wonderful: butterflies twiddle around each other like airborne thumbs. I decide to continue.

As we stroll deeper into the ivy-choked, sound-muffling graveyard, the interested old ladies find their deafness drawing them closer and closer to Matron. The hetero Americans want to be her best friends, but realize already that she will let their every question fall, colonial, into a European silence. The Japanese seem to be content in finding picturesque vignettes to left and right – the butterflies, particularly, delight them. The Two are keeping only just within sight. They didn't seem disappointed when Matron cut the Rossetti tomb from our tour. What have they come for? Another famous grave to visit? A Gothy love of graveyards, pure and simple? If I'd known anything more about Highgate Cemetery than that it housed Lizzie Siddall, I should have been able to guess.

We stop at the fortified grave of some dead Major-General whose family never these days visited. Were all dead. But once-upon-a used to take tea down in the crypt itself. Victorian tradition. Glass skylights installed for the purpose thereof. Quite pleasant, really.

At the top of the path, where it forks, Matron stops.

'Where is the young gentleman . . .?'

I walk sulkily up to her. If a 'young gentleman', then Little Lord Fauntleroy.

'The Rossetti tomb is just down there – behind those trees. It is a rather mundane little grave, really.'

And then, as if she's just made everything all right, she proceeds to make it all a whole lot worse by retailing the story of Rossetti and Lizzie – getting almost every single fact and date completely wrong.

Here are the true facts; here is the true story:

DEATH OF A LADY FROM AN OVERDOSE OF LAUDANUM 10 to 11 February 1862. The nocturnal events. Elizabeth Siddal. Lizzie. The Wife of Rossetti. A 'stunner'. 'Guggums.' Pale beautiful. The lovely wraith. The New Woman. *Beata Beatrix*. Millais' *Ophelia*. All her talk was of a "chaffy" kind – its tone sarcastic, its subject lightsome. "Took an overdose of laudanum." 'My life is so miserable I wish for no more of it.' "Accidentally, casually." 'Take care of Henry.' Dante Gabriel Rossetti. The Sablonnière Hotel, Leicester Square. 'I found a Phial on a small table by her bedside, it was quite empty . . .' She construed his every absence as infidelity.

I lie among the tall green grass
*   That bends above my head*
And covers up my wasted face
*   And folds me in its bed*
Tenderly and lovingly
*   Like grass above the dead.*

Six days elapsed before the funeral. His studio overlooking the Thames. Blackfriars. Chatham Place. A breeding-ground of death and discomfort. Manuscript-book. A little book. Bound in rough grey calf. Which she had given him. Dante Gabriel Rossetti. Hysterically penitential. Paroxysms of uncontrollable grief. Quite unmindful of the presence of others, he spoke to his dead wife as if she could hear. Placed them between her cheek and her famous golden-red hair. Entwined. Saying the poems it contained had been written to her and she must take them with her to the grave. The Bible also placed there.

Seven and a half years. Rossetti, now completely neurotic. The buried MS. Friends. It was doing no good to the dead to leave hidden in the grave the most beautiful works he had been able to produce – was it not his duty to the living, to himself, and perhaps even to literature, to recover and publish them. Swinburne. Ruskin. A certain Howell. A person out of another world altogether, a daring, reckless, unscrupulous soldier of fortune, very clever, very plausible, very persuasive, but totally destructive of delicate feeling, and almost without the moral sense. Howell. Romantic liar. Blackmailer. *Dear old boy, your letter about the poems was very kind, but it's a ghastly business.* Leaving London for Penkill. Scotland. Incidents. A live chaffinch. Nestled in his hands. Caressed him with its beak. 'It is the soul of my wife, come to revisit me.' The great bell of the castle. Violently rung. When the servant arrived. No one there. Elizabeth gave her consent. Exhumation of the passionately loved dead indeed had become quite a literary fashion, and Gabriel's whole existence was chiefly an unconscious attempt to realize literary fashions in life. *'Endless'* preparations. *'28th September 1869. In accordance with the order granted by the Right Honourable*

Henry Austin Bruce, Her Majesty's Secretary for the Home Department, for the exhumation of the body of my late wife, Elizabeth Eleanor Rossetti, buried at Highgate Cemetery: I hereby authorize my friend, Charles Augustus Howell, of Northend Grove, Northend, Fulham, to act in all matters as he may think fit, for the purpose of opening the coffin and taking charge of the M.S. volume deposited therein. DANTE GABRIEL ROSSETTI. 16 Cheyne Walk. Chelsea.' Howell. Blackmailer. *'P.S. If I recover the book I will give you the swellest drawing conceivable, or if you like paint the portrait of Kitty.'*

4 October 1869. Howell. A solicitor. Dr Llewellyn Williams of Kennington. Two workmen. A great fire. A fire of dead leaves. The best protection against infection. *'The book in question is bound in rough grey calf and has I am almost sure red edges to the leaves.'* Eased gently from her face. When the book was lifted there came away some of the beautiful golden hair in which Rossetti had entwined it. His sonnet Love in Life. Obvious reference. 'Lay all that golden hair undimmed in death.' The body was not unduly disfigured. The delicate tints of her flesh. Manuscript-book. Stained, holed and discoloured. Drenched with disinfectant and dried leaf by leaf. Later than midnight. Fulham. Howell returned to say it was all over. Already Rossetti seems to have regretted his resolution. Mental disturbance. *'I fear the truth must ooze out in time.'* Queer state of health. *'The truth is that no one so much as herself, would have approved of my doing this. Art was the only thing for which she felt very seriously. Had it been possible for her, I should have found the book on my pillow the night she was buried; and could she have opened the grave, no other hand would have been needed.'*

The volume appeared on April 25th, 1870, and was greeted on all sides with a paean of unanimous and unqualified praise. The literary sensation and the social event of the hour.

Poems. 1872. Sixth Edition.

The tour now moves on to the Egyptian Avenue – a ring of catacombs below ground-level, with the vast Lebanon Cedar (at ground-level) in the middle.

The interested old women are overtaken by The Two. Whatever interests them, we are getting closer to it.

I can't decide which of The Two is more attractive. The one who is slender but small-breasted or the one who is statuesque but stocky. Really, I want them both – either consecutively or together, I don't mind. They look unconventional enough; there might be the slightest of chances.

Some people I might mention have been living a little too long in the British Library. Books – particularly Pre-Raphaelite ones – are full of ludicrously unlikely, over-precipitate, wish-fulfilling couplings. Pre-Raphaelite heroes and heroines confront their own demonic doubles on what seems almost a daily (nightly) basis. So much so that the encounter becomes almost domestic – one's doppelgänger popping round for tea and cake, as it were.

'This is the catacomb of Mabel Veronica Batten. It also contains the body of Radclyffe Hall. Some of you may have heard of Radclyffe Hall – she was quite an accomplished writer.'

The Two look at each other in horror only semi-comic. They must have been anticipating Matronly muddle and obfuscation, but this is too much.

'She was a great writer,' the slimmer one bursts out.

'A very great writer,' the other one burstingly adds.

'Well,' says Matron. 'That is a matter of opinion.'

'It's our opinion,' says Statuesque, clearly speaking for both. 'And the opinion of millions of other lesbians all around the world.'

Now it is Matron's turn to be horrified. The word most to be avoided (particularly at this juncture of the tour) has been spoken.

The interested old ladies look at each other in bewilderment – trying to decide if this is historical enough to be safe.

'As you will see, the tomb is carefully looked after by The Radclyffe Hall Society.'

The Two take this as part-capitulation. Matron has lost her train, her patter.

'*The Well of Loneliness* was banned by the Home Secretary for a number of years, due to its controversial subject matter.'

(Expecting: 'graphic descriptions of Sapphic love'.)

Another yuck-look binging between The Two, but they decide not to call her out on this slight elision.

'The crypt is equally well cared for on the inside. Radclyffe Hall herself was recently put into a new coffin. The body isn't taken out of the old coffin – that's a bit messy. You simply build a new, larger coffin around it.'

The old ladies appreciate this goryish funereal detail, just as they will later enjoy hearing that tombstones are left off graves for a year – to allow the earth to settle. They are, perhaps, thinking a little more on the last things than the rest of us (three).

'Passing swiftly on . . .'

I hang back, trying to think of something to say to The Two – to establish between us the comradeship of the disappointed.

Then, something extraordinary: when most of the tourists are gone and I will soon have to go, too, so as not to look obvious, one of The Two (can't tell which) bangs the other up against the black door of Radclyffe Hall's tomb and starts kissing her. Just before moving off round the bend, I look back to see white hands plunging down inside black combat trousers.

Matron is now describing the great Lebanon Cedar's provenance.

I am unable to listen: half-disappointed at my clearly having no chance with The Two, half-thrilled at their sexy daring.

It doesn't take long for Matron to notice their absence.

'What are they doing?' she asks me, having categorized us as 'troublemakers'. I can see she is about to go back and fetch them.

'I think they're praying,' I say. 'At the tomb.'

'Really?' She doubts my word (the younger generation simply do *not* pray), but cannot call me a liar outright.

'I'll go back and bring them along once they're done.'

Matron hesitates but she has her schedule to keep.

'Hurry them up if you can.'

The fox cubs have been sighted, and off she goes to annex their appreciation.

I jog excitedly back to see what can be seen of what The Two are up to (or down to).

As I'd hoped (obviously) they are fucking – zips have been unfastened, hands are down inside combat trousers and fingers are up inside vaginas.

How they think they'll get away with it, I don't know (want to, though).

For a few moments I enjoy watching them – fixing the image in my mind for later, more frenzied, contemplation.

'Excuse me,' I say.

Their heads whip round.

'I don't mind at all – really, I don't. But, um, the woman taking the tour, she was going to come back and get you. I thought . . .'

Still they look, fingers unremoved.

'Shit,' one of them says.

'They won't let you hang around,' I say. 'We have to be frogmarched through by Matron.'

'Shit,' says the other.

'Sorry,' I say.

I turn to walk away from them.

'Was she really going to come back or did you just want to see?'

'Yes,' I say. 'She was coming.'

'Then she'd have thrown us out.'

'We were hoping to get left behind.'

'She was just about to come back when I stopped her,' I say.

They take their hands out, fingers not too wet, yet – as far as I can see.

'Well . . .' she says.

'Thank you,' she says.

'I suppose.'

'Yes.'

'It's nothing,' I say.

As they are zipping up, Matron comes confirmingly round the corner. She doesn't or can't or won't interpret correctly their fly-fiddling.

'There you are,' she says. 'You'll have to catch up.

You've missed the fox cubs, you know. The others are practically in amongst the Dissenters, by now.'

She waits to see that we are following her, then takes off in pursuit of her more orthodox disciples.

For the remainder of the tour, the girls and I dawdle as much as we possibly can. But even though Matron has conjoined us in disgruntlement, the conversation is still fragmentary. The Two have an unusual manner of discourse. Any comment I might make, however casual, is like a blip dropped into an echo-chamber — its resonances, however tinny, rebound between the both of them for what feels like minutes after the thing has lost any initial impetus of sense it might have had.

'I'm Gabriel,' I say.

'We are Mimi,' one of them replies.

'Both of you?' I ask.

'Mimi is our name.'

'How do you spell that?'

'We don't.' 'Me . . .' '. . . and Me . . .' 'Mimi.'

'Very clever,' I say.

'He thinks we're clever.' 'Well, we are.' 'But is it good he thinks that?' 'Should it be so obvious?' 'Isn't that a drawback?' 'Bad thing.' 'Maybe.' 'Perhaps.' 'Perhaps we should play dumb.' 'More often.' 'Sometimes.' 'What do you think?' 'I don't know.' 'Neither do I.' 'Save it up for later maybe.' 'Hold that thought.'

And they turn back to me, smiling — me not sure if they are playing dumb (or playing me for dumb) or not.

I think at first that The Two, in how they speak, are trying to disconcert me. But after a while I realize it is a passionately pursued attempt to apprehend everything at once, in the same way, together, in parallel. The Two want, as much as is possible, to be one person. A mad kind of echolalia has come into being between them. They complete and begin each other's sentences, so much so that no single sentence belongs finally to either of them. They make leaps of logic thewhich only they can follow. I try to pretend to myself that I can be accommodated within their language (that it is a discourse within which I feel relaxed), but I am terrified. I am totally extraneous to what they are saying: I might as well, I feel, be one of the graves we are passing by; something to be noticed, mentioned, bounced back and forth, giggled at, forgotten, recalled, forgotten.

I risk another commonplace.

'It's awful the way The Friends are so protective of this place.'

'We heard.' 'Yes, we heard you ask to see.' 'To see that other.' 'The Rossettis.' 'The grave.' 'The girl who died.' 'Who killed herself.' 'Laudanum.' 'Love.' 'And they won't let you.' 'Just because.' 'Only because someone else died.' 'Rossetti.' 'Recently.' 'Yes, a Rossetti.' 'Want to see it too.' 'We want to come back.' 'Yes, Mimi.' 'Sneak in.' 'Tonight.' 'All of us.' 'What do you think?' 'How about it?' 'Fuck them.' 'Fuck them all.' 'A secret.' 'It's good.' 'We have it.' 'It's a way.' 'Over and in.' 'The wall, you see.' 'Built it high.' 'They did, the Victorians.' 'Like she said.' '"Matron."' 'Keeping out the graverobbers.' 'It's in our pocket.' 'We're lucky.' 'Blessed.' 'We have the key.' 'We have a van.' 'Park it.' 'Up by the wall.' 'The key we copied.' 'A friend.' 'Want to use it.' 'Key to Radclyffe Hall's tomb.' 'Want to finish.' 'How about it?' 'Gabriel.'

'I'm sorry.'

'A van.' 'We park it.' 'Close to the wall.' 'With the key we have.' 'Together.' 'You and us.' 'Fuck them.' 'Sneak in.'

'Sneaky-peaky.' 'Like the graverobbers.' 'To prevent.' 'They had no van.' 'The very high wall.' 'We have.' 'Meet you.' 'At midnight.' 'Outside the gates.' 'Tonight.' 'Peaky-sneaky.' 'Dress up warm.' 'And bring a torch.' 'And don't . . .' 'No, don't . . .' 'Never . . .' 'Not to . . .' 'Gabriel . . .' '*Don't* watch.' 'Don't *watch*.' '*Don't watch!*'

They look at each other, eyes falling into eyes – identical, almost (as much as can be). Then they turn their gaze back on me, and speak for the first time exactly as one: 'You mustn't watch.'

The tour party is now moving away from the grave of Michael Faraday, inventor of the dynamo and discoverer of electromagnetic induction. We are standing in the jagged light that drops through the yew trees, planted to shield the unconsecrated graves of the Dissenters from 'the common gaze'.

I want – I *do* want – to see Lizzie Siddall's tomb, and to see it by night (as had Howell whilst exhuming her), and to have the advantage of sneaking in with someone else, not alone, a van.

'Yes,' I say. 'Twelve o'clock.'

They smile and kiss, lips.

'Exactly.' 'On the dot.' 'Pronto.' 'Don't be late.' 'Don't watch.' 'See you there.' 'Here.' 'Then.' 'When.'

It turns out to be a big-moony night, high-fast raggedy black-white clouds, fetidish surface winds, as if Nature had sweetly guffed a couple of miles off – perfect for our dual (triple?) purpose.

Again, I don't expect them to be there. But there they are. Twelve o'clock. As promised. And their van – a large-long American-style Winnebago. (I wonder where they got the money to be able to afford it – but there is a definite hint of disowned-posh about both Mimis.)

'Hello.' 'Again.' 'On time.' 'Good to see.'

I climb up and in.

Mimi drives further up Swains Lane and parks hard by the cemetery wall. She turns all the lights off and we sit for a few minutes in complete silence.

What strikes me most about the van's interior is its smell – or, rather, smells. For although the overall ambience is of Mimis' sweet-but-dark perfume, there penetrates through this a sharper stench of rot.

I want to use the van's loo, but don't – fearing it is there I'd find the reeking thing, whatever it turned out to be.

When we are quite sure that no-one is paying us any undue attention, Mimi opens up one of the skylights.

We climb up and out, me first.

The long flat plastic oblong of the van roof is phosphorescent in the moonlight – white tinged with a brighter green.

Mimi has brought along a rope-ladder with a plank tied to the end. One of her braces this inside the skylight whilst the other of her throws the ropey bit over the wall. Then the both of her look towards me, and it becomes clear that I am expected to go first.

'Faraday,' says Mimi. 'We should.' 'Quite.' 'Near to him.' 'You know.' 'The Dissenters.' 'Tell us it's okay.' 'Okay?'

Mimi's skins, picking up the glow of the van's roof, are inhumanly pale.

I pause before saying *okay*. Then I step onto the top of the cemetery wall and grab the ladder.

One last look, and I'm over – twisting round and round, scraping up against the stone. I reach over to grab a tree-branch in an attempt to steady myself, but the bark-dust flies into my eyes – for a moment blinding me. I make my way down the rest of the rungs by feel, which turns out to be more efficient.

Once safely on the ground, I pull out my handkerchief and dab at my stinging eyes.

'Is he?' 'Are you?' 'Faraday.' 'Down.' 'Hey!' 'Is it?' 'Shall we?' 'Or not.' 'Or what?'

Even in my discomfort, I flatter myself that I understand her weird discourse better than would most men.

'Yes,' I say. 'Yes, it's okay.'

One by one, Mimi comes down after me.

United by the brief glee of having got in, the three of us stand there. We laugh, self-consciously naughty. Matron.

'Have you?' 'We have.' 'Torch.' 'Use carefully.' 'Not to show.' 'Others.' 'Keep low.' 'But we'll.' 'Studied.' 'And the map.' 'Lead on.' 'Thataway.' 'Mmm, going.' 'Uh-huh.'

Mimi pulls out identical torches from her identical British Airways flight-bags and – sweetly together – clicks them on.

This contrived synchrony of hers is becoming spookier by the moment – partly because it no longer seems quite so contrived as before; perhaps not contrived at all.

In the graveyard moonlight, Mimi really does appear to be two versions of the same person – all the differences between her selves have dissolved imperceptible into the night.

Without saying anything further, she leads off – gliding quietly down one of the narrow paths between the over-grown gravestones.

Mimi certainly does know her way around. As I follow the twin beams of her torches through the ivy-choked trees, I wonder whether it is really possible that she's never before been in here at night. She certainly gives no outward sign of the fear that I am beginning to feel.

I am afraid of rats, very afraid – and all of a sudden I become utterly certain that the undergrowth is full of them. Every rustle that I now hear is the slick-swift shifting of a plump rodent body.

All in all, I am very relieved when we finally emerge into the moonlit clearing around the Lebanon Circle.

'Watch,' said Mimi. 'Your watch.' 'Tell us.' 'What time?' 'The same.' 'Our watch.' 'It says –' 'Half-midnight.' 'Plenty.' 'Yes, yes-ah.' 'See you in one hour.' 'Don't come back till then.' 'Back here.' 'Private.' 'Time.' 'Doing what you do.' 'You.' 'Where you do it.' 'Whatever.' 'Leave now.' 'Go away.' 'Don't watch.'

Is it my impression, or are both of her starting to say the same words at the same time? – her duologue slowly regressing into monologue.

We go together down the steps that lead to the below-ground part of the Circle, and there we part – Mimi to the left, me to the right.

As I walk down the Avenue of Death, I can still hear Mimi's babble bubbling behind me. But I am more pre-occupied with the steel-doored catacombs that are starting to wall me in. With each door-way I pass, the presence of death – of death behind each door-way – becomes more palpable. Death is the darkness that glares out at me through each square window in the steel. Death is the small noises within the night's huge silence and the huge silence over-whelming the small noises. Death is the figure I feel equally sure is and isn't an inch or two just beyond the edge of my torched vision – having joined me, begun to follow me, catch me up, catch me.

Already terrified, I force myself to keep the same even pace. Footstep. Footstep.

Mimi is no longer audible.

After walking between the obelisks I turn right, in the direction of the Rossetti tomb.

Now that I have passed through the Avenue of Death, I feel more confident. The moon casts so generous a light upon the broad path that I hardly need my torch at all. Nothing else will be as bad as the walk down the Avenue of Death – nothing, perhaps, except the walk back up the Avenue of Death.

Without becoming too transfixed, and scaring myself all the more, I try to imagine how the cemetery must have appeared to Howell, Dr Llewellyn Williams, the solicitor and the two gravediggers. The presence of five men must, surely, have introduced a businesslike tone of bravado. There was probably alcohol and tobacco. When they reached the grave, as I am about to, the first thing they'd done was light the famous bonfire. It was better for them, I think: less scary – probably. (Yet I am not about to exhume a woman's seven-year-old corpse, am I?)

I turn off the path at what I hope is the point Matron stopped us to indicate the direction of the Rossetti tomb.

My fear is now subsumed by the struggle through the undergrowth. Low-hanging branches whip backwards into my eyes. Every incline, whether up or down, causes me to stumble. Sounds which I can't identify (rats–rats–rats) surround me.

Running my torch over the epitaphs of several non-Rossetti graves, I begin to think I've got the wrong area entirely. But then I catch sight of it – recognizable from a book of photographs. Only, in the photo, the headstone had been mantled in snow.

I sit down at the graveside, trying to imagine my way further back into the night of Lizzie's exhumation.

Fire. Crunching spades. Thudding earth. Muttering. Questions. Reassurances.

But I become distracted – my mind returns to Mimi. If I understand her, she has the key to Radclyffe Hall's catacomb. What is she planning? An exhumation of her own?

Suddenly, this becomes much more important to me than the events of a century and a half ago. There is too much library coming in between me and Lizzie Siddall. Mimi, on the other hand, is there – mysterious but reachable – only a few hundred yards away.

I want to go, to see, to know.

I decide that the safest way to approach the Circle is from the opposite side to Faraday's grave.

Taking my bearings from the moon, I set off to walk parallel to the Avenue of Death. This part of the cemetery, north of the Rossetti tomb, is known as the Meadow. The trees grow more sparsely here and the undergrowth is less trip-uppy.

When I think I've gone far enough, I turn right and emerge right next to the second set of steps down to the catacombs. If the steps on the Faraday side are at three o'clock, I stand now at nine. Radclyffe Hall's tomb, I am sure, occurs towards twelve o'clock.

To ensure that I am unobserved, I walk round the top of the Circle. Ten o'clock. Eleven.

The door to Radclyffe Hall's catacomb has been swung

open, and light comes faintly out of it, projecting a wedge of flickering yellow onto the ground.

Candles – they've lit candles!

I get down on my knees and crawl to the edge of the Upper Circle. I listen so intensely that it is almost as if I've discovered another sense. I more-than-hear them – babbling and giggling and moaning and gasping. The original attraction of Rossetti and Siddall comes back to me – the hint in their story of Dante Gabriel's necrophilic passion, Howell's intimation that Lizzie, though dead, was still a seductress. Desire engulfs me, crashing down as deep-drowning surf and a million unbreathable bubbles. I scramble back from the edge and lie gasping.

How barren, in comparison with Mimi's, had been my tribute to Lizzie! What audacious accuracy in this offering of hers – this offering of herself!

No longer in control of myself, I walk round and down the stairs. I have no choice: I have to go, to see, to know.

I put my bag down so that I will be better balanced – and can run away faster if need be.

At every step, the gravel crunchingly announces me. I will be caught. I don't want to be caught. I want to be caught. I want to know what the difference is between being caught and not being caught. But the only way that I can discover the difference is to be caught.

Their clothes and bags lie on the ground, in the dark, to the side of the door-way.

I am close enough now to peer round the corner and into the depths of the catacomb.

Mimi is there, on the ground, writhing, her head between Mimi's legs, Mimi's head between her legs.

There runs through them an electricity of delight – this is

a closed circuit — a dynamo — Faraday exemplified and improved.

I think it safe to come closer. After all, their eyes are closed.

Fatally, I take a step over the threshold of the tomb — and their eyes, at once, as one, open.

Now it comes — that which I have been anticipating from the moment I stepped off the bottom of the rope-ladder: a high, ragged-edged scream. It issues from both of them, equally. Then, in an instant, it snaps off into silence.

They hustle to their feet and stand there, naked but not bothering to cover themselves.

I take another step further into the catacomb, approaching, beseeching.

And all at once they flash past me, one on either side, Mimi and me and Mimi, a delicious moment of being-between-them; and then both of her are out into the night, and are pushing shut the catacomb door, pushing hard, pushing together, and all the night seems to be pushing with them.

I throw myself against the door and strain to keep it open. Slowly, Mimi and the night force me back. For a few seconds, I halt its progress. But then I reach out to try and stick my foot in, block it, and it slams shut.

The key turns.

Now it is I, and not Death, that is looking out through the steel squares in the catacomb door.

'Please,' I say. 'Please let me out.'

The sudden calm that comes over them is the most terrifying thing of all.

'No,' they say, as one. 'You watched.'

'But I didn't see anything,' I say. 'Please.'

They stand back out of the light as they put their clothes on. They know only too well that I've seen too much of everything already.

I continue to beg, hopelessly.

'Goodbye,' they at last say. 'For ever. And ever. Amen.'

I hear their footsteps – the footsteps of only one person – crunching off across the gravel. Getting fainter, becoming imaginary, falsely returning, becoming impossible.

So terrified. Can't move. Can't breathe. Almost. Breathe. Almost. Breathing. Sounds outside. Dark there. What are they? Can't see. Outside. Inside there are candles. Four candles. Flickering. Ghostly-ghastly. Don't think of that. It sounds like. Outside. Like a baby. Like an injured dog. Like a baby, wailing. Like a dog, dying. Flickering. Shadows. Ghostly. On the ceiling. Ghastly. Where are the rats? Is that them? Can they get in? Under the door. To eat. To feast. Are they already here? Or coming? How long is night? You know. Night-long. Long until day. These aren't *natural* noises. You don't believe. In what? In hardly anything. That's untrue. What do you? I believe in what scares me. And so? What scares me right now. Which is? Yes, witches – and dogs and babies and rats. That's not like you. This isn't like me. I'm not like you. I'm not myself. Be brave. Yes, be practical. Blow two candles out. Make plans. Save two for later. How much later? Much later. Put them here and here. Far apart. Only one will blow out. Shout try shouting. What point? Bring help. Bring the devil. Don't look at the coffins. Sit here. Coffins inside coffins. Sit still. That shadow. Is it a woman? Two women. No, one. It's no-one. It's just a shadow. A shadow can be someone. Yeah-yeah. The new coffin and the old coffin. Radclyffe Hall is in the new. Mabel

Veronica Batten is in the old. I said don't look. And you – I – you – you are in her catacomb – think of something to sing – candles flickering – they won't go out – la-la-la very brave boy – they can't go out – it'll soon be light – light again – everything will be alright – let me out – don't look out – come back for me, Mimi – you're panicking – of course I'm fucking panicking – shh, quiet lalala – wouldn't you panic? – No, I refuse to panic – Mimi – Mummy – Baby – Boo!

Unhaunted

I first met Chloë online – in the *UK Women* chatroom of gay.com. When we logged on that night, we were neither of us using our real names. She had chosen to call herself Chloë, although her real name was Monica. (Something I didn't learn until later.)

A few days later, I – who had previously masqueraded as '70s Disco Queen 'Agneta' – changed my monicker to 'Daphne'.

Daphne and Chloë. We were a cybercouple, of sorts.

Chloë was witty, well read, intelligent and seemed genuinely compassionate towards other women and their problems. (How wrong about a person can one be?)

Over the course of a week, we began to 'private' each other more and more – going off into a separate chat room accessible only to ourselves.

One all-nighter led to another, and – a week or so later – we were making arrangements to meet up at The Candy Bar, London's biggest bar for gay women, along with a few more of the regulars from *UK Women*.

Come the night, and I had dolled but, so I hoped, not tarted myself up.

(Chloë later said that she'd seen I was up for it right from the off. When I asked her, *What gave the game away?* Chloë said, *Oh, come on. Just . . . everything. You were working so hard at seeming casual, it was untrue.*)

Chloë wasn't like I'd imagined her. Perhaps the gentility of her online name had misled me: I'd expected someone a little less brash, someone a bit quiet. Someone like me.

Chloë was certainly *not* quiet. She was the first of our group to become openly pissed; but, once pissed, she seemed to remain perfectly in control. I admired this. I slur after a glass and chuck up midway through the second bottle.

Yet when she got up to go to the loo, there was a hint about Chloë of débutante-learning-to-walk-with-volume-of-*Debrett's*-balanced-on-her-noddle. I found this very endearing.

Plus the fact she was just gorgeous.

When we moved on to a restaurant, I manoeuvred myself into the seat next to Chloë.

For the rest of the evening, we ignored the other *UK Women* completely.

To be honest, I lost interest in anything but Chloë the moment I felt her hand touching my knee.

I don't know which emotion, embarrassment or delight, eventually won out, but the intensity of their battle lit me up like the Disney Store on Xmas Eve.

This – this under-table touching – was the kind of thing I wouldn't have let anyone else do. But Chloë was a girl for whom one automatically made exceptions.

I was starting to think this might be really serious. In the loos, I said her name to myself in the mirror, and watched myself blush.

One firm rule of mine has always been *no sex on a first date*. (This isn't anything to do with being some kind of lesbian-variety Rules Girl. It's just, if a girl gets into the habit of showing too much interest too early on, she can end up with an impressive collection of stalkers. Clinginess is endemic out there.) And this wasn't even a first date. Yet somehow Chloë and me found ourselves in a taxi (nothing more than kissing *there*, of course). In my kitchen. My sitting room. Bedroom. We were laughing, kissing, undressing, fucking.

Chloë's public brashness continued – she did things I'd *never* have dared, outside of a long-standing relationship.

(I've certainly *never* known someone make quite such a beeline for my arse.)

It was all good stuff, though: I hadn't had satisfying-sex in months.

Chloë stayed the night, and the night seemed very short.

Over breakfast, I tried to hold back from any mention of the future.

I needn't have worried. Chloë simply barged her way into my life. She said she'd outstayed her welcome with some scary Australian dykes down in Earls Court. Could she, perhaps, stay at mine for a few days? Just until she'd sorted somewhere permanent out for herself.

At the time I felt a nigglet of worry. How had Chloë ended up without a permanent place to stay? Had she jumped out of this last one, or was she booted?

She had, or she said she had, a perfectly stable job in magazine publishing. But when I asked her about it, she was vague as *Vogue*.

Whatever, I ignored my doubts.

I said, *Yes*.

Chloë taxied over to Earls Court and, two hours later, taxied back.

Somehow, without really planning or wanting it, I'd ended up with a full-time, live-in partner.

I don't really want to go into the day-to-day details of our three months four days together. The memories aren't pleasant, and least of all the pleasant ones.

We got on pretty well most of the time – at least, I *thought* we did.

I may not be the most perceptive person in the world, but I have a fairly well-developed sense of impending catastrophe. (I should have, given the sheer quantity of catastrophes that seem to impend themselves in my direction.)

Right from the start, Chloë took *everything* for granted. Most astonishingly, she took it for granted that I was in love with her.

And because she seemed so confident about this, and because I didn't have a moment to stop and consider it coldly, I too began to take it for granted.

I *must* love Chloë, my illogical logic said, otherwise I wouldn't be letting her live just another week and then *just* another week more in my flat. Rent free.

That it (this "love") was truly out of character, for me, cautious me, seemed only to make it all the more deeply true.

Looking back, I can see now that I thought and believed it rather than felt it.

As for what Chloë felt, I really have no idea.

Of course, even on that first evening – after she'd arrived back from Earls Court with her single suitcase – she did *say* she loved me.

But it wasn't quite that simple. What she actually said, every time but one (which I'll come to), was, 'I love you, babes.'

Perhaps it was the last message sent out by my depleted

catastrophe-sensors, but something told me that the "babes" wasn't entirely sincere. Or, maybe (though this I hardly dared think) that the "babes" was the only part of Chloë's declaration that *was* sincere.

If we'd been going out for ages, and it had developed as one of the rhythms of our relationship, the verbal tics and tricks of passion turned affection, drama become devotion, then I could have believed in "babes".

As things stood, I always heard it as a catchy jingle – coming just at the wrong moment: right at the highest, most swellingest point of the rhapsody that I'd been waiting years to hear.

There were other jingles. I can hear them clearly now. At the time, however, they tended to be subsumed in the jazzy syncopations of Chloë's . . . I don't know how else to put it – of Chloë's *Chloë-ness*.

Right from day one, she was jealous of any time I spent away from her. She disguised this, not very cleverly but efficiently enough, as mock-jealousy. (At this point, with my self-delusion in full effect, cleverness was not really required.)

She began to wear my clothes. Not only comfy-leggings and baggy sweaters, *that* I could understand. But my best underwear, and *all* the time. When I called her on it, she had an explanation ready, willing and able: 'I like to feel you next to me, babes.'

However, when *I* tried to put on a pair of *her* tights, she told me straight out they didn't suit. *No Trespassing* couldn't have been flagged up any clearer.

It took a couple of months for these little pixilated pixels to assemble themselves into anything approaching a full picture. (I doubt I have that even now.)

Something else which didn't help was Chloë's continued devotion to gay.com. She paid the chatrooms almost hourly visits – on *her* laptop, maybe, but on *my* phone-bill. (And, quite often, when she could have been talking to me instead. Face to face. Or not talking – kissing.) She claimed she just wanted to keep up with old friends. But eventually I began to suspect that the parasite was on the lookout for another host organism. (I wasn't thinking about her in quite those terms, yet. She was still my infuriating Chloca-Chlola – leaving the showerhead dripping, clipping her toenails onto the living-room carpet.)

About half-way through the third month, 'I love you, babes,' metamorphosed into the even less convincing, 'Love ya, babes.'

I had started to suspect that Chloë wasn't going in to work any more. She always got out of bed later than I did, and never seemed to bring her job-worries home with her. (Sometimes I felt I brought nothing else back with me. Not even a pay-packet.)

One day, premenstrual, and needing little further excuse to give in to my suspicions, I pulled a sickie.

It was mid-morning by the time I got back to my flat.

During the Tube journey, I had imagined myself catching Chloë going down on another *UK Woman*. This, your standard-issue betrayal, would have been crushing, but not exactly unforeseen.

What I *didn't* expect to find, when I rushed in the front door, giving her no time to escape, was Chloë, sitting at the kitchen table, blithely naked, eating an apple and reciting extracts from my diary into a Dictaphone.

The *main* reason this surprised me was that I kept my

diary in a passworded file in my laptop. Chloë, so far as I remembered, hadn't been given even a hint of my diary's existence. Since she'd moved in, I'd been very careful: writing my diary entries on my desktop computer during breaks at work, e-mailing them back to myself at the end of the day. From there, once I'd downloaded them, I copied and pasted them straight into the passworded file. Even at the point of our greatest intimacy, I'd never let Chloë watch me collect my e-mail.

She turned to me very coldly as I stood there in the doorway. 'You're home early,' she said. 'Not feeling well, babes?'

It was as if I'd lifted up the lovely mossy rock of her persona to see all the spiders and cockroaches of her personality wriggling and crawling about underneath.

'It took me two weeks to work out the password,' she said.

(My password, which I'd recently changed, was 'Pepsi'. This was a reference to my nickname for her: Chloca-Chlola.)

'Very witty,' she said.

Chloë, in her caught-out insolence, was more attractive than I'd ever seen her before. She was a completely different person. Not brash at all – calculating, in total control. Even her face looked different: longer, more defined.

'You have one hour to pack,' I said.

'Jesus,' she said. 'I don't need *that* long.'

I stood over her in the bedroom – intending to prevent her from stealing anything that belonged to me.

(As if, having taken my privacy, there was anything else *left*.)

Her new icy persona showed no crack. She packed as efficiently as a nurse boxing up the few bedside belongings of someone dead during the nightshift.

'Goodbye,' Chloë said, when she'd picked up her suit-

case. 'I enjoyed it. Really, I did. I was hoping it could last —
what? — at least another month.'

'Get out,' I said.

I followed her to the door and shut it behind her.

It was only then that I realized I'd forgotten to get my flat
keys back.

For a moment I considered running out after her into the
street. Demanding the keys.

But I knew, given the state I was in, I couldn't.

I felt that I wasn't physically able to speak another word to
her. Honestly, I would have preferred to die.

Stupidly, I didn't change the locks.

There was something about not doing this that was a kind
of dare — a dare to myself.

Chloë was out of my life, and I was glad about that. But
I didn't want to appear to *myself* as anything like the cold
callous person she had revealed herself to be.

It was as if, instead, I wanted my old self, the more trusting person I'd been before I met her, to let themselves back
into my flat through the slightly insecure door.

That wasn't, of course, what happened.

The first things I noticed were hardly 'things' at all. Each
of them, in itself, seemed so infinitesimal — just one more
speck of dust in the Hoover-bag of existence — that I would
most likely never have noticed them, had they not possessed
one notable quality: meaning. Yet I even managed, to begin
with, to ignore this, as well.

Chloë, as I think I mentioned earlier, had always left the
showerhead dripping slightly. The longer our relationship
went on, the more I asked her *please* not to do this — and

the more infuriating became her failure to comply. After she left, I assumed – without really thinking about it – that the showerhead would never drip again.

But oh no.

The first time I found it dripping, I assumed that I had just, subconsciously, picked up this slovenly habit of Chloë's myself.

I made a mental note always to screw the tap up as tight as a brand-new jar of Marmite.

And nothing changed.

The fourth time I came back from work to find the showerhead sputtering every other second, I began to suspect that someone else had been in the shower that day. And not, of course, just *any* someone.

Arguments between Chloë and me had always started over domestic issues.

I was the Maid, she Lady Muck.

The things I noticed began as little annoyances, little imperfections, little messes. But, as they accumulated and their meaningfulness became harder and harder to ignore, I started to believe they were really something else: little messages.

And all of them said exactly the same thing: 'I'm not really gone. You may try to convince yourself that I am. But I'm as *here* as when I was here.'

The living-room carpet became infested with toenail clippings. My jewellery box turned into a chaos of broken links and lost earrings.

One day I came home to find a single, greasy plate in the washing-up bowl; the next, the duvet turned back and the pillow dented. A week later, the phone was off the hook – beeping like crazy.

The phone wasn't the only crazy thing. Rather than think logically, act sensibly, and change the locks, I decided to do something else – something bizarre.

I began to leave notes for Chloë to find when she snuck back into the flat.

If the messes were her messages to me, then these notes were my messages back.

Some of the notes were your average Post-It, and these I left on the fridge door; others were little slivers of paper that I slipped in between the pages of books, under pillows, behind ornaments.

In them, I said the worst things about her that I could imagine.

They weren't really even *to* her – in order to make them as hurtful as possible, I used to imagine what I'd most fear hearing *her* say to *me*.

None of the notes disappeared. Nothing *that* dramatic occurred. Yet always, when I came home, the folds in them seemed a little less firm, and their orientation (not their position) on the kitchen table seemed to have changed.

One might put this down to the paper untensing, or to slight drafts, but right from the first day of the first note, I knew: Chloë and me were communicating again. A dialogue, of sorts, began.

If I left something really offensive for her, she'd leave me something disgusting in return.

For example, the day I left a note calling her a selfish cunt, I found a recently used tampon in my linen drawer.

The next day, my note said I hoped she died alone; her response was to leave the toilet full of unflushed pee.

But when, a week or so later, I found a feather on the door-mat, I left Chloë a sincere and rather blubby thankyou.

That evening, I returned home to find the TV on and *Breakfast at Tiffany's* being shown.

She must still love me, I thought – for about ten seconds.

I became almost glad that I'd let her keep the keys. (It was *let her* now; I'd completely forgotten about *been too cowardy to demand them back.*)

This was about three weeks after she left.

Perhaps a reconciliation was possible.

After Chloë moved out, I returned to gay.com – mainly as a means of talking out some of my anxiety and self-loathing.

Since the break-up, I'd been a complete wreck.

The others were very sympathetic. They saved my life by putting up with hour-upon-hour of maudlin badly typed drivel. I changed my online name to Dumpling.

Chloë seemed to have disappeared off the scene completely. Perhaps, having fucked me over so completely, she no longer felt able to cruise the other *UK Women*.

They all took my side. Chloë was the 'bfh' – bitch from hell.

No-one seemed to have seen her or heard anything from her in person since that night at The Candy Bar.

I continued writing notes, about one a day, their hatefulness slowly decreasing.

It was about a month later that one of the *UK Women* regulars appeared in the chatroom. I'll call her Medusa.

She didn't hang around. First thing she did was say she had something important to tell me.

We privated each other, in a chatroom called *What?* and it came straight out: *Chloë is dead.*

It was either someone who didn't like me playing a gross prank. Or it was Chloë herself, logging on in this other woman's name, just to fuck me around a bit more. Or, perhaps, it was really true.

Whichever, I was grateful for being alone, at home, with only my laptop as witness.

I asked Medusa a couple of things she would know that Chloë definitely wouldn't. She convinced me fairly quickly that she was who she said she was.

My next question was coldly factual. I was crying.

When?

Two weeks ago.

How?

Hit by a motorbike crossing the road.

How do you know?

I was with her. She was my lover.

Your lover?

She moved in to mine after she moved out of yours.

Why didn't you tell me before?

She didn't want you to know where she was.

No. I guess not. Why didn't you tell me for so long about her being dead?

Grief. Anger.

Sorry.

Sorry.

Superstitiously, I had the locks changed the very next day.

I don't know why – perhaps I was trying to keep the idea out: the idea that, all this time (one whole month), I'd thought it was Chloë letting herself back into my flat, invading the smallest peripheries of my life, using tiny things to tell me huge things, and all this time it had been nothing but my own preoccupation with her.

I didn't want her to have disappeared from my life as completely as she seemed to have done; and neither did I want entirely to have vanished from her life.

Changing the locks didn't seem to help.

Two weeks later, and the shower still dripped when I came home, the bed seemed to have been lain in, the plates got dirty and moved about by themselves.

This time, though, I couldn't avoid the knowledge that it was *me* creating these things that were hardly things.

The mess-messages were mine; the meaningfulness, mine also.

Out of guilt and confusion, I was madly tricking myself into thinking myself mad.

This seemed to reach a climax a few days ago, when I began writing notes again.

But this time the notes weren't addressed to Chloë (or 'you bitch' as I'd mostly called her), they were to myself, and they were painfully simple.

For the most part, they read: 'Leave me alone. Please. Just leave me alone.'

Story to be Translated
from English into French
and then Translated Back
(without reference to the original)

The Polaroid was still a pale and sickly yellow-white, even as I hurried down the spiral staircase and out of my apartment building. As I strode towards the Metro station, the image of what I had left behind me was slowly developing. At the moment I stepped off the empty platform and onto the crowded carriage, the image was ghostly but unmistakable. By the time I took the Polaroid once more out of my greatcoat pocket, it had darkened into a full existence.

Never before had a relationship of mine, an erotic relationship, reached such unbearable intensity. Never, throughout the entirety of my sexual life, had I found myself running, in horror and outrage, away from my own bedchamber. Horror and outrage at the possibility of the outrageously horrid extent of my own possible pleasure.

I felt as though I had committed a soon-to-be-notorious murder – and that, if I hadn't quite yet, perhaps I still might.

Careless of the people around me in the crowded carriage, I examined the Polaroid.

There Edith lay – as she was still lying, as she couldn't help but still be lying – strapped by the slenderness of her wrists and ankles to the sturdiness of the iron-construction four-poster bed. There was the blindfold, the blindfold which we'd laughingly bought together only an hour or so ago. There was the gag which she herself had decided was the best, the most efficient, the most gagging, in the entire extensive shop. It was Edith, too, who had asked the matter-of-fact assistant which were the most restrictive, most painful, hand- and ankle-cuffs. All I had done, it seemed, was smile, inspect, agree, pay.

A gasp from over my shoulder startled me from my reverie. I turned and saw a beautiful young woman, ice-blonde, sculpted, her mouth open and glistening. She had seen the Polaroid.

'Sir,' she said, lowering her eyes. 'I am very sorry . . . I couldn't help –'

'What do you think?' I asked.

She looked into my face but completely avoided eye contact.

'You are making pornography.'

She might, I noticed, have invested the word *pornography* with a far greater disgust than she had. There was fascination in this young woman – and fascination fascinates.

'I'm not busy at the moment,' I said. 'Why don't you allow me to buy you coffee? We can discuss it. Perhaps you might even be able to assist me.'

She looked down and hunched her shoulders, as if about to walk into a very strong and gusting wind.

There was defiance even in her acceptance.

'I choose the place. I leave when I say. You do not follow me when I leave. If I so choose, we never meet again.'

'Agreed,' I said.

We did not speak again until we reached her chosen stop.

★

As I stood there, beside the young ice-blonde, I closed my eyes and tried to imagine what Edith must be feeling.

Antoine has been gone for a long time now, perhaps an hour, perhaps more. I am getting thirsty. This gag is starting to hurt. I wish he would come back and release me. But perhaps this is part of his game. That's interesting: I didn't know he had a game. When we were in the shop, it was I who had to make all the suggestions. If I had left it up to Antoine, we would have come out of there with a too-lacy basque and some cheap black stockings. Not quite what I had in mind. O, he is such a bashful young man. I practically had to beg him to hit me the first time. Since when does a woman have to beg a man to give her pain? Since when was a man reluctant to force a woman's legs apart, to bind her hand and foot, to gag her, silence her, not to have to endure her incessant female language? Antoine was almost as disappointing as my husband. I wonder how long he will leave me here. Perhaps he has gone back to the shop to buy some more equipment – some of the more exciting pieces he baulked at before. Such a bourgeois little prude. You could tell he'd never done anything like this – never even tied a scarf over one of his little bourgeoise girlfriend's eyes. But he soon got a taste for it. All men do. All men, that is, apart from my husband. 'O, my darling,' he will say, 'how could you ask me to piss on you?' Boys from good families! You couldn't imagine that from a ghetto-child. Hmm. That must be blood at the corner of my mouth – it tastes like blood. Yes. A taste I should know well enough by now, even in the dark. My ribs hurt quite a lot. I think he may have cracked one. If he doesn't come back in five minutes, I will piss all over his lovely four-poster bed. That will serve him right for being so boring as to leave me. Then, perhaps, he'll teach me a real lesson.

*

'May I see the photograph again?' asked the young woman, once we were seated at a table outside a café I'd never before visited.

'Tell me your name,' I said.

'Marguerite,' she said, holding out her perfectly manicured hand.

'Truly?' I asked.

'That's for you to decide.'

I dropped the Polaroid onto the table-top and slid it towards her, face up.

She winced a little, then said: 'What a lot of blood there is. I assume that it's real?'

A gendarme walked past not three feet away, his right hand on his sub-machine-gun. He smiled briefly at Marguerite and at the thought of Marguerite.

'What do you think?' I asked.

She said nothing for a moment, then: 'I can see that she is smiling – almost sneering. Who is she?'

I took a sip of my double espresso.

'Guess,' I said.

'If she were just some model, I don't think she would sneer – not unless you asked her to. And this doesn't look like a sneer that has been asked for. It is too enjoyable. So, she is either your wife or your mistress. And as you are not married' – she dipped her head towards my ring-finger – 'I am guessing she is your mistress.'

'Very good,' I said. 'Now tell me why you think I was looking at this photograph on the Metro?'

'Perhaps because you are a pervert. You like to look at these kind of images in public. Maybe you want other people to glimpse them as well. That may be part of the fantasy. Women – women you find attractive. They must see, too. Did you choose me particularly?'

'What do you think?' I asked.

Our gazes met properly for the first time. Her eyes were a pitiless, viewless snow-blue.

'I think perhaps I was wrong – you are not a pervert. You were looking at this photo because you wanted to see it, because you *needed* to see it.'

'But why would I so *need* to see it?'

'You mean right then?'

'Yes.'

'And there?'

'Yes.'

'Because you were looking for something new in it . . . or, I don't know . . .'

I could see the thought forming, the smile rippling out across her full lips.

'. . . or you were looking at it for the first time.'

'You are a real detective,' I said. 'Now, Ms Marguerite Maigret, take your deduction one stage further.'

Under the table one of her feet kicked out unthinkingly as she looked back once again at the image. Her toe knocked my ankle, very gently and pleasantly.

'I'm sorry,' she said, in an absent voice. She tried to lift her eyes to accompany this apology, but they wouldn't pull themselves away from the sight of Edith's damaged body.

'You were looking at this photograph for the first time. It is a Polaroid, so it might have been taken some time ago and then thrust into a pocket, forgotten. You put on your coat today for the first time in months. It is cold, the start of winter – you reach your hand into your pocket . . .'

Finally, she looked into my face for confirmation – but saw something entirely different.

'Your hair,' she said. 'You have spots of blood in your hair.'

'Do I?' I asked.

'Oh my God,' she said.

I reached over and took the white-framed square of crumpled sheets and injured flesh out of Marguerite's hands.

'Exactly,' I said.

We gazed into each other's eyes for a full minute: she, into my impassiveness; I, into her expanding horror.

'Where is she?' Marguerite finally said. 'Where have you left her?'

'She is in my apartment, on my bed, lying there, exactly as you see her.'

'You must go back and release her,' said Marguerite.

'Actually,' I said, 'I was thinking of visiting my parents – just getting on a train and going down there and surprising them. I really don't see them often enough.'

Her horror expanded still further.

'Where do they live?' she asked.

'A little village about an hour from Toulouse. Perhaps I could stay over the weekend. My mother is such a delightful cook. I've nothing better to do.'

'The woman will die.'

'Quite possibly.'

'In your apartment.'

'That is not in doubt.'

Marguerite stood up, magnificently calm.

'You are mad!'

'Listen,' I said. 'Unless you do *exactly* as I say, I will leave

Paris and visit somebody, not my parents, they are dead, but, wherever I go, I won't be back for five or six days at least.'

'You wouldn't,' she said.

'Come with me,' I said.

'Where are we going?'

'The train station.'

Again, as the taxi took us to the Gare d'Austerlitz, we sat in silence.

I'm dying. It must be three hours — four. I was never any good at that silly children's game of guessing the time in the dark. He can't have gone back to the shop to buy more equipment. He'd've been home by now. Perhaps he's gone to see another woman — perhaps that is his game. Not a game I want to play. I think this will be the last time I see Antoine. An hour, I would accept. But this . . . God, I'm thirsty. Even the blood has stopped flowing into my mouth. When I get to see my husband, the bruises will be old. He won't believe that I was just that moment mugged. He'll know I was hanging around for a while. I'll have to tell him I was beaten unconscious, driven to the suburbs, left for dead on a piece of waste ground. I'll have to pretend they robbed me. I won't be able to use my credit cards until I get new ones. He'll insist even more forcibly that I go to the hospital, to the police. I'll have to tell him that I was raped. O God, it will be so tedious. Really, Antoine is terrible. He has no sense of timing. This is so boring. I expect there will be terrible bruises on my wrists and ankles — which means I'll have to wear trouser suits for the next decade. How tedious. How boring.

Marguerite watched me as I bought my train ticket. She watched me as I found my seat and sat down. She watched as the clock ticked towards departure time . . . ten minutes . . . five . . . three . . . two . . . She watched my face, still impassive, as the guard blew his whistle. And then, as the last of the train doors slammed shut, she cracked . . .

'Alright,' she said. 'I believe you. You would leave. You would go. Now, let's get off this train.'

I could feel the engines starting up.

'You'll do what I ask?' I said.

'Everything,' said Marguerite.

'Exactly?' I said.

'Exactly,' she replied. 'Come on!'

The engines engaged and the train started to glide forwards. We dashed along the aisle, opened the door and leapt down onto the very end of the platform.

Another taxi, another silence.

O, my dry aching throat. O, my sore ankles. O, my rubbed-raw wrists. I hate Antoine, but he is a stronger man than I thought he was. He is more of a true sadist — taking no account of his victim's pleasure. I hadn't found this being left at all pleasurable — not until I thought how truly sadistic Antoine was being. He knows my husband will find out, but he is not afraid of involving our real lives in this. I've started to get really wet at the thought of his unflinching cruelty, his unwavering pursuit of only his own pleasure. If only some of that wetness were in my throat. And now I've pissed in his bed. I can't wait for him to come back. I will offer myself to him. I will be his slave for ever. I will say, 'Do what you want with me. Take me wherever you want.'

As we drove towards the shop, I saw a pharmacy and told the driver to stop. When I returned to the taxi I was carrying a brand-new Polaroid camera and several more packets of film.

'Load it up,' I said, and handed it to Marguerite.

In the sex shop I asked for another set of everything. I could tell that even the matter-of-fact assistant was impressed by my reappearance (only a couple of hours after my first visit) with a completely different but equally beautiful woman. How my manner had changed in the mean time. How confident I was.

Marguerite had become sullen and unresponsive. Her eyes were dull.

I'd told the taxi to wait for us outside.

Antoine is a god. I am a worm. Antoine is splendid. I am worthless. All I ask is the chance to be at his merciless mercy. Let him express his contempt for me in any way he sees fit. I will not question his wisdom. He will be my master. Let this pain be my tribute to him. Let every ache cry my devotion. O, let my abasement be total and his domination ultimate. If he would only come back. If he would only release me into my greater servitude.

For a few moments, as the taxi drove away, we stood facing each other on the leaf-strewn pavement.

'When you come inside,' I said, 'You may behave as you wish.'

'I do not know how I will wish to behave.'

'That is fine,' I said.

'This driver has seen us together,' she said. 'You are not safe. If you kill me, you will be caught.'

I looked at the departing Mercedes.

'He has seen me with you as well as you with me.'

Marguerite seemed puzzled.

'You will understand soon enough,' I said. 'Come on.'

I took her by the arm and led her past the concierge.

★

What's this? I hear the lift being called, the lift descending and rising, voices, footsteps, a male voice and a female voice, the key in the front door, Antoine's voice and the voice of a woman I've never met, footsteps down the hall and into the bedroom, a conversation, a conversation about me —

'What's her name?'

'Edith.'

'And is she your mistress?'

'Yes, she was — but maybe she won't want to be any longer. What do you think?'

'Ask her.'

'Edith, nod your head if you're still my mistress.'

O, how my neck aches as I nod and I nod and I nod. Yes, Antoine, I am yours. I am yours for ever. You have brought another woman back to see me like this. Perhaps to do other things altogether. I am in such pain: it is exquisite.

'No, she really isn't my mistress any longer — whatever she thinks. I'm going to get rid of her. I will release her. She can go. This won't happen again.'

'Thank you,' said Marguerite.

'I'm not doing this for you.'

His voice in my ear, saying: 'Listen, Edith. You have to do exactly what I say. I am going to release you. After I release you, you are going to get up, get dressed and get out. I never want to see you or hear from you again. This is finished. Do you understand? Nod if you understand.' And my neck and my heart and my soul wrenching with agony as I nod. His voice again, saying: 'Do you agree never to see me again?' I do nothing. Antoine's voice, saying:

'If you don't agree, I will leave you here until you die.' A small nod. I feel the buckles at my left ankle being undone, my right hand, my left ankle, hand. The gag being unbuckled behind my head. The blindfold being ripped away. I try to look at him, but the light — O, the terrible light.

Marguerite was waiting in my study when I came through, after I'd helped Edith — crying, begging, calling me a god, clutching the soiled equipment — into the lift.

'Let's go,' I said.

Marguerite let the manuscript page she'd been reading fall back onto my desk.

'But you are —' she said.

'Let's *go*,' I said.

'This is —'

'Yes, I am.'

'Go where?' Marguerite asked, blandly, as if she didn't know.

I held up the bag full of new equipment — the new gag, the new blindfold, the new hand- and ankle-cuffs, the new Polaroid camera.

'Wherever you want,' I said. *Wherever you want.*

tourbusting 2

I'd like to tell you about Lindsay, now, if you'd like to hear.

I think I mentioned her yesterday or the day before, when we were in that bar, uh, in, you know – that one with the . . . yeah, right. Wild, huh?

I knew Lindsay all the way through school, but we never really dated. I have my suspicions that we kissed, once, maybe – I can't remember where or when. And I can't think why. I didn't even like her then, and she was in love with – well, I'll tell you that later.

This isn't for the profile, you understand. This is just, like, between you and me. Because I *like* you.

Anyway, I can't remember the first time we met, either. Though it was probably in a corridor somewhere. You always meet the most important people in your life in corridors or on stairs. Never in rooms. Don't you think that's weird? And we would've not even – whoah, let's try that again. We didn't shake hands. We just, I guess, shrugged and said hi.

Saying that to you now makes me think I can see it all over again: Lindsay pulling the hair out of her eyes with a half-curled finger. But that's way too convenient to be a real memory, isn't it?

(Can I borrow another cigarette? I always fucking forget to buy them when we pit-stop.)

Anyway, we were just starting to form the band that later went on to make history as *okay*.

(Thanks.)

Only later did we get our famous nicknames. I wasn't yet Clap: I was just plain Brian. And Lindsay was just plain Lindsay – and Lindsay, really, was always just *plain*. She looked unfortunately like Carole King or Laura Nyro. One of those great women songwriters who you just love, and really try hard to find attractive, but just can't. Nina Simone, even. Where you love them with your eyes closed and them singing, but you can't even bear to have their poster up on your wall.

We used to rehearse over in this shack that used to be attached to a church. But the church was gone. Someone had bought it – the whole thing – and moved it to another town. It was made of corrugated iron.

And I heard, where they moved it to, they put it inside *another* church. And they called it something like 'the heart of the Lord'. Because the new church didn't feel like it had any old-time religion in it: so they drove down the road, stopped off and bought some. Seriously.

One of the walls of this shack was wood, the rest were iron. Sometimes, if you got the feedback going just right and loud enough, you could make the whole thing shake like it was going to fall down on top of you.

Lindsay was our first fan. Also, I suppose, our first groupie – though I think only two of us actually slept with her.

(I'll let you figure out who.)

When we were just banging away, sounding really trashy, she would sit there behind one of the amps – nodding her head like we were the Velvets or something. In the beginning, Lindsay was really important to us – really encouraging. When we were down, she'd say, 'Hey, you were really getting somewhere today.' She could hear things in us that we couldn't hear ourselves. She heard *through* us. I think, back then, she heard everything we've ever done since – right up to the break-up and beyond.

I know a lot of people have come along claiming to have discovered us. But it's Lindsay really that was the first. I mean, even our moms and sisters thought we were totally unlistenable.

(They listen now, alright. Sitting by their guitar-shaped poolsides in Montreal. Yeah.)

If you asked the others, if you asked Syph, he probably wouldn't even remember her. She's exactly the kind of thing he was always trying to forget.

What makes me really guilty is that we kind of dumped her early on. Like a girlfriend who's becoming an embarrassment. We had to. There was a reason. Banging away at our practice sessions in that iron shack next to the church that wasn't there any more, we were slowly getting to be quite good. But no-one knew it, and when we told people, they wouldn't believe it. In school we were actually known as 'the band that Lindsay hangs out with'. You see, association with Lindsay was making us out to look like losers. The logic went something like this: the girls thought, *They must be really sad and unsexy if Lindsay's the only girl that hangs out with them*; the boys thought, *Why go and see them play, there's no-one there but Lindsay to pick up.* And so Syph dumped her for us, on our behalf. He found some lame excuse, like she'd been stealing guitar-leads or something, and he bawled her out and threw her out and that was that.

Almost immediately, a better class of girl started to come around. In other words, getting rid of Lindsay *worked*. It helped give us a start. When we played, the girls came. And when the girls came, the boys came. They all liked the music.

I remember the first time we played to over fifty people, and that was like a big deal for us back then – Lindsay was there, standing at the back, crying: all through the gig, crying. She tried to speak to Syph afterwards, but he just blew past her – blew her off. I stopped and talked for a while.

'You're doing really well,' she said. 'You sound really tight. You're going to make it.'

And we did, in a sort of a way. We weren't the Beatles or anything. But we started to get the supports. We could headline locally. Play anywhere we liked, locally.

Next thing we knew, we had the deal, cut the record and started to go off on tours. We went to Great Britain first of all. Before we'd even toured properly at home. I've always liked Great Britain. My mom came from there. My grandmother still lives there. This music paper, the *NME*, gave us a really good review for one of our singles. 'Sea Song' I think it was. And lots of people turned up for this gig at the Marquee. Like the Television song, 'Marquee Moon'?

But you know all that shit already. I'm going to try to stay focused on Lindsay from now on.

We were away for about two months. Did Germany, Holland, Spain – or maybe not Spain. Italy. When we got back, we went into the studio to record. The shack had been knocked down, and the 'good old days' were knocked down with it. We started to get really serious about things like The Snare Sound – which is when you know it's starting to go a little wrong. Honestly, no-one cares about The Snare

Sound. Or like, 1 per cent of people do – the ones that listen on Hi-fis that cost more than they get paid in a year.

So, Lindsay wasn't around to hook up with. I only saw her again by accident. She was working in the library – behind the counter, checking out books. I went in there to get something by August Strindberg, who this English music journalist told me I'd, you know, empathize with.

(That was how come we wrote the song 'August'. It wasn't the month, it was the gloomiest fucking playwright that ever stuck a pair of cripples onstage and made them hate each other. But I guess you know that already. Done your research all the way, haven't you?)

I didn't recognize her at first. She was wearing these bottle-thick glasses. Her hair was done up in slides. Not fancy ones with butterflies on or anything. Just plain brown slides. And her hair was the same old Carole King Jewfro – you know, thick, really thick. And the slides just couldn't cope. They kept pinging out onto the books.

I stood looking at her from behind one of those turn-around things they stack paperbacks on. The sight of her made me want to cry, really. I mean, she had never looked anything like good. But it was as if she were trying *really* hard to look shitty. And nature was giving her more than all the help she'd need.

Here we come to the second thing that makes me feel guilty: I didn't speak to her that time. I found a back way out, so I didn't have to walk past the counter again.

I was feeling bad the whole way home. I couldn't stop thinking about it. What if she'd seen me? What if she knew I'd decided not to go up and talk to her? She'd think I was playing the big star.

(But then, what the fuck – I was going into a library! We

hadn't made any money then. None at all. Top-ten album, and *no money*. Believe it.)

All the band met up that night in a pizza place, and we were surrounded by some good-looking women. Syph was playing the local hero. Really, he was such a *dick*. Dropping names of people he'd seen, like, for five seconds, walking into the Executive Lounge at some airport. Like he'd jammed with them all night in the studio. And I couldn't stop thinking about Lindsay.

(Did I mention about her name? Her mom named her after Lindsay Wagner. It was as if Lindsay was doomed for ever to live in the '70s.)

So, anyway, the next day I go round to the library. And on the way I even buy her a bunch of flowers. I don't know why. I wanted to say sorry for not talking to her the day before. But I also didn't want her to know that I hadn't talked to her the day before. So I realized I couldn't give her the flowers. So I hid them behind a fence before I got there.

(Went back to pick them up later, and they'd gone. Some fucker had seen them and stolen them. To give to his poor disabled mother, I hope. (Isn't it weird the things you remember?))

I'm rambling, I know. It's the JB talking. What was I saying?

(The library – right. The library.)

It was a big yellow building. Made out of concrete. But somehow yellow. '70s yellow – like California sunshine going down on the hood of a gold Chevrolet. She was in the exact same place, and I pretended just to notice her when I went up to get the Strindberg book out. It was black and had about four plays in. One of them was *Ghost Sonata*, the play the journalist had namechecked. Lindsay was so delighted to see me, it made me feel even worse about the day before. And we agreed to go for coffee, after she got off.

(I can remember *so* many girls working behind counters who, before the band took off, I'd wanted to ask when they got off. But it never worked out – if I did ask, they never said yes. And now, when it didn't matter at all, when it meant something completely different, it was the easiest thing in the world.)

I turned up back at the library. I told her I'd gone home, but I'd just gone and sat in the park and read that weird fucking play. I was so nervous I could hardly read. I don't know why. I have no idea. I mean, this was Lindsay – Lindsay who looked like Carole King: I didn't find her at all attractive. I couldn't remember having talked to her that much, even when we were rehearsing in the shack.

She came down the concrete stairs in the sunlight. My hands were shaking, like an hour after a great show – adrenalin. I was glad to see she hadn't done anything with her hair or her appearance generally. That would have suggested she had *hope* – which would have broken my heart. I didn't want her to have any hope as far as me and loving her was concerned.

(Does that sound cruel? I meant it to sound kind. I felt really . . . compassionate towards her. God, that sounds even worse, doesn't it?)

She noticed the shaking in my hands.

'Caffeine,' I said.

'Yeah,' she said. 'I know. It's terrible. Shall we go get some more?'

We went and sat there, in one of the booths in the coffee shop. It was an old high-school hang. A few of the students knew who I was, and looked at me, but this was before anyone started coming up for autographs.

Lindsay said, 'I was surprised to see you getting that out.' She meant the Strindberg.

I explained about the journalist.

'That's very studious of you,' she said. 'It's not exactly rockstar behaviour.'

I flashed back to Syph, bumping past and cutting her at that first big gig.

'Well,' I said, 'I'm not exactly a star. I'm a drummer. Drummers are never stars.'

'Except Ringo,' Lindsay said.

As I laughed, even though it was a bit lame, I realized how much I *liked* Lindsay.

Liking isn't meant to be a particularly strong emotion: the whole liking vibe is meant to be pretty mild. But sometimes, you know, you can just be overwhelmed with how much you like someone. And at that moment I *liked* Lindsay more than I've ever liked anyone. I wanted everything to go well for her. Her job. Her life. Love.

We talked about Strindberg for a while. She'd read him, and knew a lot more about him than I'd managed to pick up in the previous four hours. Then she started to ask about what life in the band was like. I told her. I told her the old stories, but I tried to put some truth back into them. I didn't exaggerate as much as usual. I really wanted to give her some idea of what it was like, although I wasn't sure if that would make her feel bad about not being there with us. She wanted to hear, I think. I wasn't just torturing her. Thinking back, I should probably have insisted on asking her more questions. Because this coffee date – which wasn't a date – set up our relationship for what was going to be the rest of it. She would ask; I would answer.

My liking-buzz started to wear off. Lindsay's breath smelt a little, I think she'd eaten something meaty for lunch, and she had a slightly annoying way of dropping her jaw and going *Wow* whenever I said anything even remotely starry. I tried to keep liking her as hard and as much as I had when she told the joke, but it just didn't work. It was easier to concentrate on telling her the kind of stories she wanted to hear. We talked till late. I kissed her on the cheek when we said goodbye. Even half-hugged her.

I'd like to say something like *As she turned away from me, smiling, I thought, Maybe there's just a chance* –

That would be a lie. I had a girlfriend. I *thought* I loved *her*.

I saw Lindsay a couple more times before we went off on tour again.

And that was how we fell into the rhythm. I'd be gone like five, six months. When I came back round, older, tireder, more famous, richer – having had huge amounts more sex (I decided pretty soon I didn't really love that old girlfriend of mine) – I would go to the library. Lindsay would be there. It seemed like from one tour to the next, she didn't move from the Books Out counter. Her hair never got longer or changed.

In all the madness that goes on, she was the thing I clung to. I would be getting loaded in some Tokyo strip bar, and I'd be thinking about Lindsay stamping books. She was my *O Canada*.

Whenever I heard Joni or Carole or Laura, and I had tapes of theirs for the bus, I thought of Lindsay. I often wished she were more beautiful, so I could make her into my poster-girl – put her up on the wall in my head.

Sometimes, when I made it home, I'd even go to the library intending to start something with her: her goodness was so much more important than all the sluts on the road that just want to say they've banged someone in the band.

But when I saw her, standing like she always did, where she always did, I knew it wasn't meant to be.

We became like old people in our habits. We'd go out for coffee, and try and sit in the usual booth. We'd order the same thing. At some point, I'd get that same *whoosh* of power-liking. (Power-liking, I like that.) Then it would fade away. She'd ask me questions; I'd tell her what she wanted to hear. Sometimes, I sounded to myself like Syph – Kurt this, Michael that. Lindsay was my hometown reality check. She was the valve on the decompression chamber.

So, one time, when I got back from a whole six-month deal – touring the fifth album (the live one) – it destroyed me to find she wasn't there.

I mean, I was half-destroyed just by her not being at the Books Out counter. I'd always believed there were worn places in the lino where she used to stand. Another librarian was in her place. A boy. He knew who I was. When I tried to ask him where Lindsay was, he was like, 'You know *Lindsay*?'

'Yeah,' I said. 'Where is she?'

I knew he was going to ask me for my autograph. He just had the *look*.

'You don't know about Lindsay.'

'What about her?' I said.

'She left.'

'Left where.'

'Left town, I guess.'

'Left to go where?'

'I'm not sure. I can ask.'

'Ask,' I said.

He hesitated.

'*Then* you can have my autograph,' I said.

He went off. I heard him say *asshole*. Perhaps he *hadn't* wanted the autograph.

When he came back he said, 'They don't know.'

'Let me talk to them,' I said. 'It's very important that I find out where she is.'

Because, you see, in all those times we'd gone for coffee, I'd never got her number or found out where she lived. She was always at the library. I didn't need her address.

The librarian-boy goes and gets the head librarian, Miss Watts, who was like this figure of myth from my childhood. She used to be as tall as New York. (Crabs had nicknamed one of his amps Miss Watts.)

'How are you, Brian?' she asks.

We chat for long enough for it to seem polite, then I ask about Lindsay.

Pretty soon it becomes clear that Miss Watts really *doesn't* know where Lindsay went. Reading between the lines, it sounds like Lindsay especially didn't want Miss Watts to know where she was going.

I was able to get Lindsay's home address out of her.

Miss Watts asked for my autograph, for her daughter.

When I dropped by Lindsay's old place, it was an apartment block. After pressing all the buzzers, someone let me in. The elevator had piss in the corner. Her number was 44. No-one was in.

I left a note with my number.

No-one rang.

All that time I was away on tour, Lindsay wasn't behind

the counter in the library. She was living in an apartment block where people pissed in the elevator.

And that's Lindsay for you. That's all I know.

I hope she's happy, wherever she is. Whatever she's doing.

When I think of her these days, though, she isn't in the library. She's back behind the amps, reading some philosophy book. She looks younger, and better than she ever really did – like your memory of Carole King when you're trying to be kind in your mind about what she looks like.

Hey, on second thoughts, maybe you could put something about her in the profile.

Just a line at the end.

'Lindsay, if you're out there, call.'

Something like that.

Or maybe not.

(Hey, forget it. You know. Forget. It.)

Alphabed

(Sections to be read
in any order
other than the one printed.)

She lies propped up on one elbow looking across at him, trying to work out what he still means to her. She looks at the flatness of his chest and is struck once again by how widely apart his nipples are spaced. They look like broad coins made of brown-pink flesh that have been pressed flatly into the skin over his ribcage. She looks at the few pube-like hairs that form pathetic aureoles around them. She is still trying to think about what he means to her, but all she can think of are his stupid nipples. They are getting in the way. 'Look,' she says, as if by framing a word for him she could frame a thought for herself. 'Yeah,' he says, opening his eyes. She reaches over and pinches his left nipple, pretending that this was what she meant all along. He winces, un-amused. Perhaps he's half-caught-on to what she was trying to think. This could be dangerous.

He turned her over onto her front. She resisted, a little but not much. He forced her legs a little apart, so he could kneel in between them. Again, she resisted. 'Hey,' he said, and she relaxed. He was between her legs, now, looking up the bed towards the pink velour headboard. Her back was a totally present slab of flesh. At times like this, he was capable of totally losing interest in her. He forced his knees further apart, forcing her legs further apart. 'What?' she said. For a while, he waited − doing nothing. Then he stroked her cunt gently, upwards, once. She moaned, from pleasure or impatience. He lay down at her side again.

For no reason that she is consciously aware of, she begins to cry. In the moment or two she thinks about it, she recognizes whole areas of remorse within herself that she doesn't have the capacity to deal with. Not at the moment. Not at this exact moment. She senses – as she has sensed them before – darkness and density. There is a screech, not a soft sound, but half-way between white noise and feedback. Instinctively, she turns away from it – swerving into an obvious action: grabbing hold of his penis and dropping her head onto it. The taste in her mouth – of him and her and her and him, intermingling, seemingly for ever – the taste disgusts her into thinking about how little she wants to be doing this. Any of this. So she stops. 'Hey,' he says, a very long way from understanding what's just happened. Miles and miles.

D

He lay back, staring up at the dirty ceiling. She reached over and took his penis in her hand. Did this turn him on? He was no longer sure. This whole thing had been going on for so long. When he looked down he was surprised to see that his penis was still fully erect. Perhaps his body was more into hers than he knew. 'Yes?' she whispered. He wasn't sure what she meant, unless she meant what he thought she meant. She started to pull his foreskin off the head, slowly. He could smell the bedsheets around him and the pillows under him. Everything was damp. Her body against his side was almost wet. 'Yes,' he replied.

There is something comforting to her in the squalor that surrounds them: the damp sheets, the dirty room. It confirms to her that she is bad. Her forefinger strays down his side, bumping over his ribs. Abstractedly, she brings her forefinger up to her eyes and examines it, as if expecting to find a scurf-crescent of dust upon it – as if, she thinks, she were her own mother coming into this room and interrogating the mantelpiece. *Slattern*, that's what her mother would call her. *Slatternly*, that's what she is. A brief glow of the old disobedience flares up in her lower spine. If what she is doing here is something her mother would disapprove of, then it has to have *some* virtue. This thought makes her for a moment almost happy.

He turned over onto his front. She ran her hand slowly over his back and buttocks. From what he could tell, she wasn't really concentrating. Perhaps she was already thinking of someone else. Her nipples were lower down her chest than when he had first known her. 'Back,' he said, and she knew what he meant. She got up and straddled him, sitting heavily on his buttocks. He felt the wetness of her cunt-hairs in the small of his back. How long has this been going on? 'Where?' she asked. He indicated with his hand. She saw the spot and squeezed it, wiping the pus off on the headboard. When he said nothing, she lay back down at his side.

She begins to concentrate on the sheets around them. They are soft and damp. They have hairs both long and wiry all over them. They are often stained. There are white stains and red stains and brown stains. The white stains are amoeba-shaped. The red stains sometimes rub off on their hips. The brown stains are watery in some places and almost black in others. The pillows also are stained. There are make-up stains on the pillows. Both of them, not just hers. They have swapped pillows countless times. Down at the bottom of the bed there are several rips in the sheets. Her feet in stretching sometimes create these rips or slip through them. His feet in gaining purchase explore and augment them. There are thick smears on the headboard, where he and she have wiped bogies off their fingers. When she rolls across the bed she can feel small particles following her, slipping down into the dip she makes.

He got up to go for a piss. When he got into the toilet, he had to wait for a while for his erection to go down. He tried thinking about unsexy things: oranges, old men, warts, surgery. None of them seemed to work. In fact, he was surprised to discover, the thought of oranges made him harder than usual. She would be waiting for him, lying there. 'Fuck,' he whispered. He braced his hands against the toilet's narrow walls. This was not good. He looked down and noticed his penis was flaccid. Thinking of her must have done it. This was even worse. He pissed for what seemed like a long time. It was more satisfying than his last orgasm. He dripped himself off and walked back through into the bedroom without washing his hands. As he was lying down, his skin touching hers again, his erection came back.

It suddenly becomes clear to her, as she is being fucked up the arse by him, that they are playing in effect a very childish game – they are each doing their best to completely impregnate the other. (It really isn't any more mature than mud pies in the face on the beach during summer holidays.) He is forcing his spunk up into every accessible part of her body: her cunt, anus, mouth, but also her nose and ears, also through the pores of her skin. And she, in return, digs her nails into him, leaves the smell of her come and her shit on his cock, under his fingernails, across his tongue. This doesn't seem to be anything like a fair exchange. It is – really – impossible for her to compete. There is for her the threat of possible pregnancy – remote, but not negligible. All it would take for him to efface her completely would be a few days and a few showers. 'Stop,' she says, meaning the fucking. He seems to fear an argument, so stops. With relief she feels him – and other things – slide out of her.

J

An impulse to fuck her from a new position came over him. But he couldn't think of one they hadn't tried. He turned himself round so his head was near her feet. 'What?' she said. 'Yeah,' he said. Somehow she understood. That was how it worked, these days. She turned so her back was facing him. Now, this was going to be tricky. He wanted to slide it in, but everything was at a strange cutting-your-hair-in-the-mirror angle. His penis slid between her damp buttocks but not into her cunt. Her feet were close up to his face, dirty soles. He didn't want her to kick him in the face when she was coming. She tended to thrash about. No, it wasn't working. He turned himself round again and lay back.

As he fucks her she is aware of only two things: one, a distant pleasure, comparable to hearing that someone one was once friends with has struck lucky; two, the red spots across the top of his shoulders. Of the two, the spots are by far the most pressing. In an attempt to block them, she looks up at the paper globe that hangs round the single lightbulb in the ceiling. It is either dawn or dusk, and the globe is perceptible only by the lighter grey of the side it presents to the window and the darker grey of the side it hides. Her head jogs up and down slightly, making her vision insecure. From this angle she cannot see the thick white wire that the globe depends upon. It hangs like a paper version of a kind of world she might prefer to the one she actually inhabits – a world of subtle but definite graduations of tone. Monotony rendered untenable. The head-jogging stops. He has come, she now notices. Or perhaps he has just stopped.

L

He wanted to come but he didn't really want her involved. 'Hey,' he said. 'Watch.' She got up on one elbow and looked at him. He closed his eyes and started to wank himself off. Something moved up his side – oh, she was stroking him. He batted her hand away. The last thing he wanted was to be reminded that she was present. Still, he could feel her eyes touching him – particularly down over his penis. It was like being butterfly-kissed. He continued wanking himself off, trying to think of some image to come over. What TV programmes had he watched recently? Which actresses did he fancy? What songs were in the charts? Was there anyone he'd seen in the last couple of days? What about ex-girlfriends? Or that girl that he'd always seen on the bus into school? None of them was right. He couldn't be bothered. He stopped.

With a certain perverse pride she examines the bruises on her upper arms: blue, brown, yellow, green. All the strange colours that flesh employs to express its belated resentment. This is where he holds her when he holds her down. It is a weird kind of consent that she gives to this force – at the time, she resists it; before, she forbids it; after, she complains about it; but overall she knows that it is necessary. Otherwise she might smash a fist into her own mouth or buck so extravagantly that he would slop out of her. Hard as it is to credit, she does still sometimes completely lose all control. 'Look,' she says, holding her bruised arm up in front of him. 'Look,' he says, and lifts his nail-torn hips up from the bed. She miaows and makes her hand into a claw. He beats his chest and grunts.

N

He could feel her shifting across and down the mattress. Kisses started at his neck and moved down over his belly. The light coming through the net-curtains made both their bodies look grey and drug-habity. He closed his eyes. This was something he didn't want to see. Her fingers clenched round his penis. This was so boring. Her kisses reached the thicker hairs above his penis. They became more tentative. How many times had she ended up coughing her lungs up because of some manky little pube? 'Mmm,' he said, knowing it was the polite thing to do. 'Yes,' she said. Her lips moved round the head of his penis. She was tasting him; she was tasting herself. It went on for a while.

There are, she remembers, some sexual fantasies that she once had for them which they never got round to – and now, she is sure, never will. Though she managed to paint his toe- and fingernails whilst he was asleep, she never got him into one of her dresses. They would fit – that isn't the problem. It's just that he says he'd look ridiculous. She can't make him understand that it's him looking ridiculous but *not minding* that's half the turn-on. He says things like he'd have to shave his legs. 'So?' she says. And there were other fantasies as well: they never did find that empty Underground carriage or slowly ascending lift or last changing room on the right; they never bought that strap-on double-ended dildo; they never even went *al fresco*. In fact, they had never been outside London together. She sighs, quietly.

P As she was now lying with her eyes closed he was able, for a while, to watch her. He didn't think she was asleep. More likely, he suspected, she was trying to get his attention by playing dead. Sometimes, when they were in bed like this, she would play to his worst fears and deliberately stop breathing. By now, he'd become accustomed to this trick. But, to start off with, he hadn't been able to tell exactly what was wrong. He would just become incredibly anxious and believe his own death was imminent. Then she would start breathing again, as quietly as she could. His anxiety would lessen, but not disappear. Then, one day, he'd caught her at it and started beating on her chest. She exploded into laughter. If she tried that trick on now, he decided, he would try to hurt her more than usual when they fucked.

She remembers how once upon a time every touch of his skin was a delightful shock. *You forget how soft boys are*, she thinks. *Between them – between boys*. But now his soft presence, there to her left, is hardly more surprising than her own left hand. At every moment, day and night – apart from brief trips to the toilet (and sometimes not even then) – they are touching, warming against the other's warmth, sweating at the contact, becoming raw at hips and ribs. She is aware that if one day he weren't there, she would miss him – physically. But this imagined missing is a feeling she would like to try out. She wishes he might take his skin away and leave her own to her – for her to rediscover, forget, rediscover, forget. She reaches her left arm up above her head and he automatically nudges his head into her armpit. This was the response she wanted him to make – the gesture most succinctly to confirm her hatred.

He made her turn away from him, so he could inspect her back. What he'd always wanted, he thought, was not a woman but an alabaster statue that would come alive when he wanted to fuck it. Skin, close up, was about the most disgusting thing he could think of. There were moles on her shoulders – some of them little brown cauliflowers that he wanted to bite off. Occasionally, when razing her back with his nails, he had clipped one and made it bleed. They only noticed when they saw the butterfly-shaped red spots on the sheets. You could die from that, later – from leukemia. There were no spots on her back to squeeze. No fun to be had at all. He slapped her bottom and she lay back again.

The pleasure they used to give each other — as she remembers it — sometimes lasted hour upon hour. Now, it has become something begun out of brief desire and ended, as soon as possible, in deep disgust. Once, she would lie back as he constructed another language of praise, vowel by vowel, consonant by consonant, upon the unparallel lines of her cunt. Once, he could see his way through into new worlds of allure, following the hints of her flicking tongue. Now, it is all aboard for the smalltown mystery tour they have already twenty times taken. Now, their bodies are familiar laboratories in which nothing more original is bred than contempt. Once, each touch was pure exploration and improvisation. Now, preprogrammed sub-routine, Basic or C++. These contrasts make her wrinkle her eyelids up in a slow-motion flinch. He notices but doesn't say anything — certainly not what he has been thinking.

He liked her neck the most of all of her. With his hand, he made her tilt her head back so that her neck was elongated. He kissed the place where it dipped above her sternum. If that particular kiss in the particular place hadn't been one of their worst sex-clichés – like her running her fingers through his hair and pulling his head back, like him thrusting three fingers inside her just as he was about to make her come with his tongue – the action would have been almost tender. He kissed the curve upwards to her chin, but stopped short of her mouth. She strained to lift herself off the pillow, to reach upwards, to give in to his tease. But he wasn't teasing. He really didn't want to kiss her on the mouth. She fell back and so did he.

U

He smells bad. She knows this. She begins to move her face, close-up, over his skin, kissing, kissing as an excuse. She is confirming what she already knows. She scents him, up and down. There is a sour odour about his armpits. His neck has a sweeter fragrance – the back of his neck, where the hairs dip down towards the first nub of his spine. His palms have a bland aroma. His fingers reek of her – especially under the red-crescented nails. She turns away from him and instead sniffs the pillow. It has an over-aura of faintly burned hair boiled up in something sweet. Monosodium glutamate. The atmosphere of a cheap Chinese restaurant, half-way between the woks and the dustbins. It is too much. She is swimming in swirls of nausea. Now is the moment for them to be painted by Egon Schiele.

V

One of them had farted, silently, and each of them thought it was the other. 'You,' he said. It was a sour metallic, slightly cabbagey smell. Once, it would have made them laugh. Once, it would have been the perfume of their intimacy – beyond embarrassment, beyond romance. Now, though, it just made them angry with each other. The fart was an expression of their inner rottenness. It made them feel like the corpses they were. 'You,' she said. He reached across and pinched her nipple. She knew better than to retaliate in kind – he was stronger than her and happy to find another excuse to prove it. With a shrug she accepted that the fart had been hers. The smell had almost dispersed, fading into the general sourness of the damp room, their damp bodies.

She gets up to go to the toilet. He languidly tries to grip her ankle, to hold her back, to make her beg for the privilege of leaving his company. She jerks her leg away, hard enough to convey hatred. There is an argument here to be had. If he wants it, she will give it to him. He falls back on the bed with a thump that is louder than it need be. This annoys her further, but she continues out of the bedroom – nude and barefoot – into the toilet. As she pees she feels a strange gathering-up inside her, like the slow roar of a kettle boiling. She looks down into the toilet bowl, expecting to see streaks of bloody gunk. Nothing. She smells her fingers. She can't remember when her period is due. The roar in her abdomen subsides to a hiss then crackles out. The body does funny things, she thinks. She isn't able to come up with anything more adequate than that. Her mind isn't working like it used to. She stands up to wipe herself. As she drops the paper into the bowl, she tries to sense what he is doing in the other room. Walking back into the bedroom, she regrets not having taken longer – not having given herself the opportunity to steal a little more respite.

X

He is aware that, unlike most people, she is uglier asleep than awake. There is none of the usual relaxation in her face. Her lips continue to pout, like the spout of a small milk jug. Sag-lines dent her cheeks, as if she were a much older woman. In fact, this was the cruellest thing: he can imagine her five years, ten years older. And she is no longer – in this imagined future – a person he wants to have anything to do with. There are rings round her neck: one for both completed decades of her life. This number will increase. Her cheeks will become heavier and even more slablike than they already are. The lines at the corners of her eyes will be there constantly, not just at moments of hysteria (laughter or distress). He is hoping that she is asleep now, although he can tell that she isn't. He is afraid that somehow she will be able to sense how cruel his thoughts have become. If he were a decent person, he'd get out of this bed. He would be honest and end it. One of them would have to leave. But he isn't a decent person. He doesn't get up. Instead, he grips her nipple between his thumb and forefinger. She pretends to just be waking up.

Death is something she tries not to think about. She pulls the sheets up over her head, in an attempt to dark-out the thought. But the dark – fittingly – only encourages worse images. Dying while fucking. Dying while being fucked. Him dying on top of her. Her going into spasms and him not noticing. Him trying to say something final and her sobbing too loud to hear him. The one left alive – him or her – and all that would happen to them. Standing holding the telephone after dialling 999. Men and women entering the flat wearing heavy fluorescent clothing. Professional voices expressing professional concern. A complete stranger making a cup of tea and using the wrong mug. Answering questions there is no point answering. Old women glancing up and down hospital corridors. Emotions starting only at the epiglottis. Vomiting. Retching. Aching to vomit more. Only retching. Crying. Confessing. And at the end of it all, at the very end, the release – like birds flying out of the top of her head. Or his.

He reaches down with his thumb and inserts it part way into his foreskin. The sliminess that he encounters is nothing more than he had expected. This is the state that they are themselves tending towards: deliquescence. A few more days of this, he thinks, and they will flow off either edge of the bed; they will seep into and through the colourless carpet; they will stain the floorboards and wet the wiring; they will drip from the nicotine-brown ceiling of their downstairs neighbours' flat, they will obey gravity all the way down into the ground. He pulls his thumb out and draws a slime-line heart on the nearest of her buttocks. This is one of their previous languages. But, this time, she is unable to decipher the sign. 'Again,' she says. He pretends to repeat the action, drawing a question mark instead of a heart. 'Okay,' she says, and lies back with her arms held over her head.

My Cold War
[February 1998]

If I hadn't been bored and friendless in Berlin, I would never have thought to search my hotel room; and if I hadn't searched, I would never have found what I found – and I would have avoided my Cold War completely. The hotel was situated near Potsdamer Platz, part of the former Democratic Republic. Before October 1989, Doppelzimmer 834 – like every other East German hotel room – would have been bugged, would have had at least *that* glamour. But on 1 February 1998, there was nothing whatsoever of interest: a mushy-springed bed, a wood-laminate wardrobe, an old-style phone, a green-brown-grey-blue carpet. And from the streets outside, beyond the sticky net-curtains, came the sound of pneumatic drills – like Wagner's *Siegfried* multiplied and amplified. I don't know exactly why I unscrewed the white-painted plasterboard which covered the fireplace. Perhaps because my room had no television. Perhaps because the fat steel screwheads reminded me of the rivets in the side of a ship. Perhaps simply because my Swiss Army penknife had a screwdriver attachment. Anyhow, the whole thing was loosened up in about ten minutes. There were twenty or so screws, a couple of which were a little stiff. I don't know what I was expecting to find. A radio, maybe – concealed for listening to the World Service. Pornography, perhaps. Dust and soot and cobwebs, definitely. Yet behind the plasterboard the fireplace was perfectly, almost antiseptically clean. Someone had sealed up the chimney-hole and the same person, or so I guessed, had given everything a couple of coats of white gloss. Most remarkably of all, this person had left behind a clear plastic bag (one of the ones with an airtight seal along the edge) containing a vintage Leica. After only the slightest hesitation I picked it out of the shiny white grate. There was something very fulfilling in finding – if only by accident – something that had been so meticulously hidden. It was a fulfilment, of sorts: a greater fulfilment than had come my way in many months of travel. My Cold War, although I wasn't at the time aware, had already begun.

Leaving the plasterboard propped up beside the fireplace, I walked over to the bed (the room, though boring, was surprisingly large) and sat down to examine the camera. As I unsealed the plastic bag, I sniffed the air it contained. Scentless, as far as I could tell – no aftershave, no perfume. The Leica was beautiful. I don't know a great deal about cameras but I know that among photographers Leicas are universally admired and uniquely craved. 'When the shutter goes,' I'd heard one photojournalist acquaintance say, 'it makes no noise. You can take a person's photo –' Silence. '– and they will never know.' I'd also picked up the information (misinformation, it turned out: the comment refers to Praktikas) that Leicas were of two kinds, West and East German; and that the West German ones were far superior. I turned the Leica over, heavy but balanced in my hands. There were, of course, no external markings to tell me East or West. Somehow I was certain there must be film inside it: no way would someone, however eccentric or paranoid, hide a mere camera. It must contain information, images. And so I didn't attempt to open it.

I'd only been in the hotel two hours, but now I checked out – smuggling the Leica through reception deep within my suitcase. I paid – in cash, in full – for the room I would not be using and the breakfast I would not eat. No surprise was expressed at my so-early departure. The receptionist, sallow and lethargic, a woman, seemed incapable of expressing anything at all. Before vacating Doppelzimmer 834, I had screwed the plasterboard back over the fireplace – making everything appear as undisturbed as possible. Already I was behaving like a spy.

I moved across town. My Western hotel was a great deal more luxurious than my Eastern. As there was no reason for me to hold back on the money, I spent a great deal more than was necessary – and for this I got gilding, plush and an utterly dead acoustic. I'd only been slumming it before in the hope that my life would acquire some atmosphere – at second hand. (Finding an unrenovated hotel in the East had been quite a challenge; Mitte was now swankier than Charlottenburg.) But my life was in terrible need of some-thing. For six long months, my passport and I had lain side by side on the drum-tight bedcovers of Hiatts and Hiltons the whole world over. I had been everywhere but back home – a place where there is nothing but hotels. Ex-East Germany was a sign of my desperation: I hadn't really wanted to go there. No friends. No interest. But the idea of atmosphere had attracted me. I'd made one of my more fate-ful airport-decisions. The stewardess swiped my credit card. The plane took off, flew, landed. The temperature on the ground was announced as zero degrees.

By the time I had checked in, it was eleven-thirty. I found

an all-night pharmacy. As I pulled the Leica from my suit-pocket, I saw the chemist's hard face break into boyishness. 'M3a,' he said. Instantly he assumed the camera was mine, that I'd had it for years, that it was one of my most beloved objects – a pet, almost. 'Inside, the film it has?' I asked. The chemist stared at me for a moment, realizing how wrong all his assumptions had been: I felt myself becoming that which he now beheld – a barbarian, a parvenu in possession of a little piece of perfection whose impeccable quality I could not even begin (as could he, uniquely) to appreciate. '*Jawohl*,' he said, after trying the film-winder with his thumb. 'Can you to it the development make?' '*Jawohl*,' he said, this time with irony. He wound the film on to the end then popped it out of the base of the camera. One glance. 'This film is black and white. It will take twenty-four hours.' Could I trust him? If there were something incriminating in the negatives, would he call the police? Would he print off some duplicates and attempt to blackmail me? Would he refuse even to let me see or know what had been in them? 'No more so fast?' '*Nein*,' he said, heavily handing the Leica back. 'Twenty-four hours exactly,' I said. He did not smile. I stepped out from the white shop into the black street.

The next day, I felt like playing up to my ideas of atmos-phere – and so I went back to my Eastern hotel and took coffee in the drab dining room. There was no sign of the gossipy excitement and expanded curiosity that follows a visit from the police. No-one paid any undue attention to me: the night-staff and the day-staff didn't much overlap. The one person I'd spoken to before, the drab receptionist, ignored my presence completely – at least to begin with. My own suspicion was that the camera belonged to one of the hotel's customers, not one of its staff. As I imagined them, he

or she (more likely he) was someone who stayed there regularly – always requesting the same room. I wanted to ask the
receptionist if such a person existed, but my German was too
poor to pass off such an enquiry with the requisite non-
chalance. Attention would be drawn to me, unnecessary
attention. In fact, the receptionist was even now having a
word with the elderly concierge whilst looking in my direction. Perhaps she did, after all, recognize me. I nodded to the
head waiter as I walked quickly out.

Exactly twenty-four hours after leaving it, I returned to
the all-night pharmacy. The chemist handed over the paper
wallet of developed photographs. His face gave no clue as to
what I would find when I opened it. The charge for developing the film seemed exorbitant. I wanted to ask if it was a
standard rate, but decided against it: any dispute would make
the chemist even more likely to remember me – something
I was still hoping to avoid.

Just down the street from the all-night pharmacy a night-
club was open. Once inside, I found a deep booth, ordered
a beer and – after waiting for it to arrive, then waiting a
little longer for the waiter to go away – opened the wallet.
The instant I saw the photographs, I knew that I was in
danger: I had interrupted something – some mad pan-
European project. The film-roll had been twenty-four frames
long. There were fourteen exposed images. Each photograph
was of a roadsign, taken from roughly the same distance
away (I imagined the photographer pacing out the gap) – and
every roadsign was for a different European city. It was
simply unbelievable. I cannot convey the shock that these
images gave me – so simple, so repetitious. Careful not to
disturb their order (although I could always check back with
the negatives), I wrote down the following list: Berlin,

Copenhagen, Amsterdam, Luxemburg, Brussels, Paris, London, Rome, Dublin, Athens, Madrid, Lisbon, Bonn, Vichy.

It was the final two names on the list which gave me the clue I needed: Bonn, the disputed capital of Germany; Vichy, the capital of Nazi-occupied France. The photographer had already taken photographs of all the capital cities of the European Union. Now, they were journeying into history – capitals that might have been, capitals that were but failed. This second half of the project (shots thirteen to twenty-four) seemed only just to have begun. But did the number twenty-four have any greater significance? Was it merely the number of exposures on this particular roll of film? Of which signposts, of which capital cities, were the next ten photographs to be taken? Was the project's incompletion due to lack of time, or money, or was there some less guessable obstacle? I took a couple of moments to compare my recent random wanderings with the utterly logical itinerary of this traveller. Who were they? It had to be a man, surely. No woman would do something so pointless in its obedience to arbitrary rules – a woman would need an emotional motive for such a project. Examining the photographs one by one, I searched for a clue to the photographer's identity. But his shadow was not cast onto the signposts or upon the ground; his reflection was not betrayed by a single shiny surface. The photographer seemed entirely absent from his photographs. I wondered: Why signposts? Why not obvious landmarks: Big Ben, the Eiffel Tower, the Little Mermaid, the Parthenon? Perhaps because signposts are less deniable. Perhaps because I was dealing with a madman. The variations between signpost-photographs were delicious: the ground, dusty white outside Athens, grassy grey outside Brussels. London had been taken against a background of fog, Lisbon was slightly over-exposed.

Looking again and again at the photographs – slowly, quickly, now rearranging them (alphabetically, dark to light), now dealing them like cards – I slowly began to see something that should have been obvious before: in two of them (Dublin and London) the road was to the right of the signpost, whereas in all the others it was to the left. I noticed something else: a white Volkswagen Beetle appeared in the background of both these photographs.

There must be a reason for this: I tried to envisage it. The photographer's working method was unvarying – they always approached the signpost in the same way, parking at the same distance. Because of the eccentric English and Irish habit of driving on the left side of the road, the photographer's method had been slightly disrupted. And because of this, they had unwittingly included a trace of themselves in these two photographs. I had my clue: a white Volkswagen Beetle, right-hand drive and with German number-plates.

When I got back to my West hotel room, the inevitable: it had been searched. The contents of my suitcase had been tipped out onto the bed. The wardrobe doors were ripped off their hinges. The chest-of-drawers was pulled away from the wall. Even the phone had been taken apart. Luckily, I had placed the Leica in the hotel safe. Although I did not know it at the time, my Cold War had just escalated. I sat down on the edge of the double bed. How had the photographer found me? Probably he'd spotted me when I returned to the first hotel. How stupid I'd been to go back there! I ran my hands up into my hair. I could feel it turning grey, becoming brittle. Should I change hotel? If so, the photographer would be bound to follow me again. Did I want to force a confrontation so soon?

I phoned down to reception and had the concierge send up some cigarettes. When the bellboy came through the door, he glanced around the room with an expression that somehow managed to be both impeccably deadpan and deeply ironic. I had seen this young man before: he had been the one that had carried my single suitcase up to my room. He had a very podgy-pasty face and hair that, whilst being too close cropped to merit managerial censure, stood insolently vertical. He was annoying, intimidating and curiously attractive – and didn't he know it. I felt uneasy, and he knew that the longer he lingered in my unease the larger his tip would be. 'Cigarettes,' I said. The bellboy handed them over, taking the opportunity to advance further into the room, my unease. 'Is everything all right, sir?' he asked. I forced myself to tip him. 'You have lost something?' he said. 'Cigarettes,' I said. 'I lost cigarettes.' He nodded, then performed his patented discreet-retreat.

The bellboy's formality whilst in the room gave me an idea: the photographer, whoever he was, had proved himself to be a deeply meticulous individual. Yet the searching of my room had been uncontrolled, almost wild. And whilst this contradiction might not mean anything (perhaps I had merely infuriated a normally placid temperament), it *was* highly suggestive. On an impulse I turned off the roomlights, went over to the window and glanced out through the curtains. Unbelievable: parked directly opposite the hotel was a white Volkswagen Beetle.

I charged out of my room, sprinted down the corridor and pressed for the lift. It took forever to arrive – and when it did it was full of fat old men in lederhosen. They took their time ballooning out into the corridor. Once inside the lift, I pressed for the ground floor. It started to descend. So slowly – I hadn't noticed how slow the lift was before. As I rushed out into the lobby, I practically knocked over the bellboy coming the other way. I apologized, and kept on going. 'Excuse me, sir,' he shouted. 'Excuse me.' People in the lobby were looking round – old ladies. I had to turn back, couldn't just run out into the street. 'My apologies, sir. But I forgot to ask you to sign for the cigarettes. If you could just . . .' I signed the receipt. 'Thank you, sir.' By the time I burst out into the cool night air of Berlin, the Volkswagen was gone.

I went back up to my room, forlorn. The door was still open and the lights were off. When I turned them on, I spotted the unopened cigarette packet lying on the floor by the window – just where I'd dropped it before running out. I slouched over, picked it up, cracked it open. That was strange – no cellophane wrapper. I quickly counted the white circles of the filters: twenty. Perhaps the bellboy was making a few extra DMs by filling the hotel's branded packs with cheap no-brand fags of his own. I pulled the cigarettes out, intending to check the filters for the maker's name – but as I was doing so, a white oblong card fell out onto the carpet. After stuffing all but one of the cigarettes back into the packet, I bent down to pick the card up. There was a message on it, typed out on an old manual typewriter. The message (in German) read:

Tomorrow. Staatsoper. 6pm. Tristan und Isolde.
A ticket will be reserved under your name.
Bring the photographs and the negatives.
Wear your black suit. Buy a new tie: blue silk.

I had two suits: one grey, one black. Since arriving in Berlin, I had worn only the grey. The black suit, along with everything else that had been in my suitcase, now lay tipped out on my hotel bed. How had the photographer known that I had a black suit?

I thought back to the first hotel. I hadn't even opened my suitcase there. The only people who might know I owned a black suit were whoever had searched my room and the bellboy. I followed this line of thought: the bellboy was the one who had been bringing me the message in the cigarette pack; the bellboy had prevented me from running out into the street after the Volkswagen. The bellboy must know something, even if he didn't know everything. I called down to reception and had the concierge send up a double vodka. But the bellboy who brought it wasn't the same as before. This was an old man with the milky blue eyes of an alcoholic. 'Where is he?' I asked. 'The other bellboy? I wanted him.' I didn't mind being taken for a homosexual. 'Sir, arrangements can be made . . .' 'Bring him to me.' 'But, sir, he has gone off duty. I am on duty now. Would you like something else?' He winked. 'Something young?' 'I need to speak to the bellboy. Where is he?' 'He has gone home.' 'Where does he live?' 'Sir, I cannot say.' I took out my wallet and extracted a high-denomination note. 'I need to speak to him.' The old man looked from side to side, then whispered: 'Sometimes after work he goes to drink in the Stalin Bar on Bergmannstrasse. I will say nothing more.' I gave him the note and let him go.

A taxi took me to the Stalin Bar. Sure enough, the entire room was full of huge portraits of Our Great Fraternal Leader: Stalin-stern being applauded in the munitions fac-tory; Stalin-beaming paying a surprise visit to the collective farm; Stalin-businesslike boarding a chuffing steam-train; Stalin-vigilant at his desk late into the perilous night. The tables were crowded, full of young people – drinking and smoking, laughing and talking. This was the first time since arriving in Berlin that I'd encountered such a cacophony of the German language. These boys and girls were *really* using Deutsch to communicate – not just pretending to speak it, whilst abroad, to scare foreigners off from visiting their country. I felt nauseous, wanted to sit down, drink. But I went ahead searching the room for the bellboy. He wasn't at any of the crowded tables. I sat down at the bar, intending to wait and see if he would turn up later. I had nothing else to do. 'What'll it be, comrade?' the barman asked. 'Vodka,' I was just about to say, when I caught sight of the bellboy in the mirror behind the bar.

I spun round on my stool to confront him. 'Hey!' I said. Instantly, he panicked. As he dashed for the door I stepped into his path – but he merely lowered his shoulder and shunted me out of the way. I fell back, sprawling against the barstools, watching helplessly as he dodged between the tables and out into the street. Although I knew there was no way I'd be able to catch up, I ran out after him. He was already a hundred yards off, sprinting without looking back. 'Hey!' I shouted, pointlessly.

Back at the hotel I asked to see the manager. He was fat and efficient. His uniform was neatly creased but because none of the creases fell in straight lines it made him look scruffy rather than smart. He did not sweat or mop his bald brow with a handkerchief (no nervous fat-man clichés). 'Who was the bellboy who showed me up to my room?' He checked with a subordinate. 'That was Mark Felm. Have you a complaint about the service which you received from him?' 'No, but I need to speak to him.' 'I'm sure I can help you, sir.' 'Where does he live?' 'It is not hotel policy to disclose personal information about either our guests *or* our employees.' 'I'm not gay, if that's what you're thinking.' 'Sir . . .' 'Please.' 'Mark Felm only began working here yesterday. If you have any complaint to make against him, it will be treated with the greatest of seriousness. He came with the highest references.'

This was pointless. 'Do you have an envelope?' I asked. The manager handed me one, embossed with the hotel's name. I took the negatives out of the film-wallet, put them in the envelope, sealed it. 'Please put this in the safe,' I said. 'Certainly,' said the manager. 'Is there anything else?' 'No,' I said, and turned away. Upstairs in my room I smoked a cigarette, then tried to sleep.

The following afternoon, I bought myself the most beautiful blue silk tie.

Sometimes – though rarely – what one anticipates one encounters; and, rarer still, the anticipated fails to disappoint. The Staatsoper was an imposing neo-classical building in ugly stone. Black pollution-streaks ran down the statues above its entrance-way. My seat was about half-way back in the stalls, at the end of a row. And there she was – my anticipated – beautiful and aloof – sitting in the seat beside mine. Wordlessly, I sat beside her; I would wait for *her* to speak – she would be the one to set the tone. Yet it was only now, when I had looked away from her and up towards the grand gaudy fire curtain that I realized I had seen this woman before – in Berlin. But where? I couldn't remember having seen anyone so beautiful. And then I knew – because she hadn't been as beautiful the last time I saw her: she was the receptionist from my East German hotel. All the greyness had gone from her, and all the care. She shone where she had been dull, energy had replaced torpor. I turned to look at her, to confirm. Yes, I'd been correct – but at that exact moment Wagner's 'Prelude' swelled up, seasick and miraculous. The receptionist gazed steadily towards the stage, the unraised curtain. I did not seem to exist for her, not right now, not quite yet.

It has been said that *Tristan und Isolde* is the sexiest work of art ever created. I knew the opera very well, and was hoping to have established some intimacy with the receptionist during the interval – the better to enjoy the by-proxy foreplay of Act II. It was the first time my erotic curiosity had been stimulated in months.

As the moment drew closer and closer I became more and more agitated. When the lights came up, the receptionist was the first person in the entire auditorium to get to her feet. I stood up, too – along with almost everyone else. The receptionist pushed past me, then turned her head slightly. 'Follow me,' she said, moving her lips as little as possible. No introduction. No names. Hardly even a glance. Hurriedly, she pushed her way out of the auditorium. I did my best to keep up – mortally offending several camp Wagnerites in the process. Once into the corridor, the receptionist headed straight for one of the fire doors. I went after her, finding that it led directly out into the chill Berlin night. All of a sudden, we were alone. 'What is your name?' I asked. 'Come here,' she said, walking towards a darker part of the alley. Behind us, someone else came out of the Staatsoper fire door. For a brief moment the alley was lit up – and I saw two men waiting in the shadow that the receptionist had been beckoning me towards. One of the men I recognized: the bellboy; the other I'd never seen before. He was an older man, fifty plus, with hard eyes and an even harder jawline. My first thought was that it was the receptionist and not myself who was in danger. 'Hey,' I shouted. 'Come back!' They rushed me before I had time even to gasp, the old man moving with surprising speed. A rough hessian sack was pulled over my head and my hands were twistingly cuffed. I was hustled further into the shadows (I could still through the sacking make out the difference between light and dark); a sharp blow met the back of my skull and I was swallowed by the exploding pain and engulfing unconsciousness. The last thing I heard was the receptionist's voice saying: 'My name is Isolde.'

When I came round I was lying flat, being bumped and slid around, in complete darkness, a car-engine booming and road-noise hushing. Where were they taking me? The handcuffs dug into my wrists. My legs too had been put under restraint. Although actually in the dark, my head was starry with pain. After a particularly huge supernova of agony, I again lost consciousness.

The next time I awoke, I was tied to a chair in a damp cellar, being blasted with light from three halogen lamps. Isolde − if that was really her name − had just slapped me a couple of times, hard, to bring me round. My blindfold had been removed, probably by Isolde. The bellboy and the older man were standing to one side, smoking. My back was soaked with sweat. My clothes smelt of petrol. Isolde, on seeing that I was again conscious, stood up and stepped back from me. As she moved, I caught her perfume − it came to me gently as a promise (perhaps a false promise). If I were to survive this, whatever it was − a prospect that seemed fairly unlikely − then I might again, with Isolde or with some other woman, share a close-up world of scent, softness and safety. But that seemed a long way off, a memory of the future. I could not speak: my gag was still in place. Isolde approached the two men and spoke to them in a low voice. I was having trouble focusing, with the unbearable light and the sweat falling into my eyes – but I saw the hard-faced man hand Isolde a cigarette. The bellboy lit it for her, gallantly, with a flashing silver cigarette-lighter. Isolde was wearing a long raincoat with the collar turned up. After a deep drag, she walked back towards me. 'I am about to remove your gag. If you scream, no-one will hear – no-one except Mark and Melot. Mark will probably kick you in the face; Melot will do something far more subtle and far more painful. Nod once if you understand.' She had a beautiful voice, even in its harshness. I nodded once. Isolde tore off the gag.

The delight of easy air itself almost made me scream. Instead, I gasped animal for a while. Isolde smoked, her ash falling wispy-dark through the light. Despite my gasping, I wanted that cigarette. 'The negatives,' she said. 'Tell me where they are?' I was in no mood to resist. After I'd regained my breath, I said: 'They are in the safe, in my hotel.' Isolde turned to Mark, the bellboy. In rapid German, she asked him a question, to which he replied, '*Nein.*' 'Why did you not bring them?' Isolde asked. 'I didn't know . . .' I said. 'What?' she snapped. 'That they were for you,' I said. 'If I had, I would have brought them.' Isolde stood as a thin shadow between the three bright lights.

Suddenly the old man grabbed her. He was shouting in German, furious, twisting her neck. She started to gasp, fighting back. One of the lights was knocked over in the struggle. The bellboy helped subdue her. His loyalties were obvious. 'Stop!' I shouted. 'Don't hurt her!' 'What?' said the old man into the air. Then he turned to me. 'Leave her alone! I'll give you the negatives – just don't hurt her!' 'Isolde has failed. She promised us the photographs *and* the negatives. We are very angry. Mark cannot get them from the hotel safe, only the manager has the keys. But you will bring the negatives to the Brandenburg Gate, tomorrow, at midnight. Remember this. Midnight. If you and the negatives are not there, you will never see this one again. Nor will anyone else.' The old man now had Isolde completely subdued. The bellboy stepped behind me, lifted his cosh and the lights went out.

The next time I woke up, I was lying on soft wet earth in the middle of a forest. Rain was swishing into the thick pine branches over my aching head. There was no gag on my mouth or blindfold over my eyes. My wrists and ankles felt as if I'd been crucified. I tried to stand up, fell over, tried again, fell against a treetrunk and grasped it for support. This seemed my only way of progressing, though where I was intending to go I had no idea.

Blindly, I stumbled onwards, for what seemed like hours. My rescue was at first an inconvenience: I came to a place where there was a larger than usual gap between trees. I lurched forwards, my ankles screaming with agony. Nothing for me to flop against. I fell to the ground, which wasn't ground, which was harder than that, much harder. Somehow, I'd happened upon a road. Before this thought had time to sink in, I heard a car-engine approaching – then saw lights getting bigger, getting closer. I pushed myself up, exhausted, grazing my hands on the gritted tarmac. One knee, the other – and push: up: now. I was standing. I knew if I tried to get off the road I would simply fall over again, the driver wouldn't see me and I'd be run over, killed. It seemed safer just to stand there, arms out to either side, pleading for survival and deliverance. The car came rapidly round the bend – a dipping of the front left wheel the first indication that the driver had seen me. But would they be able to stop soon enough to avoid hitting me? No: no stopping, no time – so they swerved past me, the side mirror tapping my thigh. The car was a silver-white Mercedes 106e. Now that there was a possibility of deliverance, the rain on my face started to feel good. I didn't have the strength or balance to turn round. I could hear the Mercedes' gullwing door opening, upwards and outwards. German was being spoken – aggressive, male. Like a scarecrow I stood there, cruciform, unterrifying. The shouting continued. A hand was placed firmly on my shoulder. It was too much for me to bear – I fell straight to the ground, blacking out.

This time when I woke up it was far more pleasant than before. At first all I was aware of was the softness against my skin – the softness I had been promised by Isolde's perfume – the softness, as it turned out, of a pair of black silk pyjamas. I had survived. Here I was. In a large white bed. (I got up.) In a large white room. (I walked downstairs and out into the drive.) In a large white house. (I turned all around.) On the very edge of a large black lake. The pyjamas belonged to the owner of the silver-white Mercedes – a man whose name I never found out. He had dumped me at his country villa and left me for the servants to deal with. There was an English butler, a French maid and a Brazilian chauffeur. The butler dressed me, the maid fed me and the chauffeur drove me back to Berlin. (If it hadn't happened to me, I would have believed it was a dream. Thank you, Germany. After all I discover that you have a believable heart – a huge one, beating for me, for other helpless ones, too.) The white house by the black lake was two hours from Berlin – to the south. We took the Rolls-Royce, black, shiny. The chauffeur was handsome, dark-eyed and smiled slowly at my questions: 'Where did he find me?' and 'How far did he have to bring me to get here?' and 'When can I see him to thank him?' The chauffeur knew – or pretended to know – nothing of the circumstances in which his master had discovered me. 'The master likes to drive himself sometimes,' was all that he would say. The bridges on the autobahn *blip-blip-blip*ped past at over 120 m.p.h.

I hadn't woken up until four in the afternoon. We didn't set off for Berlin until six. It was a quarter past eight when the Rolls-Royce dropped me off outside my hotel. The chauffeur got out and opened the door for me, as if I were royalty; then he got back in and drove off without a backward glance, as if I were something unpleasant he'd dumped on a tip. I walked into the hotel lobby, looking out for the bellboy, Mark, who I knew wouldn't be there. Although my old black suit was now lying in a dustbin somewhere close to the Swiss border, I instinctively checked the pockets of my new black suit for my room key. (Sometimes we owe our stupidity more than we owe intelligence.) Of course, it wasn't there – but something else was: a key with a locker number on it and the words Zoo Station written around it.

The manager stood behind the reception desk. As I approached him, he looked confused by the contradictory signals I was giving out: injured face and hands, immaculate tailoring. In English, I asked him to get whatever I had deposited in the safe. It was lucky he didn't ask me for identification. The suit took care of formalities. The manager, it seemed, had misjudged me. In a moment he handed over the envelope containing the negatives. After going upstairs to fetch some money, I took the negatives to a copyshop, colour-photocopied them, put the photocopies in an envelope and posted them to my almost-forgotten home address. They came out badly but I didn't care: I still possessed them, in some form at least. It was ten o'clock by the time I'd finished this errand. With nothing else to do before the exchange, and with a natural curiosity, I hailed a taxi and told it to take me to Zoo Station. I held the locker key between thumb and forefinger, tapping it inquisitively on my lips.

I must have been developing new instincts by now, picking up Cold War habits, for I had not been in the taxi longer than a minute before I glanced through the back window to see if I was being shadowed – and there it was, two cars behind: the white Volkswagen Beetle. As we stopped at some traffic lights and it drew closer, I was able to identify the driver: Mark, the bellboy. I didn't know what to do. The taxi-driver was likely to think me mad if I told him to lose the car that was following me. Also, I doubted whether my conversational German was up to the task. The white Beetle, as I watched it, kept an even distance – never further than three cars back, never closer than one. Thinking as quickly as I could, I ordered the driver to take me back to the hotel. He turned round, and so did the white Beetle. I told the taxi-driver to hurry; I hoped he would put a little distance between us and Mark.

Once we arrived back at the hotel, I dashed out of the taxi and through the soft-carpeted lobby. Into the lift and up to my room. Without turning on the room lights or moving the curtains I looked down into the street. The Beetle was there, reversing into a parking space. I phoned down to reception and asked to speak to the manager, urgently. 'Yes, sir,' he said when – after an agonizing minute – he was able to come to the phone. 'Do you have a back entrance?' I asked. 'I can't go out the front door.' 'I'm sorry, sir. The only way to leave the building is through that door.' 'What about fire exits?' I said. 'There is the roof, but –' he said. It was all I needed. I took the lift to the top floor. The fire exit wasn't hard to find. I pushed down the aluminium bar and was quickly outside. Moving carefully away from the front of the building, I looked for some way down. There was only one: a ladder, dropping vertically into the alley beside the hotel; eight floors down. And the alley led directly out into the street, where Mark was waiting and watching. If I left that way the chances were he'd catch sight of me. With no immediate ideas of escape occurring to me, I went back down to my room.

I lay on the bed, blowing smoke-rings up at the ceiling. The sight of them dispersing and dissolving the higher they got was what gave me the idea. Out in the corridor, it was the job of a moment to start the fire alarm – smashing the glass with my elbow and pressing the black button. Bells rang immediately, horribly loudly. I ran back into my room, looked out the window. Mark, I could see, was no longer in the Beetle – he had left it behind, the driver's door hanging open. Now came the gamble: I guessed that Mark would guess that I'd have tried to find some way out of the hotel other than the front door. I guessed that he'd assume I'd found the fire exit onto the roof. I guessed that he'd cover that escape route rather than the front door. And so, I went back into the corridor, descended the stairs to the lobby and traipsed out into the street with all the frightened others. My guess was wrong – Mark was back in the car, patiently keeping an eye on both exits. But as luck had it, the crush of people vacating the hotel was blocking up the road. I took my chance and ran for it. Mark saw me, got out of the Beetle. I sprinted, turned down the next street along. I dashed left, right, right again. I ducked into a sex shop and pretended to look at lingerie. I had lost him. After waiting five minutes among the frilly things (I thought of buying something black for Isolde), I stepped outside and hailed a taxi. 'Zoo Station,' I said.

Sometimes – very rarely – one's life is altered in a moment; and, even more rarely, that alteration is for the better. I found the locker without difficulty; I opened it without hesitation. When I closed it, a few moments later, with a deliberate lack of haste, I was a different man. The locker contained two things: two brown paper envelopes, padded. I opened the top, larger one: it contained a thick stack of high-denomination Deutschmarks; I opened the second one: it contained a well-oiled revolver. Obviously, these were things one couldn't just carry away in one's hands. I locked them back up again and went off to look round the station. I found a shop selling luggage and bought myself a plain black briefcase. So paranoid had I become that I believed both the money and the gun would be gone by the time I got back to the locker. In general, I wasn't wrong to be paranoid (plots of which I was unaware were in the offing) – but in this case my paranoia was misplaced. I stuffed the envelopes into the new briefcase. In the nearby gentlemen's toilets, I took the gun from its envelope, checked that it was loaded, put it in my side pocket.

Glancing at my watch, I saw that it was almost eleven. I was hungry, despite the ministrations of the French maid. In the station café, I consumed a tasteless Wiener schnitzel with oversweetened potato salad and watery sauerkraut. A couple of beers and I almost believed that I would use the gun – if there was any sign of trouble at the bridge.

Eleven fifty-five found me approaching the Brandenburg Gate through the well-lit modern streets. All around me, people went on with their normal midnight business; I, on the other hand, was embarked upon a deadly enterprise. It was hard to believe what I was about to do – to exchange a mysterious and beautiful set of negatives for a mysterious and beautiful woman. Halogen lamps whitely illuminated the gate. There was a slight mist upon the ground. At almost exactly twelve, a thin rain began to fall. I stood there, waiting – unsure which way to look. Death could come at me from any of the 360°, or from above, or below. My right hand clutched the shape of the revolver through the expensive material of my suit – there it was, bumping solidly against my right thigh.

Then I saw it: the white Volkswagen Beetle. As it drew closer, I could see that the old man, Melot, was driving, whilst Mark sat in the back with Isolde. Her eyes flashed, wide and white with terror. A couple of times the Beetle drove past the Gate, checking that the coast was clear – and then it pulled up ten feet or so away from me. 'You have everything with you – you have all of the negatives?' said the old man, leaning out the driver's window. 'I do,' I said. 'Now let her go!' The car jerked forward, startlingly, then even more abruptly halted. The back door opened and Isolde tumbled out onto the hard cobblestone pavement. I had to restrain the impulse to run forward and help her to her feet. The old man had got out on the other side of the car. Isolde's hands were tied behind her back. Mark jumped out of the car after her and hauled her roughly to her feet. I stood in front of the Beetle, slightly to the side of the headlights. The briefcase felt light in my hand, though I knew that it contained the heft of my entire future.

'First the negatives,' said Mark, the air pluming from his mouth. 'No,' I said, 'first the girl.' 'Why should we trust you?' shouted the old man. I pulled the envelope containing the negatives out of my breast pocket. (I'd been careful not to place them inside the briefcase.) 'I have something you want.' Mark put his thick arm around Isolde's neck and made as if to strangle her. 'So do we!' he shouted in reply. 'Take off her gag,' I said. The two men consulted. Then the old man ripped the gag off mercilessly. I waited a moment for Isolde to regain her breath. 'Are you alright?' I shouted. 'Alright,' she gasped, almost as if it were not an answer for me but a question for herself. 'Should I trust them?' She looked despairingly from one to the other. 'You'll have to. You have no choice.' My heart was thumping. Now was my moment. 'Oh yes I do,' I said, and produced the gun from my side pocket. First I pointed it at the old man. On the instant, he started to cower and beg, soiling himself. Then I let Mark feel the gun's hot beam of damage and death. He instinctively hid himself behind Isolde. There was some furious whispering amongst the three of them. The only thing I could hear was Mark saying, 'Where did he get a gun?'

'Untie her hands,' I said. 'Let her come to me.' And then Isolde said my name, gently. 'Put the gun away,' she said. Mark was uncuffing her hands. 'Point it at the ground.' The old man was running for the shelter of the Beetle. 'Be sensible.' Isolde was walking towards me. 'This is for you,' I said, and tossed the envelope at Mark. But Isolde leapt in the air – far more athletically than she should have if she'd really been tied up for twenty-four hours – and she caught it. 'No,' said Isolde. 'These are for me.' Mark's hand went to his pocket: a gun, I thought. 'Get down,' I shouted to Isolde. But she was walking steadily towards me, holding my gaze, speaking slowly. 'Listen. You don't understand what's going on. Put the gun away. I'll explain.' We were linked together – the gun pointing from me through Isolde into Mark. 'Take your hand out of your pocket,' I said to Mark. Slowly, he withdrew it – along with a set of car keys. Isolde was now standing within touching distance. 'They have no weapons,' she said. 'They would never hurt you. Mark is my brother. Melot is my father. They are not called Mark and Melot. But I *am* called Isolde.' She put her forefinger over the revolver's barrel, as if over the lips of a fractious boy – saying *shhh*, saying *alright*, saying *love*. I dropped the gun to my side, trusting her. 'Very good,' said Isolde, and put her arm through mine. 'Come with me,' she whispered. 'I'll explain everything.'

I let her lead me away from the white Beetle, through the dark streets, towards her bedroom, into the morning.

This is what Isolde said as she walked with me, held my hand, took me to where she lived, kissed me, made me coffee, kissed me again, took me to her bedroom, undressed in front of me, undressed me: 'Once, a long time ago, in a different time, I had a boyfriend. His name was Richard. He was handsome and funny. He was an artist: a photographer. His subject was landscapes. But, under the old regime, he was not allowed to travel. None of us were. We were very young. He was ambitious. Because he could not travel, he wanted to go everywhere. It frustrated him terribly. And so he conceived his project: he would smuggle a camera out of the country and, by getting instructions to photographer friends and acquaintances, he would have a series of photographs taken. Each of these photographs would prove con-

clusively that the camera had been to that particular country.
It was his great idea to photograph only city signs outside
cities, not famous monuments inside them. He imagined an
underground exhibition of all twenty-four photographs. And
they would be saying, "Look, we can travel to the borders
but we cannot pass over. We have the words, the signs, but
we haven't got the images. We cannot take photographs of
the things we want to." It would be pure and political. And
so he sent the camera, a Leica, out with a friend who came
from West Germany. He took the first five photographs:
Berlin, Copenhagen, Amsterdam, Luxemburg, Brussels.
Every time he took a photograph he sent us a postcard from
that city. Then he passed the Leica on to a French photographer. She took Paris, London. Then she split up with her
boyfriend, and the camera was lost for a while. Then they got
back together, and she found it again. She passed it on to a
Spanish photographer, someone reliable, she said. We didn't
hear anything for a whole year. And then the postcards
started to arrive: Rome, Dublin, Athens. The Spaniard
explained that he had been saving the money to travel. He
was very poor, but this project had given him a reason to
work. He is now quite famous, I believe. In Athens, he met
the woman who is now his wife. Together they took Madrid
and Lisbon. Those were the first twelve photographs. It had
taken three and a half years. Richard decided that that was
enough, with the postcards, for a first underground show.
(He had a second idea: for cities that had once been capitals
but were no longer.) So, he asked for them to get the camera
back to his West German photographer friend. Little did we
know that his friend was now working in the grey area. He
set himself up to be searched at the border, all the time looking innocent to us. But the Stasi got the camera and Richard

never saw the photographs. He was arrested, when it became clear what he had done. There was a short and meaningless trial. Richard spent a year in prison. After he came out, he lost all hope. He was being watched. He had lost his most trusted friend. He said he no longer loved me, though I knew he did. And he caught pneumonia and did not look after himself properly and he died.'

Then she stopped speaking and we made love. And then this is what Isolde said, as we lay side by side, holding hands, touched, kissed, watched the ceiling go grey, kissed again, fell asleep: 'When Richard died I was distraught. I myself wanted to die, to follow him. He had died so soon before things changed. That made things worse. But it did give me the reason to live – to see if I could now complete the project in Richard's memory. I worked in the hotel, I saved, I bought a Leica, I travelled when I could, I took the twelve photographs. Then I went on to the next stage: the imaginary capitals. I had just begun. In between times, I hid the camera behind the fireplace in the hotel room that had been where Mark and I met to talk. At first, I didn't know why. There was no Stasi any more. No-one to be scared of. But I wanted to continue the conditions of secrecy. Also, I was lonely in my game. I wanted someone to join me. For me the Cold War wouldn't be over until I had completed Richard's project. I was still in mourning. But someone could help me, travel with me. But only someone who was still in the same world as I was. I knew that anyone who would search their room so thoroughly that they would unscrew the fireplace would be the one. So, I left the Leica there. And anyone who looked likely, I put them in that room. Mostly men, but not all. I had great hopes for you – from the moment you checked in. The room was still bugged from before. I had arranged with my father and my brother to perform the series of tests upon you. And you came through all of them, wonderfully. It was clear that you immediately understood where you were – that you were fighting your own Cold War. You became a spy so delightfully easily. You even managed to get hold of a gun. But now, thanks to you, my Cold War is perhaps over.'

When I woke up late that afternoon, Isolde was gone. But she had left something behind for me, a clue – in the dent in the pillow in which her head had so recently lain there now lay a postcard: Lenin, in wax or embalmed, in his mausoleum, in Moscow.

The New Puritans

Their bungalow was called Sea-View Cottage. It was located on the East Anglian coast, a few miles south of Southwold. The walls of the bungalow were whitewash white. Had it not been for the seagull shit, the slate roof would have appeared almost perfectly black. They had taken the bungalow in November. It was now almost April. A small lawn was dying slowly on either side of the crazy-paved garden path. Through the bay windows one could gaze directly out over the North Sea, towards the Netherlands. Depending on whether the tide was in or out, the garden gate was anything from twenty to eighty steps away from the water's edge. This is where Jill stood, enjoying the final ten minutes before she had to go back on shift.

Jill was wearing a navy blue coat over a woollen Breton sweater, blue jeans and Army Surplus boots. Although there had been no discussion, the three of them had adopted this as something of a uniform. At first, John had thought wearing these kind of clothes might help them blend in with the locals. Now, they realized that their uniform merely made them stick out – but only in the way that non-locals trying to fit in anywhere always stick out. And that was a good enough reason for continuing to dress this way.

Jill had become proprietorial about the beach. Apart from

the Dog-Walking Man, and someone fishing once, she had always been able to be alone here. These walks Jill called her Wind-Baths, after something Jack once said. (The proper name was Air-Baths.) Every morning for the past three weeks Jill had made an enjoyable little ritual of them – walking, in as straight a line as possible, from the bungalow to the sea. On the way, she collected pebbles, driftwood, rope, plastic. Anything that she could reach without having to step off her imaginary straight line. The beach was empty, open. The beach helped her clarify herself.

This morning the breeze felt delightfully mellow. It wasn't exactly warm, but the threatening North Sea chill was for the first time this year entirely absent.

Jill turned to look back at the bungalow. The sight of it still gave her pleasure.

Sea-View Cottage was perfect for their purposes. On the outside, it looked like any other bungalow. But the man who built it, back in 1979, had been taking the Cold War very seriously. A nuclear fallout shelter of similar dimensions to the upstairs rooms was embedded six feet beneath the foundations of the cottage. It was entered through a pair of metal doors, and down a flight of concrete stairs.

Two other white and black bungalows stood to the left and right of Sea-View Cottage: Kittiwake (after a kind of seagull) and The Old Cove (after someone with a shit sense of humour).

Jill started back towards their bungalow. She hadn't gathered anything much this morning, only a piece of driftwood of a particularly exquisite grey.

She intended to nail this to the living-room wall, as part of her collection of particularly exquisite grey pieces of driftwood.

Back in London, Jill had been a website designer. She liked to think that what she once did with Shockwave 4.0, she now did with real, physical objects. Only, she did it a lot better. And it was a great deal more satisfying.

Half-way back to the bungalow, she spotted a floppy circle stuck on top of a grey rock. These rings were all the sea left of condoms, before it shredded them completely.

Jill peeled the floppy circle off the rock and stuffed it in her side pocket. She had a nailed-up collection of condom rings, too.

Just then, she heard a car engine. It was getting louder.

She hurried towards the cottage.

By the time she reached the garden gate, the car was negotiating the last couple of hedge-hidden bends in the road.

Jill knew that it couldn't be anyone they knew. When they had left London, she and Jack hadn't exactly advertised where they were going. Or what they would be doing when they got there. Steve, and Steve alone, knew their location. (Steve was their boss.)

She hid herself in the porch, listening.

The car drew up outside Kittiwake.

Jill crouched down.

A car door opened. The engine kept running. The gate squeaked. The car moved forwards. The engine was cut off. The gate squeaked shut. Another car door opened.

"Well, we're here," said a male voice.

"Yes, we're here," replied a female voice.

They sounded young.

"This is going to be fun," said the man.

"Fun-fun-fun," said the woman.

Jill listened a moment more, as the young couple opened

the boot and began to unload. Then she slipped inside as quickly and quietly as possible.

She now had two minutes until she was due on shift. She would tell John about the newcomers when she went down into the basement. He could then pass the information on, when Jack woke up.

Just to make double sure, she wrote a message on the white board in the kitchen. *A couple have moved into Kittiwake. Caution. Meeting tomorrow morning?*

She looked over the food on the white-painted table. Since moving out of London, she had learned to bake bread. It was something she'd always wanted to do. The loaf on the table, ready for John to toast, was one she had made yesterday. The milk, butter and eggs came from a farm down the road. Even the marmalade, bought from a church sale, was homemade. Only the teabags seemed in any way industrial. She would have to ask Steve for some loose-leaf, the next time he came.

'Jill!' John shouted up from the basement.

She knew she should always be a little early for the handover. Otherwise John got angry. It was just the light had been so beautiful outside. And then she'd been delayed by the newcomers.

The car boot slamming only twenty yards away made her jump. She was no longer used to such loud, unexpected noises.

'Jill!' John called, louder.

Jill laced her fingers together and pushed them away from her until they clicked. Then she went downstairs into the basement.

The system was this: They each worked one of three eight-hour shifts: morning (7 a.m. to 3 p.m.), evening (3 p.m. to 11 p.m.), night (11 p.m. to 7 a.m.). It was important they kept the machines going twenty-four hours a day. Steve had customers waiting. Customers it wasn't a good idea to disappoint. At the moment, Jill was on mornings, Jack on evenings and John on nights. In seven days' time, when the month came to an end, they would all have two whole days off. When they started up again, Jill would be on evenings, Jack on nights, John mornings.

The machines they worked on were AMX-3000s. It took an AMX twenty minutes to make a decent enough tape-to-tape copy of a ninety-minute master. With ten machines running in tandem, they could turn out thirty videos an hour. 720 a day. 20,160 a month.

For this, they were well paid. They all cleared several thousand a month. Avoided tax. And had hardly any outgoings. The money, paid them by Steve, in cash, just seemed to stack up. In drawers. Under mattresses. None of them dared use a bank. Three months in, and already they didn't know what to do with it all.

The film they were doing at the moment was an ultra-violent Swedish hardcore movie. It was mostly gay sex, although a woman made a brief but memorable appearance. The images weren't the kind of thing any of them were likely to get off on. Although Jill sometimes had her doubts about John. At the start, she had tended to watch each video through – just to see what it was about. They soon became very monotonous. Blood was involved. And screaming. And shit. Lots of shit. She still fast-forwarded through the new tapes – making sure there weren't children involved. That had been her only stipulation.

When they first arrived at the bungalow, John had been waiting for them. John was a complete surprise, and not a particularly pleasant one. (He had almost immediately told them about the twenty-four-hour shift system.) Jill had disliked John from the moment they met. She thought him seedy. John's past was infuriatingly – Jill thought *deliberately* – mysterious. It involved drugs, in quantities vaster (he hinted) than any they had ever come across. And prison, also. For the time being, though, John said all he wanted to do was "mellow on back to grass roots". If this meant smoking dope, it did anything but make him mellow.

Despite the shift system, Jill tried to avoid John as much as possible. This wasn't difficult. Because she and Jack were coupled up, they tried to maximize their shared off-time. She took a long nap during the afternoon, then stayed up late with him after his shift was over. This left them from about 11 p.m. to 1 a.m. to hang out.

The three of them were only ever together when a meeting had been called. Usually, only John called meetings. And then, it was usually to complain about something. (The food, usually.) But the arrival of the newcomers was something they *had* to talk about. Which is why Jill had called the meeting.

Jill got up at 6 a.m., especially. She woke Jack, who had slept most of the seven hours since his evening shift had finished. John, coming to the end of the night shift, was waiting for them when they came down the stairs into the basement. As the three of them talked, he kept working – taking tapes out of cardboard boxes, putting them in machines, copying, checking, taking tapes out of machines, putting them in cardboard boxes. The machines made a loud, slightly grindy, whirring sound.

'I think one of us should go round,' said Jill, having to

raise her voice a little. 'You know, to say hello. We need to appear as normal as possible, don't we?'

'Why?' said John. 'None of us are. And I bet they're not either.'

'You know exactly what I mean,' said Jill.

'Hey,' Jack said, 'let's think about this.'

'We never let them in the house,' said John. 'We're perfectly polite and all that. But they never come inside.'

'Won't that make them suspicious?' said Jill.

'Of what?' shouted John. 'If they come in, even only into the kitchen, they'll hear that something's going on down here.'

He patted one of the machines. It continued to whirr.

'We could tell them it's the boiler,' said Jill.

Most of the time, Jack kept quiet. He knew that his attempts to peace-make only inflamed the others. John accused him of being in Jill's pocket. Jill tried to force him to agree with her. Generally, he did agree with Jill. But, because of that, he worried that John was right, and that he *was* in Jill's pocket. 'Why don't we leave it and just see what happens?' he suggested.

'No,' said Jill. 'We need a policy.'

'I agree,' said John, making one of his unexpected tactical switches. With only three of them, realignments like this were always decisive. They operated democratically, and two was an instant majority.

'Okay,' said Jack.

'I think Jill should go over and make friends with them,' said John. 'They're less likely to suspect a woman.'

'Oh, thanks,' said Jill.

'Of doing what we're doing,' John said.

They both of them looked at Jack.

'Well?' said Jill.

'Fine,' he said, still surprised they were agreeing.

'Fine,' said John. 'Then I'm going to bed.'

As soon as he was out of earshot, Jill said, 'Think he means it?'

That evening, a couple of hours after coming off shift, Jill went round and knocked on Kittiwake's front door.

When she'd introduced herself, the young woman invited her in for tea.

The kitchen was very warm, overheated by an Aga. A couple of cardboard boxes full of food were jammed against the far wall.

'I'm Molly,' she said. 'And this is –'

'Mark,' said the good-looking young man, getting up from the bleached–pine table.

They were both around twenty-two, twenty-three. Five or six years younger than Jill and Jack, and eight younger than John.

'We're just here for a week,' said Molly, after they'd sat down around the table. 'Getting out of London.'

'What are you doing here?' asked Mark.

'I live here,' said Jill. 'For the moment, at least.'

'But you're not *from* here,' said Molly.

'Not originally, no,' Jill replied. 'I'm living here with my boyfriend –' She decided at that moment not to mention John. He would just have to keep out of sight for a while.

'What do you do?' asked Mark.

Jill had to think about this. 'I'm an artist,' she said.

'Oh, really,' said Molly. 'What kind of thing?'

'I work on the beach, mostly. I collect things and put

them together. It's not very original or anything. I just do it for myself, you see.' Jill realized she was gabbling, but she couldn't stop herself. Here, at least, was something she could be honest about. 'It's good therapy.'

'I'd love to see some of your stuff,' said Molly.

'Me, too,' said Mark.

'I don't really show anyone,' said Jill.

'Not even your boyfriend?' asked Mark.

'No, not really.'

By the time she got back to Sea-View Cottage, Jill had found out all about Molly and Mark. She knew they both worked in the theatre, but only backstage. That they both – just like Jack – wanted to break into film. That Molly was two months pregnant, and that the two of them were trying to fit in as many little holidays as they could before the baby was born.

'I just wanted some fresh air,' said Molly.

'We got the address off some friends who came last year,' added Mark.

'Isn't it lovely?' said Molly.

Jill went down into the basement, where Jack and John were awaiting her.

'Well, they *seem* harmless enough,' she said.

When the meeting was over, Jack and Jill went upstairs to their bedroom. They got in under the covers with their clothes on for a cuddle. All of a sudden, they both started giggling.

'I can't believe you forgot to tell them about John,' said Jack.

Jill giggled some more. 'Well, you know,' she said, 'I

probably subconsciously wanted to punish him for being so horrible to us all the time.'

Jack said, 'So now, he'll have to stay hidden till they leave.'

'Good,' said Jill.

They rubbed noses, like they always did.

'So, you're not worried about them,' said Jack.

'As long as they don't find out what we're doing,' said Jill, 'we'll be fine.'

As Jill was Wind-Bathing and beachcombing the next morning, Molly trotted up alongside her.

'Mind if I join?' she said.

'No,' said Jill. She found it slightly disconcerting to know this young woman was pregnant, but not be able to see it.

'The beach is lovely, isn't it?' said Molly. 'So desolate.'

'I find it quite cosy,' said Jill.

'Cosy, too,' said Molly.

Jill felt all the advantages of being a twenty-seven-year-old talking to a twenty-two-year-old.

They walked to the water's edge.

'It makes me just feel so clean and refreshed,' said Molly, and stuck her arms out to either side.

As she stood there with her eyes closed, Jill took the chance to look Molly over. Molly's hair was reddish, and her skin fashionably freckled. At least, that had been the new thing in models the month Jill left London. There was an unlovely clenchedness about her face, however. It was too-hard. Vertical lines were incised on either side of her mouth. Jill knew them for what they were: speed-cuts.

'Whoo,' said Molly, when a stronger than usual gust of wind almost made her take a step backwards.

She opened her eyes before Jill had a chance to look away.

'It's not Mark's baby,' said Molly. Then she said hurriedly, 'I don't know why I told you that.'

Jill was stunned. 'Does he know?' she said.

'No,' said Molly. 'I brought him here to tell him.'

That evening, there was a knock at the door of Sea-View Cottage. As agreed, Jill answered. It was Mark. She was very aware of the whirring sound of the tape-to-tape machines.

'We were wondering if you'd like to come round to dinner,' said Mark. 'Not tonight. Tomorrow. Both of you.'

'That would be very nice,' said Jill, images of blood and shit flashing behind her eyes. This was difficult: Jack would have to switch shifts with John – that was the only way he'd be able to go out for the evening. 'I don't think we could stay very late.' Jack would have to go on nights.

'No problem,' said Mark. 'How about six?'

'Jack doesn't like to stay out too late,' said Jill. What if John refused? He couldn't. It was either this or risk getting caught.

'See you at six, then.'

Jill closed the door, keeping the whirring sound in.

The next morning, Molly again joined Jill on the beach.

'Did you tell him yet?' asked Jill.

'What?' said Molly. 'About the baby?'

'Yes,' said Jill.

Molly looked thoughtful. 'No,' she said. 'It's just too difficult. You didn't tell Jack, did you?'

'Of course not.'

'I'm *so* looking forward to meeting him. I don't want him to feel at all awkward. At dinner.'

'I didn't tell him anything.'

Molly started the conversation again.

'You and Jack eat everything, don't you? I'm going shopping today. I don't want to get anything *wrong*.'

'Oh, there's *nothing* we won't eat,' said Jill.

They both laughed.

Jack and Jill knocked on the door of Kittiwake at ten past six. Jack held the bottle of red wine. (They had promised John a crate of the stuff, to get him to switch shifts – and let him off washing-up for a month.)

It was Mark who answered.

'I'm afraid Molly isn't feeling very well,' he said, and mimed puking. 'Sorry I couldn't come round and tell you earlier. I didn't want to leave her alone.'

'We understand,' said Jill. 'Shall I go in and see her?'

'I think she'd prefer it if you didn't see her this way.'

'Hope she gets better soon,' said Jack.

'How about we do it tomorrow evening instead?' suggested Mark.

'Lovely,' said Jill.

Molly did not join Jill on the beach the next morning.

The air was wet with sea spray. A solitary seagull walked along behind her.

Jill's first thought was that Molly was still feeling sick. But then she realized that she might, at that very moment, be telling Mark the truth about the baby.

The morning seemed an odd time to do it, but you never knew with other people. If she did tell him, he'd almost certainly get into a real state. It wouldn't surprise her at all if he got into the car and drove off.

She looked back towards Kittiwake, but it gave little sign as to what was going on inside. Tufts of white smoke were ripped away from the chimney-stack as soon as they appeared.

That evening, they turned up on Kittiwake's doorstep again. Jack had the same bottle of wine. Jill had gathered some wild flowers for Molly. She it was who answered the door. 'Oh, come in,' she said.

'Feeling better?' asked Jill.

'Much,' said Molly. 'You must be Jack.'

The smell of butter-frying garlic suffused the hall.

They walked through into the kitchen.

'Hi,' said Mark, and wiped his hand on a dishcloth before holding it out towards Jack.

He was half-way through slicing a chopping-board full of kidneys.

'Mark,' said Jack.

'Jack,' said Mark.

'Sit down,' said Molly.

They began to talk, mostly about the film industry. The conversation was good, if a little awkward at times. Molly was charming. Mark was amusing, in a slightly sarcastic way. He seemed to like teasing Molly.

The food, when it came, was delicious. Stilton soup. Kidneys on a bed of rocket with garlic mash. Even the plastic tubs of Gooseberry Fool tasted almost homemade.

'It's terrible,' said Molly, as they were having coffee. 'We're only here another three days. The time seems to have gone so fast.'

Jill looked at her. She was obviously referring to not having told Mark.

'I want to show you something,' said Molly suddenly. She grabbed Jill by the hand, tugged her into the bedroom and slammed the door behind them.

Jack and Mark were left alone in the kitchen.

Mark wasted no time in leaning over to Jack. 'Molly isn't pregnant, you know,' he said. 'She lost the baby about five months ago. Just before Christmas. It sent her a little bit mad.'

'Really?' said Jack.

'I just play along with it, most of the time. It's better than having her constantly in hysterics.'

Jack thought this an odd comment. 'What do the doctors say?' he asked.

'She's in denial, plain and simple. She's been two months pregnant ever since November.'

'That must be difficult for you,' said Jack.

'I can cope,' said Mark. 'But please don't tell Jill. It's better if there's at least one person who can be completely natural with her.'

'I understand,' said Jack, thoroughly confused.

Just then, Jill came out of the bedroom. In her hands she held a half-knit baby sweater.

'Isn't it cute?' she said.

Jack was half an hour late in relieving John that night. He and Jill hadn't said anything much on the short walk home.

'Nice people.'

'Yes,' replied Jill.

'Strange.'

'Very strange.'

John was pretty pissed off at having to stay hidden the whole time.

'Don't tell me how nicey-nice it was,' he said, before

stamping upstairs. 'Because I don't want to fucking know.'

Jack knew what John would do now – head straight for his Technics decks in the living room, put on his massive headphones, close his eyes and pretend he was DJing at some superclub in Ibiza.

During the night shift, Jack decided he'd better not tell Jill that Molly was mad. He'd wait until after Mark and Molly had gone back to London.

The next morning, the beach was aslant with rain. It was colder, too. Determined never to miss a day, Jill put on her waterproofs and went out to take her Wind–Bath. The weather being what it was, she hardly expected to see Molly outside. And so, when she heard Kittiwake's front door slam shut, Jill was a little startled. But, on turning round, she saw that it was Mark and not Molly who was walking towards her.

'Morning,' he hollered, when he'd caught up. 'What are you doing out in this?'

'I don't mind it,' yelled Jill. 'How's Molly?'

'Not too bright today, either.'

'Oh dear.'

They walked towards the sea.

'You know,' Mark shouted conversationally, 'Molly and I haven't had sex since she got pregnant. Not once.'

'Oh,' said Jill.

'She just . . . doesn't want to. Says the very thought makes her feel ill.'

'Perhaps that's understandable. A lot of women feel that way.'

'Yes, but what am I meant to do?' he asked. 'Never have sex again?'

'I'm sure she'll come back to the idea.'

'I'll have exploded with frustration by then. I need to have sex regularly. It's like breathing or something.'

Jill stopped. 'Why exactly are you telling me this?'

'Why do you think?'

'I hope it's not what I think it is.'

'What *do* you think it is?'

'I'm going back inside.'

'What do you think I meant?' Mark stood in her way. '*What* do you *think* I *meant*?'

Jill tried to wither him. 'How can you be so crass?'

Mark leaned closer, so he didn't have to shout.

'It's the touching I miss, as much as anything. She never even does that any more.'

Mark was sticking his hands down the front of his trousers.

Jill dodged to one side, then back the other way. Mark, a little off balance to begin with, was wrong-footed.

She sprinted up the beach.

As she neared Sea-View Cottage, she saw Molly standing on the porch in her dressing-gown.

Molly waved and smiled.

Jill spent most of her shift feeling furious with Mark. But, when she calmed down, she began to feel sorry for Molly.

If she told Molly about Mark, she might leave him. And if that happened, the baby would lose its father.

Who was she to risk making that happen?

She really wanted to tell Jack. But Molly had looked so vulnerable, standing on the doorstep.

Jill decided she'd tell Jack all about it, after Molly and Mark had left.

★

In the afternoon, when they were in bed together, Jack asked Jill what she thought of Molly.

'She's very nice,' said Jill. 'Why do you ask?'

'I don't know,' said Jack. 'She's just a bit young to be pregnant, isn't she?'

'Perhaps it was an accident.'

'Perhaps.'

They were silent for a while.

'What do you think of Mark?' Jill asked.

'I'm not sure if I like him very much.'

'Why not?'

'He seems a bit creepy.'

Jill felt very relieved. 'I agree,' she said. 'There's something indefinably nasty about him.'

'Do you think they think it's odd, us not inviting them back for dinner?'

'Let them think whatever,' said Jill. 'They'll be gone in two days.'

About two in the morning, just as he'd finished changing over another twenty tapes, Jack thought he heard someone knocking on the front door, knocking hard.

But John was upstairs. If it *was* the door, then he'd get it.

The knocking came again.

John was probably DJing, wearing his big headphones.

After closing up the basement, Jack went to investigate.

Molly was there, wearing only a dressing-gown. She didn't look at all mother-to-be.

'Can I come in?' she said.

Jack didn't seem to have a choice. John was in the living room. Jack led Molly through into the kitchen. 'Noisy, isn't it?' he said, meaning the whirring sound.

'Don't worry,' said Molly. 'I won't stay long.'

'It's the boiler.'

Jack sat down, terrified that at any moment John would come through to fetch another beer from the fridge.

'Are you alright?' asked Jack.

'I'm fine. I'm fine. I just had to come and tell you.' She hesitated. 'This morning, on the beach. I think something happened between Mark and Jill.'

'Something, what?'

'Well, it's pretty obvious that they're attracted to each other, isn't it?'

Jack thought about this for a moment.

'I saw them *kissing*,' said Molly.

'No,' said Jack.

'I did,' Molly said. 'He thought I was still asleep, but I looked out the window and saw them.'

'I don't believe you,' said Jack. He felt quite convinced that this delusion was another sign of Molly's madness – along with believing herself pregnant, she had started to believe her boyfriend was serially unfaithful.

'But it's true,' said Molly, a little too loud for comfort. Even with headphones full of Euphoric Trance, John would hear.

'I think we should get you back to bed.'

'Why don't you believe me?'

'I do,' said Jack. 'I'm just sure it didn't mean anything. Come along.'

He put his arm around Molly and led her to the front door. While they'd been talking, the whirring sound of the machines had ceased. Luckily, Molly didn't seem to have noticed. Her torch was on the doorstep, lit but pointing into the concrete.

'I'll come with you,' Jack said.

They walked down Sea-View's garden path, through the gate, along a dozen yards to the right, through Kittiwake's gate, up the path.

Before they'd even reached the door, Mark had yanked it open. 'What's all this, then?' he said.

'Molly just —' But Jack didn't know what to say.

Molly elaborated the lie for him, '— wanted to talk to Jill about something.'

'Yes,' said Jack. 'I was just walking her back. Quite innocent.'

Molly turned as she went in the door. 'Thank you, Jack,' she said. 'And say thank you *so* much to Jill, too.'

'I will,' said Jack.

By the time he got back to the machines, Jack reckoned he'd lost about twenty minutes.

The tapes which had been stacking up for a fortnight were due to be collected the following night. The routine was this: Steve, accompanied by either Geoff or Keith, arrived around midnight in the van. They took two and a half hours in total to unload the blank tapes and then load up the finished ones. They were usually well away before it started to get light.

Jack felt anxious about collection day all through his shift. He already knew he couldn't mention anything about Molly's midnight visit to Jill. He was sure that Molly had been lying, though she might not herself know it.

During the night, Jack had started copying a new movie. He watched it through at normal speed on their quality-control machine. It was the hardest porn he had ever seen: camcordered in a concrete bunker of some sort, five ugly men raped an ugly woman, and then each other. He could see the woman trying to fight back, even though she was obviously smacked off her tits. The violence was homicidal.

He wanted to tell Jill not to watch it, but he knew that — if he did that — she would slam it on the moment he left the room.

The shift passed very slowly.

When Jill came to relieve him, he gave her a big kiss. She looked at his box of uncompleted tapes.

'I dozed off,' he said, before she asked.

During her sleepless night, Jill had almost decided to tell Jack about Mark's clumsy pass the previous morning.

For the first time since they had arrived, she'd not gone out for her Wind–Bath. She hadn't wanted to risk meeting Mark alone again. In some ways, he'd ruined the beach for her.

Jack went to bed.

But he couldn't sleep. After half an hour, he went back down to see Jill. She had been watching the new movie, and was obviously quite sickened. 'I have to tell you something,' he said. 'You have to promise to keep it a secret.'

'Yes?' asked Jill, putting the tape on pause. 'What?'

'Promise.'

'I did.'

'Molly isn't pregnant,' Jack said. 'She just thinks she is because she lost another baby.'

'Rubbish,' said Jill.

'Mark told me the other night, when we were round at dinner. You were in the bedroom. Looking at baby clothes. Molly's a bit mental.'

'She's not.'

'Well, you don't have to believe it. I just wanted to tell you, so you knew.'

Jill thought for a moment about returning the favour, and telling Jack about Mark not knowing the baby wasn't his. But if there wasn't a baby, or even if Jack just believed there wasn't, then that didn't really mean anything.

'You're nuts,' she said, and kissed him. 'Go back to bed.'

That evening, Molly appeared on the doorstep. Jill answered when she knocked.

'Hello,' said Molly, a little formally.

'Hi.'

'We wondered if you'd like to come round to dinner again. Tonight's our last night. I know it's a bit short notice. We'd like to see you both again before we go.'

'Oh,' said Jill. 'Lovely.'

Molly beckoned Jill to come outside. They went a few steps down the garden path. 'I told him,' said Molly.

'My God,' said Jill. 'How was he?'

'Much better than I thought it would be.'

Jill didn't know what she believed any more.

'He says we can always have one together in a few years' time.'

'Does he know the father?'

Molly blushed, very convincingly. 'It's his best friend from school.'

'That's terrible,' said Jill, at that moment believing it.

'I know,' said Molly, naughtily. 'Can you come around seven?'

'We'll be there,' said Jill.

'We can't go,' said Jack when Jill told him. He was still a little worried about letting Jill and Mark spend any more time together. Even though he knew Molly was mad, he thought there had been some truth in her suggestion that the two of them were attracted to each other. The fact that he himself fancied Molly seemed somehow to confirm this.

'We have to,' said Jill. 'Anyway, they'll be gone tomorrow morning. What harm can it do?'

'Steve is going to be shifting half a ton of extremely hardcore porn into the back of his van tonight,' said Jack. 'What *harm* is it going to do?'

'We'll just tell him to keep it quiet.'

'They're *bound* to notice.'

'What do you want to do? Tell me.'

'Phone him. Tell him not to come. Tell him to come tomorrow.'

'He won't do that,' said Jill.

'We'll tell him the police are sniffing around.'

'He'd just come to see for himself.'

Jack knew this was true.

'I'm going for a walk,' he said.

'You haven't got time,' said Jill.

'Do you want to get us caught?' shouted Jack. 'Do you know what will happen if they catch us with this stuff?'

He picked up a tape and hurled it towards the bedroom wall. Frustratingly, it landed flat, dropped to the floor, and didn't shatter.

'I'm *going* for a walk,' Jack said. 'Don't worry – I'll be back in time.'

Jack was half-way down the garden path when he spotted Molly. She was standing right in front of Sea-View Cottage, looking down the beach. There was no way he could get round her without her noticing. He thought for a moment about going back into the bungalow. But he was too angry with Jill for that. He needed to walk away from her for a while. He needed, perhaps, to let himself think that he might never go back.

When she heard the latch of the garden gate being lifted, Molly turned to see who it was.

'Jack,' she said, apparently relieved.

'Molly,' said Jack. He intended to walk straight past her, and on towards the shoreline. Without being rude, of course.

'I was waiting for you,' Molly said. 'I was hoping you'd look out and see me standing here.'

'Did you?' said Jack.

She took a couple of steps towards him. 'You were so kind when I came round last night.'

'It was nothing.'

'No,' said Molly. 'No, it wasn't.'

She was now close enough to touch him, which she did. She reached out with one of her hands, and gently stroked his cheek.

He flinched away. 'Get off,' he said.

'Mark's busy cooking,' said Molly. 'We could find somewhere to go.'

'But you're pregnant,' Jack said.

Molly took another step forwards. 'You know that's a lie,' she said.

'Fucking hell,' said Jack, backing away. 'What the fuck is wrong with you?'

Molly followed him.

Jack tried to turn round, so that he could run. But the sandy ground gave way beneath him, and he fell on his side.

Molly jumped on top of him. 'That's more like it,' she said.

With her groin, she pressed down on his hips. When he reached to try and push her off, she grabbed his wrists.

'Don't,' said Jack, warning violence.

Molly was surprisingly strong. Jack struggled, but Molly was able to ride him.

'Let *go*,' he shouted.

'Only if you kiss me.'

Without waiting for a response, Molly pushed her face down on his. Their teeth clicked sharply together.

'Fuck,' said Jack.

Molly pressed down again. He could feel her tongue licking along his lips.

He tried again to push her off, and this time he succeeded – but only because she let him.

She landed, quite hard, on her back, on the grass.

As he scrambled to one side, he heard her saying, 'Beat you.'

After a second to get his breath, Jack stood up. 'You are sick,' he said.

She closed her eyes and pretended to sunbathe. 'Would you mind?' she said. 'You're standing in my light.'

For a moment, Jack thought he wasn't going to kick her – then he kicked her.

His toes caught Molly's thigh. She doubled up, and he guessed he'd dead-legged her.

He bent down. He was about to start apologizing when he heard her whisper, 'Now that's more like it.'

Jack was only a few steps away from the porch when Jill opened the door.

'I'm sorry,' she said.

'Let's go inside,' he said.

'I said I'm sorry.'

'Okay,' he said. 'Apology accepted. Inside.'

He felt himself on the point of shoving her back. She was looking dangerously out over the beach.

'We need to get ready,' he said.

She took a final deep breath, and turned back inside.

Just then, Jack saw Molly standing up from behind the garden fence.

He almost leapt through the door into the bungalow.

Jack and Jill took another bottle of the same red as before round to Kittiwake at seven o'clock.

'Come *in*,' said Molly.

'How *are* you?' said Jill.

'Oh, very well,' said Molly, looking directly at Jack.

They walked through the hall and into the kitchen.

Jack felt Molly pinching his bum.

'Hi,' said Mark, who had just been prodding something in the oven.

'Smells lovely,' said Jill.

Mark kissed her on both cheeks, and she was in control enough to let him.

'Make yourselves at home,' said Molly.

They sat down in the same places as before. Jack immediately felt Molly's toes crawling up his calf. He reached down and pushed them away. They started again, at the ankle.

'It's not quite as elaborate as last time,' Mark said. 'I'm afraid we're using up the last of our food – so, it's baked bean surprise.'

'Lovely,' said Jill.

★

The meal was torture for Jack and for Jill. Molly kept pestering Jack beneath the table, with both feet and hands. Jack tried to ignore her pinchings, strokings and fondlings. Mark sent yearning looks in Jill's direction. Jill tried her best to avoid them. Jack, even whilst being distracted by Molly, couldn't help but notice what Mark was doing. He looked at Jill, to see if she reciprocated. Jill caught Jack looking at her a couple of times. She knew what he was thinking. To reassure him, she directed all her conversation towards Molly. This only made Jack's under-the-table situation more desperate.

The food was fairly disgusting: undercooked potatoes on top of lukewarm baked beans and half-cold spam.

After they'd finished eating, Molly took Mark's hand and said, 'We've decided that, if the baby's a boy, we're going to call it Jack, and if it's a girl, we'll call it Jill.'

'I don't know what to say,' said Jill. She avoided the eye contact Mark kept trying to make.

'That's very sweet,' said Jack, who was a little more used to treating Molly as the nutter she was.

Just then, they all heard an engine approaching.

'I wonder who that is,' said Mark, and went to the back window.

Molly joined him there. 'It's a white van,' she said. 'It's coming this way. Is it some friends of yours?'

Jack looked anxiously at Jill. 'It might be,' she said.

'Well, don't you know?' asked Mark. 'You must have arranged it.'

The van's lights raked through the candle-lit kitchen. The horn beeped three times, making everyone jump. Jack and Jill, looking at each other desperately, heard the engine switch off.

'It's a man,' said Molly.

Jack leaned over to Jill and whispered in her ear, 'What do we do?'

'He's coming this way,' said Mark.

'He looks very tough,' said Molly. 'He's wearing a leather coat.'

Jack got up out of his chair and crossed quickly to the window. He was just in time to see Steve disappearing behind the side of Kittiwake. For a moment, everyone stood still. Then the front door opened. Steve walked into the kitchen, leaving the door open behind him.

'Molly,' he said, nodding. 'Mark.'

They nodded back at him.

'What?' said Jack.

'Oh,' said Steve. 'I see you lot have already met.'

'Do you know them?' said Jill.

Just then, John came through the open door. He walked straight into the kitchen.

'About time,' said Steve, angrily. 'You and Molly grab ahold of her. Me and Mark'll get this one here.'

The Waters

There was nothing unusual about the layout, design or detail of Elyot's two-bedroomed midtown apartment – at least, not in relation to conventional, physical architecture: as for emotional architecture, however, things were very different: for Elyot's apartment, on the 150th floor of a 300-storey block, was directly beneath that of his ex-girlfriend, Vivian, and directly above that of his maybe-perhaps-future girl-friend, Valerie. There was a simple explanation for this: Elyot worked from home – the second of his two bedrooms being an office: and the only time he ever went out (except for odd visits to friends) was when he went to buy milk from the vending machine or for a walk in the nearby park: the only girls he ever met, therefore, tended to be taking the elevator. 150 floors – or 149 – were too many to ride in silence: talk took place: introductions were made: topics negotiated: goodbyes said. Rhythms of intersection began to occur: patterns of coincidence were noted, repeated: acci-dents became arrangements: times became dates. This is what had happened with Vivian and him: this is what Elyot hoped would happen with him and Valerie.

The front door opened into a short hall which led directly into the living room, the biggest single space in Elyot's apartment. When he looked out of his floor-to-ceiling window, he could gaze towards an identical building opposite. Both, however, were covered in mirrored glass, so neither – unless it was night, and the blinds unclosed – could see anything of the other's insides. Down below, at the base of the block, the sidewalks were wide, uncrowded and edged with thoughtful trees. Although it was only five years old, the city was in perfect taste – which was why Elyot had decided to move there. The living room was dominated by a long, shallow fishtank full of neon tetras, nothing but neon tetras. Each of these small darty fishes had down both its sides an electric blue and a fiery red stripe, eye to tail. Elyot loved his tetras, and kept their tank snail-free and glassily spotless. He was fascinated by their particolored stripes – so dull when the light was off, so impossibly bright when on. The fishtank separated the recreation area of the living room from the breakfast bar. Here, Elyot had made waffles with Vivian: here, he hoped to make waffles for Valerie. The bedroom, office and bathroom all led off from the living room. Elyot was less interested in the décor of his furnished world than Vivian had wanted him to be: the walls were still set upon the colors selected by the apartment's first occupant: the bedroom was dark red, which felt quite historical: the office was green, the bathroom, yellow. Throughout, the apartment was equipped with state-of-the-art it. Elyot was lonely there, and loved the place as no other in his life.

The elevator doors pinged open as Elyot turned the corner. It had told it to arrive, just in time for Elyot to get in. He was breathing quickly, having rushed to shower and change – it was ten to four: he was late: he needed milk.

Elyot was a tall young man with straw-blond hair and fairly standard blue eyes. His parents had not been people of great imagination or virtù: they had made him as special as they thought necessary. Elyot stepped into the elevator: it began its descent.

Valerie had moved the previous year into the apartment below – at the exact same time Elyot was breaking up with Vivian. After several prostrate months, glass to ear against wood of floor, Elyot had come to learn his new neighbor's habits – the audible ones. She showered every morning, singing along to the songs it played her. She had a kettle which whistled, and which had he not loved her would have annoyed the hell out of him. She slammed her front door when she left for work but was very quiet when she came back in. She liked to watch old movies and shout back the lines she knew by heart or knew almost by heart. Most importantly, she came home every single day – excepting weekends – at five minutes to four.

He didn't need milk: he had plenty: but she would never know that: he wasn't planning on inviting her into his apartment, to look inside his fridge, to see the milk cartons – that wasn't going to happen today, tomorrow, or even this month. He *would* ask her on a date, however. Things, to tell the truth, hadn't been going very well, so far. He sensed hostility – unprovoked. Valerie had perhaps met an ex-boyfriend in an elevator. Elyot was in love, impatient. He knew, in his heart, how wonderful life would be when Valerie had taken him into her heart. The problem was conveying to her exactly how perfect their being together would be – minds meeting, hearts interpenetrating. What did most to increase Elyot's impatience was Vivian. These days, if they coincided in the lobby, one of them – alternately – would await the next elevator: if they both by accident got into an over-crowded early morning downer, one of them – alternately again – would get out. This wasn't so bad: with this, he could cope. It was the fuckings-overhead he disliked: her apartment and his had the exact same layout, and hence her bedroom was positioned directly above his. He remembered being there with her, and fucking her there: but never quite as violently or as frequently as the fuckings he now overheard (or underheard): or in fact felt – for the thudding was sometimes enough to ripple the water in his bedside glass. Elyot knew Vivian's promiscuity was malicious, and therefore pathetic. When it occurred, he deciphered it as a message, Morse-like: I still hate you: I still love you.

As he was a little late today, he ran out to the vending machine.

At five minutes to four, Valerie came round the corner of the block, swinging her satchel in the early summer sunshine, swinging.

Elyot flashed his palm, pressed the button: *thunk* went the carton of milk, landing. He started back towards the apartment block, ahead of Valerie but slower. As long as she didn't stop to buy milk or cookies, Elyot estimated a fifty-fifty chance of things working out – elevatorwise.

They did: he reached the elevator just before her: she arrived beside him with sufficient swish for him naturally quite naturally to turn round. 'Oh, Valerie, hello,' he said. They had gone beyond *hi* a few weeks ago. The most glorious of their conversations had occurred when the elevator broke down, and they fell to talking about how long they'd lived there and what each of them did. Another man had been present, a doctor, Vladimir, who – they learned – had lived on the top-but-one-floor since the week after the block (and the city) were opened. He was proud of this, like it meant something. If Vladimir hadn't been there, Elyot

would probably have taken the opportunity – after she was
safely out of the elevator, and so not going to feel threatened
– of asking Valerie out on a date.

'Oh, hi there,' Valerie replied. Valerie, of course, was
beautiful: her hair was an oriflamme of orange, and sparks
flew, blue, in her eyes.

'Milk again,' Elyot said, holding up the carton. She knew:
she must know.

'You could always buy two,' said Valerie. Worryingly,
Elyot could not make out whether this remark was flirtatious
or dismissive.

The elevator arrived. He was glad he didn't have to reply
to her suggestion. His two answers were neither of them
right: one, *It gets me out of the apartment*, sounded nerdy: the
other, *I like the vending machine*, sounded autistic.

'149, as per,' she said, for Elyot was where he wanted to
be – nearest the buttons.

He didn't say, *I know: I know* might be construed as
threatening. Of course he knew.

After puffing her cheeks out a little and holding her breath
a moment, Valerie sighed. Unsure whether this was a state-
ment or not, Elyot dared: 'Long day, huh?' The dull hiss of
the elevator prevented silence.

'Not long,' said Valerie, 'just hard.' She worked with
people, arranging things.

They were passing the fifteenth floor. It wasn't a
particularly fast elevator. More dull hiss.

Floor twenty-seven. Too many thoughts, too many floors
already gone. It was a great day, they were still alone. Usually,
someone intruded in the lobby, and the rise was blandly
small-talky. Once, Vivian had joined them. There had been
no speech then. The two women didn't know one another.

Elyot was about to ask, 'I was thinking of catching a movie this evening – I wondered if you might like to come?' When – *ping* – the elevator stopped. Two people Elyot had never seen before got in, pressed 300 and continued talking about the roof garden.

As the elevator rose towards 150, Elyot went into total decline. He would never ask Valerie out: she would never even have a chance of saying yes. When they reached her floor, Valerie said bye and got out. Elyot watched the retreating back of his love narrow to a slit.

In his absence, whilst Elyot had been failing, or not even risking failure, <u>it</u> had taken two messages from Ezra – Elyot's voluble best friend. The second of Ezra's messages was urgent. Elyot ignored them both: taking off his outdoor shoes, in something of a trance, and strolling thoughtless across the living room for his usual check on the okayness of the tetras. It was just *now* that he felt the damp. The rug sagged up slightly between his toes and for a moment – so thought-deep was he – it occurred to him that he might actually be in the bathroom imagining himself by the fish-tank as a better way of filling his mind with Valerie. He knelt down to touch the rug, and felt his kneeling knee go moist. His dismay at the possibility that the fishtank had started leaking was interrupted by the first drop, which fell – as if the prank of a mischievous friend – down the collar of his short-sleeve shirt. It ran cold, half the length of his spine – like a shiver made liquid. He stood and looked up. On the ceiling above his head a transparent nipple of water was slowly forming, squeezing itself out through itself, until – soundless – it fell onto his forehead, again as if intended. Still looking upwards he stepped back until the rug beneath his feet was again dry. This took him only a couple of steps. He put his left fingertip (he was left-handed) into the still-formed droplet above his eyebrow – lifted and carried it into sight. The water glinted brightly, as if there were a sword-fight going on inside it. He considered tasting it to find out more about it, but decided not to – not until he'd found out more about it. First, he would go and have a talk with Vivian: her motives seemed clear – not content with sensational fucking, she was now deliberately overflowing the sink in her breakfast bar. For a moment he considered the possibility that she had fallen in the shower, hit her head, bled, lost consciousness and drowned, blocking the plughole and causing water to go everywhere: but he dismissed this almost straight away – for one thing it was too good: for another, her shower was directly above his – the water should be running down there, too. He went to check, saw nothing amiss. It was less confrontational, Elyot decided, to go upstairs and talk to Vivian directly, rather than have it contact her. From the kitchen area, he fetched a large bowl: after placing it directly beneath the water-nipple, he went out the front door.

Elyot walked up the one flight of stairs in bare feet. He and Vivian had spoken only once since they split up, that too-late night when they had attempted to reclaim and return the things they owned, disowned. 'I have a list,' the conversation began, 'So have I,' it ended.

Elyot knocked on the tall pale wood of Vivian's door, identical to his own except for the ten-higher number. No response. He used the doorbell. Nothing. He abused the doorbell. Nope. She really *hadn't* come in yet, or really *was* being evil.

Back in his apartment, Elyot saw the drip-bowl was about an eighth full. He listened to the interval of the drips: it was

round about eight bars – thirty-two beats. He messaged
Vivian, quite without fury. He talked to the Building
Manager, called Ford.

Ford, fifty, was choice-bald and eccentrically muscular.
His voice implied cigarettes, which his smoky uniform and
dirty nails confirmed. Ford's machismo was outdated but still
had the power to disconcert the young. Elyot had never felt
comfortable dealing with Ford, feeling that he only encour-
aged the Manager's contempt by giving him generous tips at
Christmas.

Ford got back to him within half an hour, saying Vivian
had been contacted and was coming home.

After another half-hour, Ford and Vivian called in on
Elyot. Elyot said hi, and together they took the elevator up.

'Please,' said Vivian, and went with Ford into her apartment. Elyot stayed behind in the corridor. He wondered
whether there was anything in particular Vivian might
not want him to see. His picture, maybe. A few moments
went by.

'Thank you, Vivian,' said Ford, walking with his head
turned away from his direction.

'And?' asked Elyot.

'No problem here,' said Ford.

'No leak,' said Vivian, without visible anger.

'I'm sorry,' said Elyot, 'sorry for getting you home from
wherever, but there's a leak in my apartment – and it *is*
coming down from you.'

Vivian seemed to have told Ford about their ex-ness, or
perhaps he'd known already – either way there was knowledge in the man's crumple-faced smile as he gently said,
'Let's go and take a lookie down there, shall we?'

'Goodbye,' Elyot said to Vivian, but got no response.

Elyot followed Ford into the elevator – Ford took it always, as a matter of building company policy: Elyot led Ford into his apartment, and all the way through to the fish-tank. He knew a while before he got there that something was very wrong: the nipple of water had disappeared from the ceiling and the rug was entirely dry: the bowl remained on the floor but was empty of even a drop of water. Upon Ford's face the smile grew broader and even more widely comprehending. 'Listen,' he said, 'she's a lovely girl but don't humiliate yourself like that again, okay?'

'But it was *there*,' said Elyot, pointing, 'and it was wet.'

'You're a proud but foolish man,' said Ford. 'Goodbye.' And Elyot showed Ford out, without attempting further persuasion. He stood in the hall for a moment, afraid of what he might find when he re-entered the living room. Of course, when Elyot eventually returned to the fishtank, he found the carpet again wet, the bowl half-full of very cold water. Outside, the going-down sun had turned the mirror-glass of the building opposite the fiery orange color of Valerie's hair. Without hesitation, Elyot this time dipped his fingers into the bucket and drew them out dripping. He let a few drops drip into his open mouth, and was surprised at how bracky they tasted.

Unwilling to give up on this thing, or to allow his very virtùous carpet to be ruined, Elyot contacted Vivian. 'Yes,' she said, not allowing him to see her.

'Take a look at this,' Elyot said, and pointed up at the nipple of water on the ceiling. Conveniently, a large drop formed and fell. Through it, Vivian looked at it. 'Very clever,' she said, 'now leave me alone.' She cut out. Elyot was left baffled: Vivian thought he was using it to construct fake visuals. Perhaps she even thought he wanted to draw her downstairs into his apartment – when, in fact, he could think of little he would like less.

Elyot sat down upon his couch for a minute or two, watching the drips form and fall. His apartment felt unusually chilly, despite the air-conditioning which most of the time was blandly attuned. Then he had a terrible thought: the water would start to drip through his floor and into Valerie's apartment. That would be the worst. He decided to do what he could to prevent this: he rolled up the rug and stacked it in a far corner. Then he laid a couple of thick white bath towels in its place, and repositioned the emptied bowl beneath the water-nipple. It would be okay like that, for a while at least.

Later on, when it started closing his blinds, he told it to stop. Angrily, he told it not to close his blinds ever again without asking him first. He went over to the window and looked across at the apartments opposite. Quite a few of his favorites had left their blinds undrawn, and he watched their inhabitants without caring if he himself was seen. The apartment directly opposite his own was dark, as usual – though he sometimes believed he saw movement there, behind the pot plants.

The fucking-overhead started up earlier and worse than usual, that evening. Elyot knew that Vivian was thinking of him with each and every crunch.

Ezra, frantic, called and called again. 'I'm getting worried about you,' he said, 'should I come over?' Still Elyot had it blank him, and did not speak back when he spoke. 'I'm hurt,' said Ezra. 'Are we still friends? Call me.'

Ten o'clock, Elyot took himself out for a walk. At night he tended to avoid the park, but there was nowhere else to go. He snuck out the door as silently as possible, not wanting to let Vivian know how futile her unheard revenge would be.

Elyot stayed a long time, sitting on a bench under a tree, hoping to miss the second fuck as well as the first.

Entering the lobby on his way back, Elyot saw Valerie waiting by the elevator. As he walked towards her, he took great pleasure in her posture – the way she stood *properly*. Her body seemed simple and sensible, satisfyingly so. He wanted to put his arm around her. He knew it was a body he could live with a long time without finding any aspect of it ludicrous. 'Hi,' he said, as he came to her side.

'Oh, hi, again.' Her recognition was gratifyingly instant. She was carrying a brown paper bag. He wished he'd been for groceries, too. Conversation would have been so much easier in the store, and on the walk round the block. But – 'Been out?' she asked.

'Just to the park,' he said. Oh no, she'd think he was a loner. Just as he was about to deny himself, she said, 'I do that, too. It's a good place to go when you want to be – quiet.' The elevator arrived. The door closed, without anyone else having got in. The intensity was unignorable: they were inside a new room, together. 'I like the trees,' she said. 'Particularly. They're very . . . well done.' Then she giggled slightly and added, 'God.' The *God* had been a foot-note to herself. These were good signs. Elyot found her awkwardness lavishly encouraging: second only, he felt, to pretending to spill her groceries. The elevator continued its ascent, still uninterrupted.

'Yes,' he said, 'the trees. I know what you mean. And the spaces between them, too.' A silence that threatened per-manance overtook the hush of the cables. Then she said, 'But I don't always feel 100 per cent safe, at night.'

'Oh, I do,' he lied. 'It's pretty fine up this end.'

'Not under the trees,' she said.

'Maybe not.' He couldn't avoid what had to come next. 'Well, if you ever want to go, but feel a bit scared – I'm only upstairs.'

'I know,' she said, quickly.

'Of course,' he said.

'That came out all wrong,' she said. 'Can I start again?'

'Surely,' he said.

She coughed and went formal: 'Thank you for that kind offer. I will definitely take you up on it.' The elevator reached 149. Their idyll fractured with a *ping*.

'See you soon,' was all Elyot dared.

'Sure,' Valerie replied.

He knew it was love because he'd forgotten the water-nipple entirely. The bowl was full to overflowing. Vivian was still fucking, or pretending to fuck, but he didn't care any more. Valerie knew and liked and admitted and trusted him.

He emptied the bowl and replaced it with a bucket. He took a sleeping pill, then another, then went to bed, joyous. The thumping and grunting from above became almost comically soothing.

The cold woke Elyot around 3 a.m. He had never known it be so cold inside his apartment, not even when they once a winter turned the heating off to test turning it back on again. Being sur-oceanic, temperatures in the city never went below freezing. Elyot had it turn the lights on, first to a gentle dimness. The picture on the opposite wall, an image of the fishtank in real time, neon tetras floating bright, seemed blurry. Elyot rose out of bed, the sheet still around his shoulders: there was a definite chill in the room. He asked it to put the lights on full, and was stunned to see the

room retain its hazy whiteness. He walked out into the living room, but the mist was even thicker in there. As he
moved, he could feel it gathering clammily upon his skin.
He remembered his childhood nightsweats and wondered,
of course, if he might be dreaming. Going back into the
bedroom, into the closet, he found some warm clothes, put
them on. Then he asked it to wake Ford.

Ford was nothing if not efficient, even more so when
angry – he made it to Elyot's apartment in fifteen.

Elyot went to open the door after hearing Ford's knock,
but as soon as he opened it a crack he felt the room around
him warming up. By the time the door was fully open, the
apartment behind him was entirely free of mist. 'Yes,' said
Ford, 'and tonight's problem is?'

'Could you stand there just one minute?' Elyot asked,
holding up an index finger.

'Sure,' replied Ford, for whom sarcasm was a vocation.
'Nothing I'd like better.'

Slowly Elyot closed the door, and slowly the apartment
filled with mist. Elyot felt nauseous. He reached for the door
handle and turned it, the mist remained: he opened the door
by as small an amount as possible, the air began immediately
to clear: he inched the door open wider and wider, the mist
evaporating as he did so: by the time it was fully opened, the
apartment was as it usually was. Ford, however, was not: his
smile was rictal.

'Once more,' said Elyot, knowing that several festive
seasons would have to pass, with their gifts and thank-
yous, before his relationship with Ford was fully repaired.
He closed the door, turned away from it and took a step into
the mist. He wondered for a moment whether the whole
mist-experience wasn't merely it playing a perceptual trick

upon him. But <u>it</u> didn't do that: <u>it</u> wasn't allowed to: probably, without his permission, <u>it</u> couldn't. Suddenly Elyot turned around, interrupting himself mid-thought, lunged for the door handle, yanked it open. More suddenly still, the mist evacuated itself from the apartment. Elyot and Ford stood face to face. 'Come inside,' said Elyot.

'Thank you,' replied Ford, and attempted one last pleasantry. 'Had me worried back there, buddy.'

Ford stepped over the threshold and Elyot shut the door behind him. The apartment remained entirely free from mist or inexplicable phenomena of any sort. Elyot hadn't had time to think of another problem with which he could confront Ford: and so, he began apologizing for what had happened in the afternoon. This he did in such a way that both of them knew a large amount of virtù was being transferred from him to Ford.

'I'm sorry,' Ford said, 'I can't do anything for you. If the girl doesn't want to see you again, I'm not going to get involved in anything.'

The virtù was coming back, rejected. 'No,' said Elyot, stemming its flow. 'Really, I just wanted to say it won't happen again.'

Ford smiled, accepting the virtù. 'You could've waited till the morning to tell me.'

'Drink?' asked Elyot, enjoying the restored warmth of his apartment.

'No, I think I'd,' said Ford, and yawned, 'better head.'

Elyot showed him to the door and watched as he walked down the corridor and round the corner to the elevator. A chill ran up Elyot's back as he closed the door. The short walk into the living room was through a dense white mizzle.

★

By the following morning, the mizzle had thickened to a drizzle. Elyot slept through, beneath his usual blanket and a couple of added-on overcoats. Around dawn, he walked through into the living room. Automatically the lights came on. Elyot looked out towards the apartment block opposite, and thought he saw movement in the apartment directly opposite his own – a scuttling away. However, he forgot it almost immediately as the lights chose this moment to fuse – with a pop. The only lightsource left in the apartment was the long strip within the fishtank.

Elyot got dressed and headed out for a walk around the block, to warm up and take some time to think. He was not so much terrified at the thought of going mad as annoyed that his madness should be taking such an uncomfortable and inconvenient form. Being normal-mad wouldn't, he thought, make all that much difference, even to himself.

On reaching the vending machine, he bought himself for comfort a carton of milk. The purchase reminded him of Valerie, and the thought of Valerie in turn gave him an idea: perhaps Vivian and Ford couldn't see the drizzle because they found him, Elyot, unsympathetic: perhaps someone unprejudiced, or even predisposed toward him, wouldn't have the same problem. Elyot hurried back through the lobby, hoping to catch Valerie before she left for work.

'Sorry to disturb you,' he said, after she answered the door. 'Do you think you could come take a look at something in my apartment?'

'Sure,' she said, more amenable than he'd anticipated. Her hair was still wet from the shower that, this one morning in a hundred, he'd failed to hear her taking.

He stood back from her closed front door as she did whatever she was doing: putting a few final things in her workbag, probably.

As they walked upstairs, Valerie asked, 'What is it? It isn't anything creepy-crawly, is it?' Elyot had decided to tell her the truth. This, he hoped, would enable her to join him in seeing the drizzle. 'I think there's something weird going on with my apartment,' he said, 'it's really damp.'

'You mean the air-con?' Valerie asked, adorably perky.

'More than that,' said Elyot. 'You'll see.' And then, silently, 'I hope you'll see.'

When he opened the door to his apartment, Elyot was – for the first time – delighted to see that the drizzle was still there. In fact, it had if anything thickened to something resembling a rain. An inch or so of water lay across the hall floor. He sploshed a few steps in, deliberately wetting his trouser-bottoms, turned round in triumph to Valerie, and said, 'You see.' She was about to cross the threshold, and ruin her expensive shoes when – 'No!' cried Elyot. 'You'll get them wet!'

'Wet?' replied Valerie, looking towards the floor. 'But it's –' Before he could stop her she took a step into the hall. 'It's not wet.'

'Oh,' said Elyot, realizing.

She looked at him, hard. 'Is this some kind of game?' There was indeterminacy: she wasn't sure whether or not she quite wanted to join in.

'Come here,' said Elyot, and led the way. It was full-on raining in the living room. Elyot felt his hair being battered down against his head. He looked at Valerie, and was distressed to see that whilst her own hair was still shower-damp, it wasn't downpour-drenched.

'It's wet in *there*,' Valerie said, and pointed. Elyot's momentary hope died when he followed the line of her finger to the fishtank.

Valerie moved towards the neon tetras: she was about to step directly into the thickest column of water falling from the ceiling, right beneath the spot where the water-nipple had yesterday been. Elyot couldn't prevent himself from trying to prevent her getting drenched, even though it was already obvious to him that she was staying dry. Grabbing her by the upper arms, he pulled her a couple of steps back. She screamed, and he let go of her – guiltily retreating towards the window. 'Jesus, you frightened me,' she said, her hand grasping her throat. 'What are you doing?'

Elyot saw just how much of her trust he had lost, by touching her unasked. 'I'm sorry,' he said. 'If you can't see it or feel it, then something's obviously wrong with me.' He had been trying for a while to stop himself shivering, but this had only caused all the small judders to accumulate: something like a fit now convulsed his body, rippling him from hips to head. Disconcertingly, this made Valerie scream again, and start gradually to back away from him. 'I think,' she said, 'I'll just be, um, going along now.'

'Yes,' said Elyot, 'go – that's a good idea – and please forget this ever happened.'

She backed her way through the hall and felt for the door handle with a blind hand. Elyot reached to open it for her, and she screamed for a third time. 'Get away from me,' she breathed. He straightened up, too close to her. '*Get* . . . *away*,' said Valerie. He retreated all the way into the living room, hands up in surrender.

'I'm sorry,' he said, to a slammed door: 'I'm sorry,' to

her running-away footsteps: 'Dammit,' to her probably permanent silence.

After an hour's regret, Elyot asked _it_ to contact Ezra – who was available, as always, and agreed to come over straightaway: no explanation required.

Ezra was thin, spike-bearded, acerbic by inclination but gentle when gentleness was required. His clothes were ragged, an affectation which Elyot forgave him. If Ezra gave him a direct order, Elyot usually obeyed it – and usually benefited thereby. But when Ezra disapproved of something, or somebody, Elyot might ignore him, but always felt guilty. And Ezra disapproved of Valerie. She was so much of an Elyot-fantasy, he said, that she couldn't be proven really to exist.

The waters in the hall were up to Elyot's ankles when he opened the door for his best friend. 'It's bad,' he said. He could tell from Ezra's gaze, from the fact it fell upon himself rather than upon the torrent falling from above, that his friend couldn't see anything either. Elyot got Ezra a soda, got himself a coffee: they arranged themselves on the couch.

'So what is it?' asked Ezra.

'Valerie,' said Elyot. 'She thinks I'm mad.'

'Why?'

'Because probably I probably am.'

'And again why?'

Elyot told Ezra the whole story, right from the first drop. As he did so, his friend threw the occasional glance round the to-him dry apartment.

'You're sure it doesn't feel any different than usual?' Elyot asked, interrupting himself about half-way through.

'Well, it does feel a little bit colder than usual,' Ezra said, 'but maybe I just think that because I've been sitting here watching you shivering.'

'It feels to me like the ice-compartment,' said Elyot.

'Then let's get out and go to mine, then,' said Ezra.

The moment Elyot stepped outside his apartment, he felt entirely warm and dry. He did a small dance, hopping over and over the threshold, in and out – warm, cold: dry, wet. 'Okay,' he said, satisfied.

Ezra lived towards the bottom of an apartment complex two blocks away. His zone had been built to house a more bohemian community than Elyot's. 'Would you like me to call anyone?' Ezra asked, after they had been sitting there watching <u>it</u> for a couple hours.

'Call Valerie,' said Elyot, 'explain.'

Ezra smiled, his moustaches tilting upwards. 'I do believe you,' he said, 'surely I do – but even *you* admit it's only happening in your head.'

'What do I do?'

'About Valerie or about the rain in your apartment?'

'Both, I guess.'

'Try not to think of Valerie too much,' said Ezra, 'and sleep here tonight.'

The next morning, Elyot felt unable to stay away any longer from his apartment – whatever state it was now in. He turned down Ezra's offer to accompany him. The lobby was almost empty: the elevator journey, although upwards, felt like an unending plunge. He was approaching Valerie, passing her, rising above her. They were estranged.

On opening the front door, Elyot saw dryness – his apartment looked normal, was warm. He felt the hope swilling around in his stomach, like a beer-breakfast. Stepping over the threshold he pulled the door shut behind him, and a huge black wave smashed through from the living room and slammed him back against the pale wood. Salty water invaded his mouth, and he choked as he tried to spit it out. After he found his feet, he found also that the waters were now up to his armpits. They were gushing so thickly from the ceiling that it was hard to find gaps in which to breathe. He cupped his hands over his mouth, forming a small cave into which air could flow.

Spitting out the last of the salty taste, he half-waded half-swam through into the living room. The waters in here were surprisingly clear, although they were churned to white by the heavy rain from the ceiling. A couple of cushions from the couch were floating over in the corner. A few other things bobbed along on the surface: utensils, containers, shoes, pictures. Over the horizon of the waters, Elyot could see the apartment block opposite.

After a minute or two of looking around, Elyot realized that if he stayed in his apartment for very much longer the waters would rise above his head and he would drown. Panicked by this thought, he fought his way back through into the hall. He took hold of the handle and pulled it, but the front door wouldn't open. He tried tugging, yanking: the door stayed shut. It was obvious: the pressure of the waters, pressing against the door on the inside, was stronger than he was. He was trapped, and – if he did nothing – only a short time away from drowning. Desperately, he tried ordering it to open the door. When there was no response, he calmly told it to contact Ford. It did not reply: it seemed if not dead then non-functioning. This was a new state, one very hard for Elyot to cope with. It had accompanied him everywhere, in various versions, periodically updated, every day of his life: and although he had often resented it, for its intrusiveness, its slowness, he had never contemplated life without it. He mourned it, for a good moment.

The waters had risen another few inches, making it necessary for Elyot to start swimming. Above his head there was about a foot and a half of air between him and the ceiling. These were filling up at the rate of about an inch a minute: and as the waters' incursion had been accelerating from the moment it started, Elyot calculated he had fifteen or so minutes left in which to do something. After considering his options, whilst swimming on the spot repeating the words, 'Okay, okay, we can deal with this,' Elyot swam off towards the bedroom. The waters falling upon his head, like chucked buckets, made it difficult for him to see: he felt his way, therefore, fingertips touching the slimy walls. It seemed as though algae had already started growing upon them. The bedroom floor was now a dark green, and when Elyot plunged his head beneath the waters to take a look at it he saw small fingers of seaweed, sprouting. This panicked him, again: he didn't want to be sucked under by the clingy green growths. He breaststroked, high in the water, across the bedroom. The closet, where he had expected to find his baseball bat, was wide open and completely empty. Luckily, he found the baseball bat almost immediately: floating among other buoyant objects in the far corner of the room.

Bat in hand, he swam back to the front door, and wasted ten minutes of vital time trying to smash it down. Underwater, it was almost impossible to create enough handspeed to make a decent hit. The pale wood was sturdy: the hinges held: small dents in the surface were his only reward.

In despair, Elyot swam through into the living room. His

head was very close now to bumping against the ceiling. 'I wonder who'll find me,' was his thought. He made it over to the window, and looked out towards the apartment block opposite. (He was already feeling a nostalgia for air, and he hadn't even drowned yet.) In the window directly opposite his, a young woman's face was visible – just above a horizontal line, beneath which her room appeared to be darker, greener. She caught sight of Elyot, and waved her hands excitedly. Elyot did his best to wave back – he pressed the baseball bat against the glass and swished it from side to side. The young woman got the message. She pointed at the waters rising in her living room, then shrugged. It was touchingly comic. Elyot took a deep breath and, braving the seaweed, submerged himself completely: then he pressed himself up to the window and did a huge shrug in reply. He looked across – underwater – towards the young woman, who seemed to be laughing. He wanted to get a message to her: 'Escape from your apartment before the waters trap you.' He made pushing-away gestures with his free hand, but the young woman failed to interpret them. When Elyot resurfaced, the top of his head was pressed hard against the surface of the ceiling. He sucked his breaths in through gritted teeth.

With the baseball bat still in his hand, Elyot considered his options. If he did nothing, the waters would rise to cover his mouth and nose, and he would certainly die: and if he smashed a hole in the window, the waters would just as surely shatter the entire pane and sweep him out into high mid-air: but there was, in the smashing scenario, the slightest chance that he'd be able to hang on to something within the room, and wait for the waters to gush out. He decided the chance was worth taking. Rather than try to swing it underwater, he used the baseball bat as a battering-ram – big-end on. He gave the window a couple of smacks, and a thick crack in the glass darted off to one side. He put his head underwater and checked he'd seen this correctly. When he resurfaced, the air pocket was almost gone. He took three of his deepest breaths, and then submerged himself – perhaps for the last time. Another two slams, and a spiderweb of cracks had appeared in the window-pane. He started to pound, becoming frantic for air. The web dented in the middle. He bash, bash, bashed – but the head of the bat just would *not* puncture through. Elyot felt lightheaded but drowning wasn't as he'd imagined it to be: he did not feel in any way strangled. His lungs seemed relaxed and ample with air, though Elyot knew this couldn't be the case. With each bash he bashed against the glass, more bubbles spurted from his mouth – until no more came, even when he tried to force some out. 'I should be dead by now,' Elyot thought. He tried breathing, and found that he could – or rather, that breathing was now an option – he didn't have to, but he could if he wanted: the waters were incapable of drowning him. With a little more time to do it, Elyot worked on deepening the dent in the glass. After about a minute, the bat punctured through. Fast as he could, Elyot swam back from the hole, grabbing hold of the fishtank's legs: expecting to see a great sideways geyser of water, he looked out the window. But the waters weren't moving. He let go of the fishtank and pushed himself over for a closer look. In the effort of saving his life, he had entirely forgotten the young woman: a glance confirmed she was still watching. He passed his hand over the area in front of the hole, but felt no suction: the waters were staying flush with the plane of the glass. Elyot put his mouth to the hole, and tasted the sweet dry air of the city.

He spent a minute in the pleasure of mere breathing, eyes closed. When he looked out again towards the young woman, he saw she had smashed a hole in her own window – a hole large enough to poke her whole head out of. Elyot used the baseball bat to chip the edges off his own hole, making it about a foot in diameter: still no water flowed out: he stuck his head through and looked 150 stories down: the sight, and the feeling of the force of all the water behind him, almost made him sick.

'Hey,' the young woman shouted. 'Hey, you made it!'

'I thought I was going to die,' Elyot shouted back, in triumphant ragged gasps.

'You were under such a long time.'

'I can breathe the water!' he cried. 'I can breathe it.'

'Wow,' the young woman called back.

'I'm Elyot,' he shouted, 'who are you?'

'Jerry!' she shouted back, 'with a J and a Y.'

'Hey,' called Elyot, 'great.'

The two of them took a moment looking at one another. They were strange images, the white oval of Jerry or Elyot's face sticking out of the side of their building, as if they were the building's face, smiling. 'Pheoo-wee,' Jerry shouted. At the same instant, they looked down, towards the street, to see if anyone was looking up at them. As far as they could tell, they had passed unobserved. The sidewalks were evenly interspersed with walkers. Elyot next looked over the rest of the apartments in Jerry's block: one or two of them looked a little misty, but hers was the only one with a visible water level. 'I need to get out – I can't open my front door,' Elyot shouted. 'Is it still working for you?'

'Yes,' Jerry cried. 'Do you want me to speak to your Building Manager?'

'He's called Ford,' shouted Elyot. 'Tell him to come up with the spare keys – and an ax.'

'I'll come over, when I've called.'

'Oh God yes,' said Elyot, and shouted out his apartment number.

He went back inside and swam around for a while. Now he knew it wasn't going to drown him, now he knew himself to be undrownable, the seaweed had ceased to terrify. When he dived up close, he saw barnacles had begun to attach themselves to the skirting board. The lid of the fish-tank had come off, and the neon tetras were swimming freely about the room – although they seemed to retain some loyalty to the area of the tank. The tetras seemed to have multiplied – though this, on top of everything else, was an added impossibility: they were all female.

After about ten minutes, Elyot heard a gentle knocking on the door. He freestyled through the hall. Ford was probably trying to get him to answer, before he used the key – before he axed the door down. The knock came again: Elyot knocked back, three equally spaced times. Three knocks, equally spaced, replied: Elyot scraped twice with his finger-nails: two scrapes came back. Elyot waited. There were five, six knocks. Impatiently, Elyot reached for the door handle: he intended just to jiggle it a few times, to demonstrate his helplessness: but to his astonishment, the front door opened as soon as he turned it. A figure was standing there, rippling slightly: the waters had again failed to gush out – it was Vivian. He saw her mouth fall open, her hand leap up to cover it. Her face turned into a widening circle of astonishment. She took a step back. Elyot realized he was floating about a foot off the floor: even if Vivian couldn't see the waters, she was seeing something pretty freaky. Vivian's mouth moved, as if she were speaking – but Elyot couldn't hear her: he swam forwards, and stuck his face out into the air of the hallway. '– been all over it, but I'm sure you're the first person it started to happen to. Almost everyone else who's got it has just got the mist or the rain . . .'

'Vivian,' said Elyot, 'what are you saying? I couldn't hear you.'

Vivian looked annoyed. She'd already made her apology once, and wasn't sure if she had grace enough to go through it a second time. 'I'm *sorry* I didn't believe you,' she said, 'about the water . . . It's happening in my apartment – and all over the city, too. But you were the first: I'm sure you were the first. It was asking for any information, and I told it just now. I think someone is going to come to speak to you about it.'

Just then, Ford and Jerry came together out of the elevator. Gosh, Jerry was thin. The imminent danger of gangliness in her overlong limbs made her, to Elyot, instantly endearing. With sceptic Ford in view, however, Elyot half-expected the waters to recede: instead, he continued to float there – it was Ford who went two amazed paces back. 'You know, I didn't believe it till I saw it,' he said. 'Not till I saw it with my own eyes.'

Jerry came up close, until she was standing right beside Vivian. 'You got the door open,' she said, amazed.

'It just opened when I tried it,' Elyot replied.

'And who's this?' asked Vivian.

Elyot introduced them, making a point of calling Vivian his ex. She looked as if she wanted to have an argument about this, which for Jerry only confirmed it. Ford approached with great hesitation, still talking to himself. 'It told me,' he said, 'it really did.' He reached out with his forefingers and stroked the surface of the water. Vivian copied him, once she saw it was safe. Jerry too reached out – but her hand passed through until it came to touch Elyot's hand. 'Do you want to come in?' he asked her. She nodded, very sharply. He swam back: she stepped through. Only for a second did he worry that she might drown. He saw Ford reach out to make a grab for her, but miss. He saw Vivian stepping back in disgust. Jerry, still with his hand in hers, was now floating alongside him. More people got out of the elevator and came down the corridor towards the door. There was a reporter, a cameraperson: two Fire Department people: there was Valerie. Elyot turned to Jerry and gave her a large shrug. He pointed at Valerie then pointed a couple of times at the floor. 'Downstairs,' he mouthed. Jerry gave him the a-okay fingersign. The reporter held out her microphone toward the surface of the waters: the light from the camera speared into the apartment like sunbeams seen from above a coral reef. Everyone in the corridor seemed to be talking at once – shouting to get Elyot's attention. Valerie and Vivian stood side by side, making identically imploring gestures: looking, now he saw them together, shamefully identical. Elyot shut and locked the door upon all of them: he wanted to be alone with Jerry.

Ignoring the loud thumping that started up on the door, they explored together the expanded spaces of the rooms. Jerry chased the neon tetras in a shoal behind the couch. Elyot turned upside-down and mimed a slow-motion swing with the baseball bat. It was much more fun, being under-water with another person – and knowing you were neither of you going to drown. They sensed rather than heard the fact of wood splitting. When they turned into the hall, they saw the shark's-fin of an ax blade sticking out toward the top of the door. Carefully pressing himself against the side wall, Elyot went up to the door and rapped against it with his knuckles. The ax was pulled out and didn't come back. Elyot reopened the door, and stuck his head into the air of the corridor. Jerry semi-hid behind him.

'When did it all start?' shouted the reporter, getting in first.

'Are you alright, sir?' shouted the Fireperson holding the ax.

'We need to talk to you, sir,' said a man in a blue uniform, who hadn't been there before.

'I'm sorry, Elyot,' said Valerie, 'I should have believed you, but I didn't.'

'We need to talk,' said Vivian.

'I'm fine,' said Elyot. 'Go away. I don't want to talk to you – to any of you.'

The man in blue stepped forward. 'Actually, sir, whether you talk to them or not is a matter for your own conscience – but you are, I must tell you, obliged by law to speak to me.'

'You're a cop?' asked Elyot.

'No,' the blue man said, 'I'm from the Water Department.'

The interview took about fifteen minutes, throughout which the reporter held her microphone out towards Elyot. At one point, a red light came on at the top of the camera, and Elyot realized that most people in the city would be watching and listening to him. 'Hi, Ezra,' he said. He could almost sense them asking their its to find out more about him, the ones that were interested – 25 per cent, he guessed. Valerie and Vivian stood to one side, conducting a whispered conversation behind cupped hands. A couple of days ago, this would have been, of all sights in the world, the one most horrifying to him. But after everything that had happened, finding Jerry, or being found by her, Elyot didn't care at all: they could discuss his good points and his failings as much as they liked. Ford had retreated to behind the reporter, standing on tip-toe to look at Elyot. The questions the Water Department man asked were all about the water: When had it started? Where had it seemed to come from? What did it feel like to be submerged in it? How many cubic feet of water, approximately, would it take to fill his apartment? He handed Elyot a test-tube with a rubber stopper in the top, and asked if Elyot could do him a sample. Elyot faked an uncomprehending grimace, and got a laugh from the cameraman. 'Of the water,' said the Water Department man, playing along. But when Elyot handed the filled test-tube back, it was empty. There seemed no way of transporting the water beyond the boundaries it had chosen to set for itself. The Water Department man was about to step into the apartment, bringing with him a few pieces of test equipment, when the red light on the camera dimmed: the reporter said, 'We've gone to a weather report.' She put her finger in her ear and said, 'Oh my God.'

'What's happened?' asked Ford.

'It's started raining,' she said.

'And?' asked Valerie, unimpressed.

'And there aren't any clouds,' the reporter said. 'And the rain isn't coming from anywhere they can see – it's coming out of nowhere.'

By the time the Water Department man had entered, tested and exited the waters, Ford, Valerie and Vivian had left: Ford, gone to other apartments: Valerie and Vivian to dissect Elyot privately. Elyot wasn't sorry to see them go: the sight of them together made him think less of himself.

The red light came back on for the Water Representative's announcement. 'At this stage it's difficult to make
any definite statements about this substance – it appears to be
liquid but breaks the most fundamental law of liquids: that
of finding their own level. It is highly saline, and supports a
wide variety of marine life. It also,' and here he turned to
indicate Elyot and Jerry, 'appears to support human life as
well. Which is a relief. All I can say, therefore, is do not be
too alarmed. I'm sure there's a rational explanation for all
this. We're getting to work on it.' The reporter did a piece
to camera, after which the red light went off. She turned to
Elyot. 'When we come back,' she said, 'would you mind if
we took a look around your apartment?'

Elyot thought of the seaweed. 'It's a bit of a mess right
now,' he said. 'Plus, it seems as if this stuff fused my lights – I
don't think his camera will like it.'

'We'll take that chance,' said the reporter.

'In ten,' said the cameraperson.

'Do whatever you want,' said Elyot, then turned to Jerry.
'Shall we go out for a walk?'

She nodded, and they left the reporter to take her one
small step.

The elevator journey was awkward – Elyot could see Jerry
was thinking about Valerie and Vivian. But just as he was
opening his mouth to say something, she said, 'It's okay –
I don't want to hear.' She looked smaller out of the water,
her skin less pale. Elyot was already aware how comfortably
she would fit beneath his arm, for ambling. Getting to
know her, he felt, would be all about reconfirmation, not
discovery.

When they reached them the streets were full of rain,
panic and joy. About three inches of water were already

being sloshed across the sidewalks by passing cars. Elyot and Jerry looked up towards their apartments – a beam of murky white light could just about be seen moving around inside Elyot's. A lot of the other apartments in both blocks now displayed water-lines at some level of their windows. 'Do you want to get anything to drink?' he asked Jerry. 'Or eat?'

'No,' she said, 'I don't want anything, really – apart from this.' She turned her face back to the blue cloudless torrential sky and opened her mouth: it was raining so hard that it took only a minute or so for her mouth to fill with water. She then reached for Elyot's hand, pulled herself towards him, and began their first kiss, letting the waters flow from her mouth into his.

They went for a walk in the park. Grown men were taking the opportunity, perhaps final, to twirl their umbrellas and kick their way through puddles. One in four was singin' in the rain: it seemed an identifiable mania, like St Vitus' dance. Elyot and Jerry sat themselves down upon a bench and watched the world go by, go mad. Every so often, one of them filled their mouth with water and let the other kiss-drink them. They held hands, and watched as the waters rose over their knees. The park ducks were in Elysium, some web-footed version of their Day of Judgment having finally come to pass.

'I look out towards your building quite often,' said Elyot, 'and you live in the apartment right opposite – so, how come I've never seen you?'

Jerry seemed, for the first time, embarrassed. 'Because I never let you: I hid.'

'Hid?'

'There's a couple of pot plants –'

'Oh yeah –'

'– which I used to hide behind, if you looked suddenly. Otherwise I'd just keep the lights off and stay back in the shadows – wearing something dark.'

'For me?'

'Of *course* for you.'

'And for how long?'

'Well, I don't know if I want to tell you that,' she said, linking his arm through hers. 'It might give you too much of an advantage.'

'Tell me,' Elyot said, 'you must have wanted to talk to me all that time, so tell me now.' He was very conscious of the one thing he wasn't telling Jerry – the year he'd spent listening to Valerie. It was almost certain that she knew, though – she would have seen.

'A year,' said Jerry. Elyot was amazed: he wanted to say, 'Me, too,' but stopped himself. He knew exactly how she must be feeling – how the slightest deviation by him from what she'd imagined might endanger the whole thing. He himself had *known* Valerie was entirely adorable, it had been there in every tinkle of sound she made. He knew how easily any out-of-character discovery about her would have downcast him.

When it began to get dark, Elyot and Jerry sloshed back home to his apartment. The door was open but the reporter and her cameraperson were gone. Elyot and Jerry closed the door upon the world, locked it.

Hardly had they begun to kiss than they felt a surge pulse through the waters. They opened their eyes, and saw that they had been pulled half-way along the hall. Whilst they were looking at one another in astonishment, a second pulse came – stronger than the first – and swept them into the living room. It felt as if they were just under a huge wave, cresting, breaking before spreading itself out onto a long beach. The third pulse came, and the water seemed for a moment to become denser and darker. Elyot let go of Jerry and began to swim against the current. A fourth and a fifth pulse went by. The both of them had managed to grab hold of the legs of the fishtank. They watched as the sixth pulse swept through the room, smashing all the floating objects up against the window. Most of the neon tetras were there, too – heads toward the current, shimmering. The seventh pulse, the strongest so far, broke their hold upon the fishtank and swept them into the middle of the room. They expected death, but were unable to speak, so clung to one another, making touch eloquent. The next gentle pulse took them through the glass of the window, which did not break but did not impede, and out into the air, 150 stories up. They did not fall, neither did they rise.